The Dali Deception

Adam Maxwell

A Lost Book Emporium Publication 2016

First published in 2016 by The Lost Book Emporium

ISBN 1533480273
978-1533480279

www.adammaxwell.com

10 9 8 7 6 5 4 3 2 1

For Eve

The Dali Deception

18th September

Almost 3 weeks to go…

one

Violet Winters pretended not to look at the security guard leaving the Kilchester Metropolitan Museum and Art Gallery. Even in the early evening, the sweeping steps of the gallery were teeming with people finishing their working days. People going home, arriving to attend a concert, to go to restaurants. The life blood of the city getting right in the bloody way.

Violet peeled a five pound note from her pocket and handed it to the Big Issue seller who sat at the foot of one of the ornate columns. The young lad took the note Violet offered and began rummaging in his pockets. Violet's hair was dark, almost black, and cut into a long bob that almost touched her shoulders as she shook her head. "Keep the change," she said, looking over the shoulder of the kid. "In fact, you can keep the magazine too. I've already got that one anyway."

The Art Gallery towered behind them, refusing to allow anyone, least of all Violet, to ignore it for long.

"What happened to the woman who used to sleep here?" asked Violet.

The kid shrugged. "I been here a year. Maybe a bit more. She died, I heard."

"I used to see her a lot," said Violet. "She was pretty young. Well, not young-young but, you know, not old enough to die…" She trailed off.

"Happens," the kid said. "Living on the streets."

"Do you mind if I ask you something?" Asked Violet.

The kid shrugged again but held a little tighter onto the fiver in his hand.

Violet, leaning in a little closer. The kid smelled cleaner than she expected. "Can you see someone down the street?"

The kid frowned. "What sort of someone? You being followed?"

Violet nodded. "Perhaps. This someone would be taller than everyone else."

The kid nodded slowly. "Yeah, I see someone. Over down by the newsagent. Brown hair, tied in a pony tail?"

Violet nodded.

"You shouldn't encourage them, Miss," a man in a crisp, inky-blue uniform said.

"Oh, I don't know." Violet turned to face him, weighing him up as she spoke. "Three pay cheques and it could be any of us."

The security guard shrugged, his mouth turned down at the corners. "I suppose," he said and started to walk away.

Violet moved off too, then changed direction and gently bumped into the security guard.

"I'm sorry," she said, glancing at her shoes.

The security guard smiled and side-stepped, moving on his way.

Violet glanced behind her again. She adjusted the strap of her handbag on her shoulder as it became tangled with the strap from the tubular courier bag she also carried. The tall figure was gaining so she moved faster, swimming through the crowd until she ducked down the alley that ran down the side of the museum. Out of the crowds her heartbeat quickened. The only footsteps echoing between the museum and its neighbour were her own, until the unmistakable sound of a second set joined. How far? Forty metres? Twenty?

Halfway down the side of the museum was a second, smaller alley. It was no longer used by the museum and the rubbish lay in piles, blown there by the wind. This was where she was comfortable. Out of the crowds, in her element. Violet reached into her bag and took out a small, leather make-up case and a hairbrush. As she lifted the bag up she noticed how battered it had become. It was probably time to get a new one, but this one had served her so well.

The owner of the pursuing footsteps came around the corner but stepped carefully to remain in the shadows. This was quite an achievement given that the figure was around six feet ten inches tall.

"So you got my message then?" Violet said, fiddling with the leather cord that held the make-up bag closed. She placed the bag on top of a large bin and carefully put the hairbrush next to it. Gently unrolling the material, revealed three panels, each containing a variety of the tools of her trade.

The figure nodded but said nothing.

Violet took the tubular courier bag from her shoulder and pulled it over her head, letting it fall diagonally across her body.

Still the figure remained silent.

Violet rattled the handle of the door she stood in front of but it didn't open. She laughed a slightly manic laugh and reached over, taking the hairbrush once more and beginning to pick at it, feeling between the bristles. "Well I guess this is it then."

Another nod and... was that a smile?

"Right," Violet said. And then that laugh again. Like a staccato Syd James. "Before we do this... come here..." and darting forward, heading straight for the figure, then picking up speed, running now, until she was just a couple of steps in front of the figure and launching herself into the air.

Violet leaped forward and caused the figure to stagger backwards as she landed with her arms wrapped around their shoulders and legs hooked onto their hips.

"Did you miss me then Katie?" Violet grinned then planted a kiss on the cheek of the giantess.

Katie hadn't changed but whenever they went any time without seeing one another, Violet tended to forget how incredibly tall she was. And she was. Really, really tall, but not in a large and lumbering way. She had a grace that belied her height and, if you could see them up there, her features were fine, with a thin, straight nose pointing to lipstick-free lips. She smiled, and her hand, which was bigger than Violet's head, instinctively darted up to cover her smiling mouth. A silent laugh escaped instead as two little puffs of air from her nose. Violet let go and dropped to the ground and Katie, seeming intent on exaggerating the effect of the childish behaviour of her friend, reached down and ruffled Violet's hair with her hand.

"Now keep an eye out, will you?" Violet said, an urgency creeping in to her tone and a seriousness to her expression. Katie nodded and strode to the edge of the alley, watching for anyone who might spot them, and Violet went back over to her make-up bag.

"Okaaaaaaay," she said under her breath. "Let's do this shit then, shall we?" She glanced up at the door once more. There were two locks: a regular lock that had probably come fitted on the door and another newer deadbolt. For extra security.

Violet ran her hand over the tools in the first two panels of her make-up bag, her fingers skimming over the light metal of the lock picks and tension tools until they reached the third panel. The bump keys. She stared at them for a moment then slid one out, squeezed it into her palm, the sharp, metal points digging in ever so slightly. In her other hand she took the hairbrush.

Checking that Katie was still on guard, Violet moved to the door and slid the bump key into the first lock. She felt the butterflies of excitement rising in her stomach and took a breath. She needed this. Being away from Kilchester had been irritating, but being away from the life had been excruciating. She turned the bump key just enough to put pressure on the mechanism, then gave it a whack with the hairbrush. In one smooth motion, the bump key turned the rest of the way and the lock was open.

Violet smiled and glanced back to her friend. Katie nodded at Violet, who turned back to the second lock.

Another deep breath and then the key slid into the deadbolt. She tested it with her fingers, found what she judged to be the right amount of pressure then

Whack

The sound of the plastic on the metal echoed around the alleyway but the lock didn't give. Violet pictured the inside of the lock – the pins that stopped it from opening were not quite catching. She changed her grip on the bump key; the pressure exerted was minuscule but she altered it ever so slightly and

Whack

She felt the mechanism become lighter: two, maybe three of the pin stacks had caught; just one more

Whack

And the lock gave. Violet turned the bump key and, once she was sure no-one was directly inside, made a click-click-click noise with her mouth. Katie recognised the signal and followed quickly, moving like a shadow down the length of the alley as Violet gathered together the remainder of her kit. With one final glance to ensure they had remained unobserved, the two of them stepped inside and silently closed the door.

two

"Thanks for coming," Violet said, putting her hand on Katie's upper arm. Katie raised an eyebrow and let the corners of her mouth twist upwards just a little. Violet gave her friend's arm a squeeze. "Bloody hell, Katie! Have you moved into the gym?"

Katie rolled her eyes and started down the corridor. The scuffed, grey linoleum was almost worn through in places. The strip lights flickered, moving the shadows of the peeling paint and giving the walls the impression of having scales. Here in the bowels of the museum things were very different from the exhibition spaces the public swarmed around.

"Anyway," Violet continued, padding slowly down the corridor. "Enough about you. I suppose you'll want to know about me?"

There was a noise somewhere ahead of them and the pair froze, staring into the strip-lit distance.

Violet counted to sixty in her head and, when no other noise came, began to walk again. A little slower than before.

"You heard what happened, I take it?" Violet whispered.

Katie held up her thumb and forefinger a small distance apart.

"Percy Parkin. The prick." Violet gritted her teeth as she spat his name.

6

The two women reached a door. Katie instinctively positioned herself with her back to the opposite wall and kept lookout. Violet placed her palm on the door and pushed. The door swung open and she proceeded, her eyes flashing around the stairwell beyond, comparing what she saw with the blueprints she had studied, replacing in her mind the lines of the drawing with the solidity of peeling, damp walls.

She waited, but there was no-one in the stairwell. Not at this time of day. The only thing in there was the smell of the damp. And the two of them. She beckoned to Katie, who moved silently to her side.

"We were inside. So close to getting the goods," Violet shook her head at the memory as if the act of doing this might dislodge it and send it crashing down the stairs. When nothing happened she began to climb. "I started to get a bad feeling about it. But you can't just say 'I've got a bad feeling about this' can you?"

Violet glanced back at Katie, who raised an eyebrow and smirked.

"Well, okay," Violet conceded. "Maybe you can if you're Han Solo but normal people who aren't, you know, in movies…"

Katie packed away her smirk. Almost.

"But a bad feeling I had. So I told Jenny, who was dealing with the alarm system, I told her to go and double check. For my peace of mind, I told her. And she complained, dented her pride a bit I think. But I thought she could warn us."

After four flights of stairs, Violet had to catch her breath. She paused on a landing and watched Katie silently loping after her.

"How come you aren't out of breath then?" Violet asked. Katie ignored her and picked up the pace; her long, long legs taking the next set of stairs three then four stairs at a time, turning the corner and moving faster and faster until she was out of sight.

"I hate fit people," Violet muttered, a wheezing, tiny tortoise to Katie's six feet ten inch hare.

Violet reached the penultimate floor and, still panting, pushed open the door to find Katie sitting on a chair on the other side.

"All clear?" asked Violet.

Katie nodded, that smirk back on her face. She reached into a pocket of the black cargo pants she wore and pulled out a bottle of water, which she tossed to Violet.

Violet caught it and unscrewed the lid. Katie stood up and, with a flourish, twirled the chair around herself and behind Violet. She gave a gentle shove, and Violet toppled into a sitting position.

Violet took a gulp of water. "I'd forgotten how irritating you can be when you get yourself in gear," she said.

Katie smiled sweetly.

Violet stood up. It was time for some payback.

"This way?" she asked, and gestured towards a corridor. Katie followed the gesture and, as she did so, Violet started sprinting in the other direction. The second Katie realised, she bolted after her, the two of them hurling themselves down the length of the corridor until they skidded to a halt, grinning like idiots, a couple of hundred metres further along.

Violet opened her mouth to start speaking again but Katie placed her hand over it. Katie's hand, like the rest of Katie, was very large indeed and wrapped around most of Violet's face. To ensure Violet could still breathe Katie placed her index finger on the bridge of Violet's nose and her three remaining fingers under her nose. Experience had taught Katie this would prevent the embarrassing moment when you accidentally suffocated the person you were trying to subdue. One oversight, one time, that requires ten seconds of mouth-to-mouth and you have yourself a reputation as heavy handed...

With the sound of approaching footsteps beginning to echo louder, the pair froze. Fun though it was to catch up and to lark around, in this situation Violet knew when to talk and when to shut the hell up.

They waited, the sound of their breathing suddenly drowned out by the sound of shoes tap-tapping down a nearby corridor.

Katie glanced over her shoulder and, noting the room number, shoved open the door. With her hand still clamped firmly over Violet's mouth, Katie stepped backwards, moving into the room and dragging her companion with her.

Violet made a quiet *mmmph* noise.

It had a questioning tone to it which Katie chose to ignore. The footsteps were getting closer.

Violet opened her mouth and licked the palm of Katie's hand.

Katie recoiled, her hand flying free of Violet's face, and that laugh again, two little puffs of air from her nose. Her hand instinctively went up to cover her mouth but she realised before it was too late. Reaching out, Katie wiped saliva on the shoulder of Violet's black motorbike jacket.

The footsteps began to recede into the distance.

"This is the place then?" Violet asked, knowing the answer to the question.

A seriousness descended on the room like a fat man sitting on a beanbag.

Katie nodded. It was time for them to get to work.

three

The small ante-corridor they found themselves in was large enough to accommodate three people standing shoulder to shoulder. It was, therefore, something of a squash when Katie began to do some impromptu stretching.

"You're bored, aren't you?" asked Violet.

Katie raised her hand to her mouth and pretended to yawn.

Violet dropped to her knees in front of the door and unfurled her make-up bag. Quietly clicking her tongue against her teeth, she glanced between the door's lock and her tools. A second later she'd made her decision and plucked the tension wrench from the bag. Like the pick she held in her right hand, it was a tiny, delicate thing.

They weighed nothing in her hand, but she rubbed them with the tips of her fingers and thumbs. A reverential gesture before inserting them into the barrel of the lock and beginning to feel her way around.

Katie sighed and rolled her head from side to side, causing her neck to click. Violet's eyes flicked towards her and she fixed a stare on her companion.

"It's a weird one," Violet said, trying to construct a mental picture of what the tools were telling her about the lock's insides. "This could take a while."

Katie's shoulders fell and she let out another sigh for good measure.

"So do you want to hear the rest of this story or not?" Violet asked.

Katie shrugged one shoulder as she nodded her head.

"Excellent, that's what I like to hear," said Violet. "And another thing." Violet gave one final prod with the lock pick and then used the tension wrench to turn the lock. "We're in."

She pushed the door and stepped from the cramped ante-corridor into a climate-controlled storage area.

"You can tell me how wonderfully talented I am now if you like." Violet flashed Katie a grin and Katie rolled her eyes in return.

"Suit yourself," said Violet. "Now... where was I..? So I'd told Jenny to go and double check the alarms because I 'had a bad feeling'."

Katie nodded, a seriousness entering her expression.

Violet sensed it and her tone changed. She started again, rewinding the story back to its proper origin. Percy Parkin. Violet's now ex. Though ex what? That was probably a good question. Ex-boyfriend certainly. Ex-fiancé? Not quite but as good as. And, of course, her ex-partner was also the ex-fence of any stolen property anyone might wish to shift.

Because Percy had had a tip off. Too good to be true. And of course if something appears to be too good to be true then, inevitably, it is. Unless you, or one of your crew, has a deep desire to end up behind bars.

Except, of course, you trust your partner, don't you?

Don't you?

And Violet had. At that moment, for her, Percy could do no wrong. Little did she realise that he was about to hurl himself from that pedestal and out of her life.

Busting in and busting out of a diamond wholesalers. That was the job. She had thought he was joking when he told her. She had replied that they should rob the coffee shop they were sitting in and told him it was because 'Nobody robs coffee shops, pumpkin.'

But it had turned out he was completely serious. It wasn't a hare-brained scheme he had cooked up after watching too many Tarantino movies. In fact, he knew a bloke who knew a bloke...

It often started that way, of course, that much wasn't new. And she had chalked up her original bad feelings to the fact that the robbery went so badly in the movie. But they were professionals, not actors. This wasn't scripted, it was real life.

"And things were about to get seriously fucked up for us," said Violet to Katie, closing the door to the room as Katie entered. Although, as it turned out, this was less of a room and more of a vault. A blanket of cold air blasted down from an air conditioning unit suspended from the ceiling. Katie surveyed the area, looking over the tops of the shelves and storage containers but finding no-one.

Violet closed her eyes, searching her memory for the location of the item she was looking for. It came to her as she moved forward, Katie in tow.

"Percy said he could move the diamonds," Violet went on. Katie raised her eyebrows. "Not any diamond. There were some specific stones that were easier for someone of his status as a mid-level fence to move. The ones he'd had the tip off about.

"So we weren't going in there on some smash and grab mission. It was planned. It was controlled. At first.

"Jenny had disabled the alarms before we got inside so she was trailing around whilst other people did their thing, and she was royally bored. A bit like you right now, I suppose. Anyway, she started flirting with Will, this short fat guy who was our inside man. But he wasn't responding."

Katie shrugged, confused.

"Will was this sweaty, horrible, greasy, hairy little man. He was fat, he smelled really bad."

Katie's lip curled.

"Exactly," Violet said, her pace quickening and her eyes flashing left and right, looking, searching. "Never felt the touch of a woman, I bet. What an odd phrase. The 'touch of a woman'."

Violet ran her fingers seductively along the back of Katie's hand.

"Do anything for you?" she asked.

Katie shook her head.

"I must be having an off day then," Violet concluded. "But Will... I don't know. At the time I think I just wanted to concentrate and Jenny's flirting was irritating me but... I dunno. Now that I think back I wonder if somewhere in my head something was telling me that there was a piece out of place. And that was why I gave her a task.

"All I had to do, it was simple really... All I had to do was get into the case that held the diamonds. One last lock. And if the alarm was disabled just scoop them up and go. Like I said, I trusted Jenny so the alarm was off, getting her out of the way was never really about that. Of course, Will had gone to follow her. But this is the part I can't explain. I stopped him."

Violet held up her palm and Katie came to a dead stop, her thin eyebrows descending into a familiar look of concentration. A silence overtook them for a second, without the echoes of conversation, but then their ears attuned to the background thrum of the air conditioning. Violet shook her head, shaking out whatever thought she had. They moved off once more.

"I stopped him by handing him my tools," she continued. Katie held up Violet's bag and waggled it in the air. "Ah yes," said Violet. "Just like that. I kept asking him to pass me this, hand me that... All the while fiddling with the lock. Of course, I'd had it open before Jenny left the room but that was beside the point. Will just got more and more uncomfortable. And more and more sweaty."

The corners of Katie's mouth turned down and half a frown formed in her brow.

"Looked like he'd pissed in his pants," Violet said through a grimace. She stopped walking then continued, "Hang on. This is the one we're looking for."

She gestured toward the cabinet in front of them then lifted her tubular courier bag up over her head and loosened the lid. From inside she took two pieces of paper. They were ridiculously small given the size of the container. The tube itself was perhaps a metre or so long and the pieces of paper it contained no more than twenty centimetres along their longest edge.

Katie stooped to read what was written on them:

13

'This object has been temporarily removed for cleaning and study.'

And in the bottom right hand corner was the logo from the museum.

Violet handed the small cards to Katie with a smirk. Katie proffered the make-up case but Violet shook her head, instead reaching forward and pulling at the handle on the metal casing. With an alarmingly loud grinding noise the container opened.

"Who'd bother locking these? Imagine if you worked here, it would be a right old pain in the arse if you had to unlock every single one. Their laziness, however, is our gain…"

Inside the metal drawer was a small canvas which was almost as minimalist as the paper Katie held for Violet. Its shortest edge was perhaps thirty or so centimetres long, its longest no more than fifty. And it was completely blank.

With some reverence Violet lifted the canvas from the drawer and held it aloft. Delicately, slowly and precisely, Violet rolled the blank canvas until it was tight enough to fit into the courier tube. Gently, she slid it inside, took one of the 'removed for cleaning' signs, then placed it in the metal drawer and pushed it closed.

Katie was about to walk away but Violet stopped her.

"I've got a plan," she said with a grin as she reached forward, pulling at the handle of the next drawer. The pair winced as the cacophony of clanking filled the air. Inside the drawer was another blank canvas.

Violet reached forward to remove it. "And this is exactly what I need to make it happen."

four

Violet closed the drawer and flipped the courier tube over her head, letting the strap fall across her body from shoulder to hip.

"Come on," she said, and the pair set off at a jog. Well, Violet was at a jog; Katie kept pace just by lengthening her stride.

"That was the moment in the job," Violet whispered, "when you really don't want to get caught."

Katie looked over at her and then pointed at the ground.

"No, not this job," Violet began before a thought crept up on her. "Actually, yes, just like this job. You've got the goods, but you haven't got away yet, and you don't want to get caught en flagrant délit."

Katie raised one eyebrow.

"I've been reading," Violet retorted. "I'm well-read now. It means red handed." She glanced over to her friend, who responded by rolling her eyes.

"Which you already knew. Well, fine. Up yours," Violet paused at a crossroad in the museum stacks and glanced around. "Anyway, Will stayed, holding the tools for a minute and then off he trotted after Jenny. At the time I thought Jenny would be well out of the way so I figured it would be okay to let him go…

15

"Turned out afterwards that Will caught up with her. Bludgeoned her with his baton."

Katie stopped and stared at Violet, letting her jog off ahead.

Violet skidded to a halt as she reached the door she was looking for and stared down the corridor at Katie's imposing silhouette way behind her.

"I've thought about it a lot and I don't think I could have known," Violet's voice echoed down the long corridor. "I couldn't have known."

Katie nodded before pointing towards the door but Violet shook her head, instead opening it and waiting for Katie to walk through. Violet dropped to her knees and retrieved her picks, effortlessly re-locking the door behind them.

Katie pointed to the door opposite the one Violet had just locked and this time Violet nodded. Interlocking her gloved fingers, Katie cracked her knuckles then dropped her foot back, bracing herself. Violet squinted, knowing what was coming next. Katie erupted, stepping forward and slamming her palms simultaneously above and below the position of the lock on the door.

The door, which was entirely unprepared for such an assault, exploded inward, its frame shattering, sending shards of wood and plastic spiralling through the air.

Violet clapped her hands slowly and deliberately. "Good show, old girl. Jolly good show."

Katie reached up and touched two fingers to her forehead in a mock salute, but the serious expression had not left her face.

"I could have done with your help on Percy's job." Violet walked through the shattered frame and looked around, getting her bearings once more. "Sometimes you choose the wrong people."

Katie stood outside the room. Waiting. Listening.

"You know how long you've got, at that point, before they arrive with their flashing lights and give you a lovely new set of bracelets. I mean, you don't know it know it. You just... you know... know it, don't you?" Violet's voice was beginning to become more faint as she ventured slightly further into the room. Katie remained where she was.

"I phoned Percy. Couldn't get a word in. He thought I was at the police station already, using my one phonecall on him. Just kept trying to get me off the line. I was going to shut him up, but then I realised there was no way he could have known about the police. I got the feeling you get on a roller-coaster, you know, when you hit that point and it feels like the bottom of your stomach gets sucked down and out of you?"

Katie frowned and shook her head.

"Of course you don't. Anyway, I waited for him to stop talking, then I told him I hadn't been arrested. That I wasn't going to be arrested. And he says, 'Fuck, really? You haven't been arrested?' and the tone of his voice, he can't believe it. And then there's another voice in the background. A woman. I hear her screaming at him 'What do you mean she hasn't been–' and then he hangs up. And... well, you know the rest about Percy.

"So I knew that I had enough time to get out of there but... fuck... you should have seen her, Katie... Jenny was a bloody mess." Violet's head poked around a set of shelves and into view for a moment. "But with actual blood."

Katie nodded and stared. Violet stared back for a moment, the events replaying in her head. She hadn't felt anything like that before. Violet had always been supremely confident. She was the brains of the operation, it was her plans the team executed and they always worked. Except that time they didn't. When she left Kilchester, she left vulnerable and with her confidence hanging in tatters. The vulnerability hadn't lasted long. Violet had used her time away to rebuild herself, and it had taken time, but she had come back a stronger woman.

"There was a cleaner's cupboard. It was locked but you know me... So I dragged her in there, then I used a cloth, some bleach and cleaned the floor where he'd left her. Cleaned it and dried it off with some paper towels and then locked us both in that cleaner's cupboard.

"You could hear the police come and then go again. There was a first aid kit and... I don't know anything about that sort of thing but my phone still had signal in there and I Googled the best I could. Made her comfortable. And this was... Saturday. So we were in there until it all died down. On Monday.

"At first, it was like in the movies. She'd been knocked out or whatever. She was in and out of consciousness and she was talking here and there. Not so loud you could make out what she was trying to say. I thought... well, I thought I was saving her from being arrested. Saving both of us."

Violet loitered where she was, half way around a corner standing fifteen metres away from Katie. Even from that distance Katie could see Violet's expression change, her brow furrowed as she stared downward.

"Anyway..." Violet said eventually. "I found what I was looking for here."

"Run," Violet said as she triggered the museum alarm system.

And they ran.

20th August

7 weeks to go…

five

"Please, Miss Winters, take a seat. Can I get you a drink?" Brad Fegan's right hand instinctively moved to his left lapel. He squeezed it gently between his thumb and forefinger, smoothing it out. He loved the feeling of the moleskin fabric and was on the verge of developing an interesting series of tics all based around the stroking of various parts of his jacket.

"Call me Violet. And yes, I'll have a Long Island iced tea." Violet looked around, taking in the grandeur of the restaurant then, feeling a little underdressed, began smoothing down imaginary creases in her skirt.

Fegan nodded to the waiter attending their table and he moved away purposefully.

"Have you been back in Kilchester long?" Fegan asked.

Violet smiled and shook her head slightly. "No, I just got in this morning. I only have one meeting and then I'll be back on the train out of here."

Fegan raised two bushy, black eyebrows in mock-surprise as the waiter returned and deposited a drink in front of each of them.

"Will there be anything else, Sir? Madam?" the waiter oozed obsequiously.

Fegan ignored the waiter, his eyebrows still raised, waiting for Violet to continue.

Violet stared back, letting Fegan play his little game.

The waiter coughed.

Without breaking eye contact with Violet, Fegan beckoned the waiter who leaned closer.

"Fuck off," he said quietly.

The waiter nodded and off he fucked.

"You hate this place so much?" Fegan raised his left hand and slowly rubbed at his breast pocket in a way that probably wouldn't have been entirely appropriate in a restaurant of this calibre. That is, if there was anyone in the restaurant except for Fegan and Violet.

"No," said Violet, staring past Fegan to the empty tables beyond. "It's a lovely place, it's just... complicated."

She lifted her drink to her lips and sipped lightly at it.

"Oh, do tell," said Fegan, leaning forward eagerly. "Do tell."

Violet leaned forward, letting a few strands of hair fall across her face, then fluttered her eyelashes a couple of times. With her index finger extended, she slowly moved her hand from the polished gold cutlery on the table, across her body and up to point at her pouting lips.

"Fuck off," she said quietly as she finally met his gaze. "You asked me here and it wasn't to talk about why I will or will not be staying in Kilchester. And you know anyway, you knob."

A vein in Fegan's neck pulsed one, twice, before he burst out laughing.

"I like you, I really do," he wheezed, caressing the cuff of his coat. "And I have to know – did you actually make off with any diamonds in the end?"

Violet took a sip of her drink. They certainly hadn't skimped on the rum. Or the tequila.

Fegan flicked one of his eyebrows in anticipation.

Violet tilted her head slightly to one side and waited. The alcohol stung her mouth as she savoured it.

"You want me to tell you what happened?" She rapped four long but unpainted nails on the placemat in front of her, then shrugged. "Okay then. We'd had a tip off. The fence, my then boyfriend, told us exactly where the items were. It wasn't a smash and grab, it was a... erm..."

"Duck and pluck?"

"Is that a thing?"

"Duck the police, pluck the diamonds. If it isn't a thing then it most certainly should be."

Violet nodded and took another sip of her drink. It was entirely possible that this was a set-up. That someone was recording the whole conversation. She stared at Fegan, his nervous tics dancing through his fingers as he touched parts of his coat repeatedly.

He caught her studying him and placed his palms on the table in front of him.

"This isn't a sting," Fegan said, staring at her calmly.

Violet dabbed at her mouth with a heavy linen napkin for no other reason than to see it stained with her dusky red lipstick.

"If I really believed it might be a sting then I wouldn't have come," she said. "But I'm here so... you show me yours and I'll show you mine."

Fegan scanned the room, looking for loitering waiters or waitresses.

"There's a painting one of my clients wants. But it's complicated," he said.

"Which is..."

"...why I need a person of your particular proclivity," Fegan interrupted.

"And how did you find out about my skills?" Violet retorted, a little too quickly. She took a breath, picked up her drink and sipped. Damn if there wasn't a whole lot of alcohol in there.

"I worked with your mother," Fegan said.

Simply stated, no frills. Less likely to be a lie, Violet thought. Or he knows that and it's a trick. She took another moment to weigh up the man. Thick black hair, streaked with white. He's older, might have been going bald if he had different genes, so that fits. She knew his name, his reputation. In their profession there weren't many who stuck around as long as he had. His name was enough for it to draw her back to Kilchester.

But tempting is different to trustworthy.

"She may have mentioned me?" Fegan had stopped stroking his coat. This was his pitch. He was selling the job, selling himself to her.

Violet half-nodded her head. "And my father, I suppose you've worked with him too? Perhaps you should just get them on board instead of me?"

"Your mother stopped working after she broke her leg. And why would I need your father? This is not a job for a conman, even one as accomplished as your father." Fegan sipped at his water, his eyes twinkling. "Did I pass the test?"

"Yes, yes," she said impatiently. "You can't be too careful, though, can you?"

Violet watched as Fegan once again scanned the periphery of the room for wanderers then leaned back and began fondling his lapel.

"Tell me about the painting," Violet said. "You'll want to tell me all about it, won't you? Who does it belong to at the moment?"

Fegan barked a couple of belly laughs. "At the moment! At the moment it belongs to Rollo Glass, the chairman of the Kilchester Bank."

"A banker. So presumably the security is…"

"…your worst nightmare."

"And the painting itself?" asked Violet.

"Tell me why you left Kilchester," said Fegan blankly.

Violet stared at him for a moment, weighing him up before she spoke again. This was how he wanted to play and if he was going to finance the job then she had to play along.

She nodded and took a breath.

"I left because I wanted to keep my head down."

Fegan nodded. "And I appreciate you popping it over the parapet."

"And I wanted to keep my head down because I was betrayed by members of my own crew. And by my treacherous fucking ex."

Fegan gave that belly laugh again. "Betrayed by your lover?" He sucked air through his teeth.

Violet didn't flinch, just waited for him to stop, the feelings welling in her stomach again. Another deep breath.

"We were inside. The security had been disabled. I was up to bat. All we had to do was get into the containers that held the diamonds."

Fegan leaned forward, studying her face, savouring the story.

"I took off my coat just to be comfortable to pick the locks and Jenny – did I mention Jenny? She was the brains of the operation. Knocked out the alarm system. She picked up my coat and put it on. Said she was cold or something like that.

"But then my phone rings and it's my ex.

"'Surprise!' he texts. And a picture of a bag full of diamonds. Next thing I know two massive heavies are storming out of a janitor's room towards me and Jenny. I started scrambling backwards and she's watching me with this look of confusion on her face…"

Fegan was frowning with concentration, staring at Violet, his mouth hanging open.

"I was pointing and… I don't know if I was shouting but one of the guys shoves a knife into her as she starts turning around and…"

Violet stopped talking.

Fegan traced his finger from the far side of his glass clockwise to the side closest to him, the condensation parting for a moment and allowing the droplets above to pour down into the gap.

"But you escaped?" he said eventually.

Violet nodded.

"And I guess that means it's my turn to show you mine?"

Violet nodded once more. She leaned forward, sliding her drink to one side. "If I come back to Kilchester then I'm not coming for some half-arsed job. If I kick in the doors of this town then I'm kicking them wide open…"

"Scores to settle, all that melodramatic poppycock?" Fegan rolled his eyes.

"All that shit," said Violet. "And I am prepared to do it. For the right job. Enough time has passed."

"And this ex…" said Fegan. "Is he likely to take another shot at you?"

"Try to kill me?" Violet stared over Fegan's shoulder out into the street, watching the people bustling by, all of them happily oblivious. She had to balance the truth with the bravado that she could pull off the job. Being away had given her time to think about the situation. If wanting her dead was Percy's sole purpose then he would have sent someone after her when she retreated. After all this time she was resigned to the fact that he was probably too inept to try anything else.

"No," she said, finally. "It wasn't about me being alive or dead. It was about the job."

Fegan nodded. "Usually is."

"But if I come back then I'll need to deal with the situation in some way. Two birds and all that…"

"One stone," Fegan said. "Well, that's where it gets interesting," he grinned. "Because the painting I want you to steal is actually blank."

six

"Salvador Dali?" said Violet. "You want me to steal a Dali? That's blank? If it's blank how can it be a Dali?"

"Did you know that in the 1960s Salvador Dali realised that if he signed a blank sheet of paper he could sell it for forty dollars?" Fegan had finally summoned the waiter and in front of the pair of them now sat several plates of tiny, neat objects of undesignated origin that neither of them were touching. "With one person sliding a piece of paper under his pencil and another person taking the finished article away he could sign one every two seconds. This meant that he could earn seventy two thousand dollars in a single hour."

"But," said Violet, beginning to see the fatal flaw in Fegan's scheme. "If he was signing that many then he would have flooded the market. You would be lucky if they held their value, let alone..."

Fegan raised a finger to his lips and shushed her.

Violet resisted the urge to snap off his finger and drop it in his drink, fixing a fake smile across her face instead.

"You are a very perceptive woman," Fegan continued. "The actual number of papers he signed... some say it was as high as four hundred thousand... the Dali camp puts it rather more conservatively down at the fifty thousand mark."

"And yet," interrupted Violet, unwilling to be shushed. "Even fifty thousand would make them worth less than this plate of..." she glanced back down at the plate. "What exactly are they supposed to be?"

"Buggered if I know," replied Fegan before picking one up and inspecting it. "And yes, you are ahead of me, which is incredibly rude since I'd gone to the trouble of preparing a whole monologue which–"

"Which is now a dialogue."

"Quite."

"Which you will now bring to a rapid conclusion if you wish my interest to be sustained." Violet had had quite enough of indulging Fegan's love of his own voice; either he showed her how it was worth her while or she would head to the station.

"Greed," said Fegan with a flourish.

"Sorry?" said Violet.

"It's all about greed," continued Fegan. "Dali was even kicked out of the surrealists for it. They said he was too bloody greedy, gave him the moniker 'Avida Dollars', an anagram of his own name which literally means 'greed for dollars'. The irony of which, given the nature of our current conversation, is not lost on you?"

"What is lost on me is the part where you want to pay me a great deal of money for me to put myself in harm's way for something I could grab from eBay for twenty quid." Violet snapped.

"Very well," said Fegan reluctantly. "The point... is that every greedy idea stems from something. The mass-producing of pencil signatures came from an event way before. Dali had been commissioned to produce a painting on canvas but he had fallen ill. On the appointed day the client had travelled to Dali's studio to collect the painting and Dali was still in bed. One of his aides went to raise him and in the meantime the client wandered into the studio. The foolish fellow spotted the untouched canvas and by the time Dali arrived had convinced himself that the great surrealist had left the canvas blank deliberately."

"You have got to be kidding?" said Violet.

Fegan shook his head, "Not a bit of it. The story goes that Dali looked on whilst this idiot heaped praise on the blank canvas then congratulated the artist on his intellect and vision. The man handed over the money for the canvas but before he left, Dali couldn't resist pushing the poor bastard a little further.

"While the man looked on Dali instructed his aide to mix paint and then signed his name, in oils, in the bottom right hand corner. Lastly he told the man to leave his studio because the painting would not be dry for another week."

Violet laughed and picked up something from the plate between them. She examined whatever it was and then changed her mind and carefully put it back.

"Avida Dollars," Fegan puffed up his chest.

"So this is Dali's first," said Violet.

"And the only canvas. Every other one is on paper. At least every one we're aware of."

"Okay, now I almost like the sound of this," said Violet, finally warming to the job. "So how exactly do we pull this off?"

"That's down to you, my dear, but I'll tell you the terms I've been given. Some of them I have no doubt you'll like, some of them you will object to, but they must all be met. The bad part first. The mark cannot know that you have taken the piece."

"So I'll need a forgery? Of a signature? That's not so bad. I can probably live with that."

"You'll have to. Also," Fegan interrupted, "the nightmare security is made worse by the fact that the flat the banker owns, the flat that contains the painting... it's underground."

"Oh for fu–" Violet began.

"A bunker of sorts. One way in–"

"One way out," Violet chorused.

"Those are the bad bits. The question is, does that pose a problem?" Fegan leaned forward.

Violet stared at Fegan for a moment, relishing the opportunity to make him sweat, to have placed almost all his cards on the table and to be waiting for her. "I can live with the bad bits."

Fegan clapped his hands.

"I'll need a crew." It was a statement.

"I had no doubt you would," said Fegan.

31

"And money for them, for setting the whole thing up, equipment," Violet continued.

Fegan smiled and nodded.

"And the money to pay for the forgeries, too."

Fegan's left eye twitched almost imperceptibly but he smiled through it and nodded once again.

"And what price are you offering for me to perform this miracle for you?"

Fegan stopped smiling.

3rd September

5 weeks to go…

seven

Zoe Zimmerman wasn't like the other children, and she never had been. Of course she wore the same school uniform as all of the other kids spilling out of Kilchester Central Comprehensive School, the same black blazer. She even wore the same garish blue and yellow striped tie that was, of course, tied in the same non-conformist way as all the other girls in the lower sixth-form so that the knot was precisely three times as wide as it should be and only three inches of the tie poked through to hang down.

But Zoe wasn't like the other girls and boys. She was very much an odd sock.

If you'd been walking down the other side of the street looking for Zoe at that moment, and, as it happens, somebody was, you would have had a great deal of difficulty in spotting the girl. Zoe was practised. Zoe blended.

Mostly.

None of the other children spoke to her. She didn't make eye contact, just pushed a lock of her shoulder-length auburn hair behind her ear whilst letting another fall forward over her right eye. Camouflage. She glanced behind her, checking to see if anyone had noticed her. Of course, none of the other kids had, they were too absorbed in their own social bubbles. Pulling the strap of her heavy satchel up a little higher she quickened her pace and began to draw away from the pack to cross the road towards the library.

A half a dozen or so other children broke off, to shouts of 'teacher's pet', 'swots' and 'fucking nerds' from the more cerebrally challenged.

Kilchester, as a city, housed some architectural gems. The pillars and colonnades, the spires and steeples, from the gothic to the Victorian; you could scarcely walk three hundred metres without the sorts of stonework that stood shoulder to shoulder with the most beautiful listed buildings of London and Edinburgh.

The library was not one of those buildings. Kilchester library hadn't so much been designed and built as summoned into existence through satanic ritual. The grey concrete jutted out of the ground as if the devil's own Lego set had been thrust through the earth's crust. Counterpointing the angular Lego were thin triangular shards of windows grinning like teeth across each of the four upper floors, giving the impression that the library may in fact be made from two sets of disembodied jaws. If that wasn't bad enough the space between the library's teeth was covered with patches of pebbledash, which had eroded over time and now appeared like the patches of Satan's spew.

Zoe's eye's flicked upwards to the familiar building as she entered through the single sliding door. She moved quickly through the corridors to the back of the library, where the stairs to all floors guided anyone who wasn't interested in 'general' fiction or getting a book stamped by a real, live librarian.

"Excuse me." Zoe approached the desk of the librarian on the second floor in the children's section of the library. "I booked a computer."

"Oh, hello dear," said the librarian with a smile. "You here again? They must give you an awful lot of homework at that school."

Zoe smiled and nodded in recognition before once more pushing her hair behind her ear.

"I think there's someone using your usual computer," the librarian continued. Zoe's face dropped as the librarian looked at a piece of paper on the counter in front of her. "Oh, no, my mistake. Computer four is free. I'll get today's password for you, love."

A moment later and Zoe was crossing the picture book section of the library, heading towards the best seat in the house, the one computer with a view. Whilst every other workstation was dropped next to the nearest plug point and facing the wall, Zoe's spot offered a view of the bustling high street. It was nice to see life flowing by as she worked. And best of all it was tucked around a corner so no-one could see what you might be up to.

"What on earth are you doing you horrible little boy!" A woman bellowed into the picture book area and barrelled into Zoe, knocking her bag from her shoulder in her haste to leave. "Oh, sorry," she muttered, picking up Zoe's bag and handing it back to her.

Zoe snatched the bag and stomped off to finally take her place in front of the computer. Glancing over her shoulder to ensure she was unobserved, she slid her satchel to the floor and slipped out a small, grey box. Zoe turned it over in her hand. It was, perhaps, the size of a pack of cards but, unlike a pack of cards, the side of the box had a single, square opening. Zoe plucked a wire from her blazer pocket and, with practised skill, plugged one end into the computer and the other into the box.

The computer's screen flickered for a moment, collapsed in on itself then jumped back into life.

Except it wasn't quite the same.

Zoe's fingers clattered across the keyboard, only stopping when her hand darted over to the mouse. Within a couple of minutes she was up and running. If anyone had walked past they would have seen Zoe the schoolgirl surfing the web, looking at videos on YouTube, occasionally checking the library catalogue and typing random nonsense into a word processor.

Which was, of course, exactly what Zoe wanted them to think. She definitely wouldn't have wanted them to see that she had tapped into the security feed of the bank opposite the library and was streaming it in the guise of YouTube. Or that the word processor she appeared to be using was transmitting her keystrokes to allow her to dip in and out of the bank's network, particularly the cash machine that sat just inside the lobby. And there was no doubt that she would have had some difficulty explaining that in the library's 'catalogue' the space that should have displayed *Author, Title, ISBN* instead showed the words *Name, Card Number* and *PIN*.

Those were the sorts of things that someone would struggle to explain in polite society.

eight

Zoe Zimmerman wasn't like the other children. And one of the primary reasons for that was because none of the other children at Kilchester Central Comprehensive School were in the habit of hacking into bank's computer systems and stealing people's card details before cloning their cards and taking their cash.

There was also the fact that none of the other children at the school were twenty two years old, either.

When she had been in the lower sixth form it hadn't been a great deal different. When she walked with the other kids she was ignored in the same way she was today. With one notable exception. But then you would expect other kids to notice you when you had the police escorting you from the computer labs.

Fortunately for her they never did manage to prove anything in the eyes of the law. In the eyes of the teachers, however, it was another story. They knew there was only one child capable of framing dear old Mr Coleman.

As it happened, Zoe was guilty of everything the teachers suspected her of doing. She had indeed created evidence that Mr Coleman had been up to no good in chatrooms on the internet, but she was younger then and hadn't really realised how quickly what she thought was a pretty funny joke would escalate.

Escalate it had and as a result she had been thrown out of school. So Zoe had worked hard, studied hard and over the next five years honed her skills and became one of the most talented and prolific hackers the north of England had ever seen.

The incident with dear old Mr Coleman hadn't left her entirely cold; she had been affected by it. Not that she actually regretted it, but she'd felt, after watching several crime films on the television, that she should have some sort of code. At first she would kid herself that it was because she wanted to be a noble criminal, only stealing from those she believed deserved it in some way. But it wasn't really for that reason.

Yes, she did have a particular type of target and yes, she tried to justify that each one deserved to be a target. In fact it just gave her an excuse to exercise more of her hacking talents. It was petty theft. With showboating.

So she would spot someone on the street on their way to the bank. Smile please, you're on CCTV and...

Click.

She's got your photo and the first search can start (also potentially useful for identity theft further down the line).

You take your purse or wallet out of your pocket and slide your card into the cash machine. Don't forget to cover your PIN as you type it in...

Oh dear, you forgot to cover your PIN, we've got that on CCTV too – thank you.

Or, alternatively...

Well done, you covered your PIN, but unless you REALLY try to obscure what it is I've watched so many people enter PINs I can guess them with 97% accuracy just from watching the back of your hand.

Now the biggest risk for Zoe comes as she dips into the bank's network. Stay hidden, drop in, just for a second and... Thank you very much, I've now got your Name, Account Number and Card Number.

Time to find out if you've been naughty or nice... and off Zoe would go, into the ether, searching databases, newspapers, police records, public files, private files, drawing up a picture of you as a person from your digital footprint. Well... not just your digital footprint but also the footprints that have kindly been left behind in the snow by any organisation you've ever been in contact with.

And Zoe would blast through them all with ruthless efficiency until she made the decision.

Are you naughty or nice?

This particular man fell at the first hurdle. He was a banker. And that was enough for Zoe. She didn't care if he was counter staff or a city toff. Works for a bank. Ruined the country. Fair game. And on to the list he went, ready to be robbed at her leisure at a future date.

How long she kept this up for varied. Sometimes she set herself targets, sometimes she just found the one person who pissed her off. If she did, she would pack up shop and move on to stage two.

Sometimes... Zoe stopped in her tracks as she spotted a familiar face heading into the bank. It was the woman who had shouted at the kids in the library – only now she was, for some reason, child-free. Zoe couldn't resist. She tapped a button, took a photo of the woman's face and waited for her to put her card into the machine. The woman was third in the queue and Zoe drummed her fingers impatiently on the desk as she stared down the YouTube page, waiting for her quarry.

Finally, after what seemed like hours but had, in fact, been less than two minutes, the woman put her card into the machine. The first thing Zoe noticed was that the woman moved fast, the card in, the PIN entered, the cash amount requested, all happened in a flurry. She *was* fast. But Zoe was faster. In and out. She had the details and she flipped screens.

The woman had taken out three grand. Was that even possible? Well she had done it so Zoe guessed it must be. She grinned, knowing that was the sort of person that she loved to scam. But her grin fell from her face when she saw the name of the woman.

Zoe.

Zoe Zimmerman.

Zoe Zimmerman panicked, simultaneously pulling the plug on her carefully constructed set-up and scrabbling around inside her bag. Her purse. Where was her purse? This woman had been here and now she was there and she had stolen her fucking purse.

It was gone and, moments later, so was Zoe, shoving her belongings haphazardly into her bag as she sprinted through the library, down the stairs four at a time, barely keeping her feet from falling over each other as she sprinted out the front of the library and caught sight of the bank. But the woman was no longer inside.

"SHIT!" Zoe screamed at the top of her lungs. "SHITSHITSHITSHIT!"

People were staring, but Zoe didn't care. She spun in a circle, whipping her head left and right when she finally spotted the woman once more. And she was walking towards her.

"Hi Zoe," said Violet, holding out a purse that was stuffed with cash. "I believe this is yours."

Zoe's mouth opened. And closed. Then it opened again.

"My name is Violet Winters. You might have heard of me?"

Zoe closed her mouth and nodded slightly.

"I've being doing some research and I've heard about you too," Violet continued. "Judging by what just happened your reputation is justified."

People were beginning to move on now. The crazy shouty girl wasn't doing anything interesting so they began to wander off.

Zoe blushed slightly at the compliment.

"Fancy going for a drive?" asked Violet, still holding out the purse.

"Yeah." Zoe finally snatched the purse and shoved it in her bag. "Alright."

"Come on then... we'll need a car first. A really expensive one." Violet smiled.

Zoe grinned back and tapped her satchel. "That shouldn't be a problem."

5th September

Still 5 weeks to go…

nine

Violet pushed down the accelerator and immediately she and Zoe were pinned back in their seats as the car hurled them forward.

"You look like you're gonna puke," said Violet with a grin.

"I will if you keep doing that," Zoe frowned and stared out of the window.

"Six point five litre engine the rental guy said," Violet replied. "Whatever that means."

"What it means is that maybe you shouldn't have worn heels as high as that to drive it." Zoe's hand went to her mouth and the colour drained from her face.

"Nought to sixty in less than three seconds, the bloke said." Violet's foot slipped from the accelerator and the car lurched, the seatbelts locking. "He didn't say much about driving in heels. Although he looked the type."

"I can see the Ferraris do not suit madam," Zoe trying to sound posh and putting on a deep voice. "I think the Lamborghini Aventado may be the perfect choice."

Violet laughed and slowed the car down as they took the exit from the motorway. "Anyway, you better not vomit in the car, I need both of us to remain unsullied by your lunch."

Zoe relaxed a little, touching a button to lower the window. Everyone on the pavement was gawping at the car. At her. She blushed, punched the button to raise the window and turned away.

"Sooooo..." said Violet. "I have to ask... What's with the whole schoolgirl thing? I mean you've got to be... what? Twenty-two?"

"Twenty. And a bit." Zoe shifted in her seat, adjusting the seatbelt against the dress Violet had instructed her to wear. "It's camouflage. And it works. No-one is going to look for a hacker in the kids' section of the library. The rest is... it's..."

"Window dressing?" Violet nodded and checked her side mirror. Some joker in a BMW was itching to get past them. She slowed down to wind him up. "So how the hell do you hide those bad girls then?" Violet fluttered her fingers towards Zoe's chest.

The BMW was revving his engine and ducking out to see if he could find a point in the road to overtake.

"Sports bra. Industrial grade," said Zoe. "I get them specially made by a team of cross-dressers I keep locked in my basement."

Violet hammered out her staccato laugh. "Well, you've certainly developed a reputation, young lady."

Zoe raised her eyebrows.

"People up the chain have noticed you. They just didn't know how in God's name you were pulling it off."

"But you did?" said Zoe.

Violet said nothing, just eased the car to a halt at a traffic light. The engine idled with a noise that sounded like a tractor playing a sousaphone.

Zoe stared at her.

Violet watched the pedestrians start to cross the road.

Zoe couldn't take it any longer, "Okay, I give up. How did you work it out? It's obviously not that you were a better hacker than me because – well... you wouldn't need me if you were that good. So how the hell did you work it out?"

"I started from the bank," said Violet simply. "I started from the bank and looked at where I would go if I were going to rob the place. Where the surveillance would start. Once I had that figured out I just worked backwards until I found you."

"So you reverse engineered my disguise?"

"If you say so. Not to blow my own trumpet but I figured I'm a pretty smart cookie. If this was the way I would have pulled off the job, and you were doing something vaguely similar, then at the very least I wanted to meet you."

Zoe smiled with pride. She desperately wanted to impress Violet, to be allowed to be part of whatever job she had planned. The traffic lights changed from red to green.

Violet didn't touch the pedals, just sat in silence for a second before turning back to Zoe. "But the schoolgirl thing..."

"I've been approached three times," Zoe interrupted. "Three different gangs. The first two when I was still at school, sixteen and... these men were..."

"I've probably met them, I can imagine," said Violet. "But you were sixteen?"

"I can handle myself now but then I just panicked. The only way I could lose them was to learn how to blend in. Back into the crowds of school kids. Plus my sister Agatha always says I look about twelve so..."

"You kind of do. In a certain light."

There was a honking of horns behind them as Violet continued to ignore the green light. A crowd had begun to gather on the pavements on both sides of the road.

"Twice already today you've proved to be exceptional at all that computer malarkey and I would love to have you on the team. If you'd like."

Zoe stared, her eyes widening. This was it, the moment she'd been praying for since Violet had revealed who she was. She waited a split second, trying to play it cool, and then blurted, "What's the job?"

The blaring of horns stopped for a moment and was replaced by the slamming of a car door. Glancing in her mirror, Violet could see a man striding from the BMW towards their car.

"All in good time, darling." Violet placed her index finger on her lips. "Are you in or are you out?"

Zoe began to speak but the heavy *clunk* of the driver's door opening interrupted her. Violet had timed opening the door so that it coincided with the BMW man drawing level with the car.

She extended her arm out of the car and he stopped in his tracks.

She *tutted* and then snapped her fingers three times in quick succession, and the man came scuttling up to the car.

"Help me please," she said, affecting as posh an accent as she could muster. She winked at Zoe and the man leaned forward into the cockpit of the Lamborghini to see two beautiful women inside. "I said *help me please!*" Violet snapped her fingers one more time and the man gently took her hand.

Violet swung her legs out of the car, which was so low that real concentration was required not to break the illusion and show all the onlookers the colour of her knickers.

"Pull!" she barked.

The man gently pulled and Violet extricated herself from the car and drew herself to her full height which, given the four and a half inch heels she was wearing, was a damn sight taller than usual. Looking at the man for a moment, she knew that the choice of outfit had been perfect. If the little black dress, stilettos and too much make-up worked on Mr BMW it would certainly work on their next target.

Getting back into character, she sighed and finally made eye contact with the man. "You were... toot tooting."

He broke eye contact and didn't say anything so Violet continued. "Why, please?"

"Erm – well... I thought..." he began.

"You thought what?" she shouted. The crowd were all staring at them now. "That your dick was bigger than mine because of the car you drive?"

"Buh," was all he could manage.

Violet rolled her eyes and held out her hand. BMW man took it gently and reached forward to kiss it. Violet slapped him in the face. "No!" she shouted. "Help me back into the car."

The man did as he was instructed. Violet closed the door of the car and slammed the accelerator. As she did the lights flipped back from green to red, leaving the unsuspecting BMW driver to face the same abuse he had tried to rain down on Violet.

"Well?" asked Violet.

"I am soooo in," said Zoe.

ten

Lucas Vaughan stared across the road at the imposing Victorian terrace opposite, struggling to see through the bay window of his own office. The walk back had been uncomfortable, mainly due to the dire quality of the shirt and suit he was wearing. He squinted in the bright sun and scratched at the collar of his polyester shirt. Finally he spotted what he had been looking for: the two marks sitting in the reception area waiting for him. He took a deep breath. For some reason he felt nervous. And that wasn't right. This was the day: the culmination of all his hard work, all the hours he had put in. He took a deep breath as the pedestrian crossing turned from the red man to the green man and he walked slowly across the road.

It was because of the money he felt like this. Or rather it was because of the lack of money he felt like this.

Usually he would rent an office, dress it, employ a secretary. Usually he would get some samples of... well... of whatever the hell he was supposed to be selling. Usually he had three or four times more money to invest up front. Now every penny he had rested on the sale of an X-ray of an orang-utan's chest.

Lucas began to lengthen his stride. They were sitting in reception with his secretary, he told himself. There is absolutely no reason to be nervous. The marks have come back to buy the X-ray.

And what marks they were. Lucas always had a sixth sense for finding the perfect target. He knew the places they went to relax, the bars they would drink in, the restaurants they dined in. And Lucas was a member of all of these places many times over. After all, you never knew when you would need to be someone else. It always astounded him how easy it was to appear different: a moustache, a beard, a pair of thick glasses, a pair of round glasses, a dark-haired wig, the list was... well actually the list wasn't much longer than that.

He would reach the stage where he went in so often he recognised the staff. It was strange, he noted, that no matter how he changed his appearance they never recognised him. Either they really didn't know it was the same person in a different wig or, more than likely, they just weren't paid enough to care.

Unfortunately, in chasing money you also had to spend money and unfortunately he had been going through something of a dry spell. The cupboards weren't simply bare, they had been licked clean to the point where he had splinters in his tongue.

Reaching the office entrance he began to piece together his character for today. He reached forward and touched the carved golden plaque he'd had made.

Logan Price & Associates
Dealers in Obscurities & Ephemera

There was a time a couple of years ago when he could have afforded for the plaque to have been made of metal instead of plastic.

It was time. Lucas took a deep breath. After today he would be back at the top of his game. And...

He hurried through the porch and, as he strode through the office door, swept the blond hair of his wig out of his face. "Miss Nicholson," he began.

Miss Nicholson, a bird-like woman in her early twenties, raised a hand as if at school. "Mr. Price," she began, her voice thin and unusually high in pitch. "The gentlemen..." she waved over at the two men seated on a sofa against the opposite wall.

Lucas pretended to do a double take and threw a big, warm grin across his face. "Mr. Redford," said Lucas and grabbed the man by the forearm as he rose to his feet, shaking his hand vigorously.

"Mr. Price," Redford nodded back.

"Mr. Beeks." Lucas released his grip on the first man and grabbed the hand of the second, pumping it just as hard. "Please, please, come through to my office. I trust that my secretary has made you comfortable?"

"Er, no. Not really," said Beeks, a small rotund man with a wisp of grey hair that seemed to float above his otherwise bald head.

The three men began to make their way towards the door to the right of Miss Nicholson's desk.

"We've been here seven minutes," Redford glanced at his watch. The watch, Lucas was happy to note, was a beast: huge, metallic and very, very expensive. He resisted the urge to fall back on his old pickpocket ways and ushered the men through the door. "And not a sniff of a cup of tea."

Beeks shook his head. "Not what we expect."

"Not at all, what were you thinking, Miss Nicholson?" Lucas turned back to her and glared.

Miss Nicholson pursed her lips and gave a tiny shake of her head, her feathers ruffled. He wasn't surprised. If you want loyalty you had to pay for it and he had been promising to pay her last week's wages for three weeks. He wasn't even really sure why she kept turning up. But he was bloody glad she did.

"Gentlemen, please take a seat," he continued. He could feel himself relaxing into the role.

Beeks lowered his overfilled frame into one of the chairs and Redford crammed his bony backside into the other. Lucas smiled and picked up the phone on his desk.

"Would you care for a beverage?" Lucas managed somehow to stay just this side of smarmy.

"Chai Tea," Beeks said with a snort. "With milk. For both of us."

Lucas pressed a button on the phone and a digital ringing could almost be heard coming from the outer office. After three rings it was answered.

"Miss Nicholson, would you be so kind as to fetch our guest some tea?" said Lucas.

"Mr. Price, do you realise that I haven't been paid for over three weeks?" she replied, her voice high and shrill. Lucas glanced up at the men who were gazing around the office. Thank God they couldn't hear her.

"That's right, yes. As you know, there is going to be a delivery later this afternoon." Lucas covered the mouthpiece and whispered to Beeks and Redford. "She's concerned that you might want Darjeeling and we've run out."

"This afternoon, eh?" Miss Nicholson's voice was thin but it was still angry. "Those horrible men you're with are paying you then, are they?"

"Yes, yes. That's two cups of Chai Tea for our guests."

"We don't have any tea. We don't have any money for any tea. I drank the last cup of tea this morning so the only tea bag we have is in the bin."

"Perfect, well if you could stick the kettle on and brew that up that would be wonderful."

"What? Really?"

Lucas hung up before she could irritate him any further.

"So... gentlemen," he began, relaxing back into his chair, the only one in the room that offered any comfort whatsoever. "How is the restaurant business?"

"Moving forward," said Beeks.

"Slowly," added Redford.

Lucas nodded knowingly. He knew nothing of the restaurant business but he knew much of knowing nods. He added a sage-like rub of his chin. He would have rubbed his beard but this outfit hadn't called for the addition of a beard.

"And part of that slowness is down to you, Logan Price," said Beeks tersely.

"A very large part," confirmed Redford.

"Our business partner is very anxious to get the place open and start making money," Beeks continued. "The bar is stocked. The chef–"

"His work is exquisite." Redford smacked his lips. "And I am

56

quite the epicurean, Sir."

There was a knock at the door and Lucas called over for Miss Nicholson to come in. She entered carrying a tray with three cups, a milk jug and a teapot which, thankfully, was not as dirty as Lucas remembered.

"Thank you, Miss Nicholson, if you could pop it down on my desk I'd be grateful." Lucas waved his hand at the desk then, turning back to his gentlemen guests, said "I have some very good news for you both."

"That was what you said last time we were here, Mr. Price," Beeks snapped. "I wasn't even sure that we should give you the benefit of the doubt but..."

"Certain stories have come to light about a gentleman of your description," Redford interjected. "Stories that do not impress ourselves or our employer."

Miss Nicholson laid the tray on Lucas' desk before turning on her heel and fluttering out of the office.

"A misunderstanding, I'm sure," said Lucas. "There are many gentlemen fitting my description in Kilchester. And many fitting yours, Mr. Beeks, and, if I might be so bold as to say, yours too, Mr. Redford."

Beeks tried to interject but Lucas stood up and turned his back to them. "But I'll wager none of those people have what I have in that filing cabinet over there." Without turning around Lucas raised his right hand and pointed to the filing cabinet in the corner of the room. "Do either of you take sugar?"

Lucas began to feel his powers returning; he was back on top of his game. These two idiots were ripe for the picking. He would sell them the fake and then, if he was in a good mood, he might actually stand by his promise and pay Miss Nicholson.

The consensus came back that neither of the two wanted sugar. Which was probably for the best given that he had none. Lucas poured the tea into the first cup; there was a slightly unusual smell and he suddenly snapped back into the moment.

The tea bag. From the bin. Oh shit.

He poured a second cup and...was that something floating in the tea? He glanced at the third cup but decided he would pass, given the nature of the brew. Something outside caught Lucas' eye, something fast, yellow and noisy growled past the window.

He shook his head and lifted the milk jug, adding a little to each cup then turning to his guests. Lucas wasn't sure the smile he had balanced under his nose was convincing anyone.

Beeks and Redford took their cups of tea and began lifting the putrid liquid to their lips. Well, he'd had a good run, hadn't he? That it ended in this way wasn't the worst thing that could have happened. He gagged slightly at the thought of the horrid liquid sloshing down their gullets and finally sat back down in his seat to face the music.

eleven

"This is quite simply—" Beeks began loudly.

"The most wonderful Chai Tea I have ever tasted," said Redford in amazement. "I have never tasted its equal."

Beeks nodded. "We may have to pressure you into revealing your supplier so that we can have it in the restaurant."

Lucas opened and closed his mouth a couple of times but nothing in particular came out. Eventually he mustered a short, "Miss Nicholson is quite the secretary."

"So, what have you got in that filing cabinet of yours for us then?" Beeks sipped at his ashtray-infused brew happily.

There was a noise in the outer office, slamming doors, raised voices. Lucas closed his eyes. It was all going so well. For those twenty seconds, right there, it went well and then... More shouting. Miss Nicholson saying that someone isn't allowed to go in. Oh shit, who was it? Someone had caught up with him; that much had to be true. But how the hell did they find him here? Beeks and Redford frowned at one another but neither stopped drinking.

Lucas stood up and was about to launch into something when the door flew open and a woman walked in.

And what a woman. Lucas' eyes widened, his hand went

instinctively to straighten his hairpiece.

She stood in the doorway, a true femme fatale: the Jackie-O sunglasses and black dress. The three men stared unblinking at her. She slunk into the room swinging an attaché case, her ruby stilettos clicking on the polished floor.

"Why won't your staff park my car?" she barked at Lucas. "I've left it outside. The keys are in the ignition."

"Buh," Lucas began. "Wha?"

"It's yellow. Quite low to the ground... erm – oh, what did the man say it was called? Lamborghini." Violet took off her sunglasses and put one of the arms into her mouth, pouting as she did so. "Do be a dear and tell the little girl to sort it out will you?"

Lucas glared at Miss Nicholson as she stormed out in silence.

"Logan, darling, it's so good to see you." Violet tottered over to the desk, sat herself on the corner and crossed her legs dramatically. She leaned over and kissed him on the cheek. "Do you have what I came for?"

Lucas didn't have a clue but he could see both Beeks and Redford were quite happy, sitting there sipping their terrible tea and trying to catch a glimpse up this woman's dress.

"I was in the middle of a meeting I'm afraid," said Lucas, finding his feet. She was someone in the game. A conman. A conwoman. Like him. But a woman. In a fucking Lamborghini? "Would you care to wait in the office with my secretary whilst I conclude my business with these gentlemen?"

"With that ghastly secretary of yours? Certainly not. Don't mind me, though. I'll wait here. You don't mind do you, gents?"

Beeks and Redford flushed with embarrassment and shook their heads.

"I think we'll be done here in a few moments." Beeks stopped staring at Violet's chest long enough to glare momentarily at Lucas.

"Yes, I don't think we'll be here much longer," added Redford without bothering to avert his leering gaze.

"Gentlemen." Lucas sat back down in his chair. He was a professional. First he would handle the situation with Beeks and Redford and then he would handle the situation with this strange interloper. "And lady," he nodded to Violet, keeping his eyes on the tea drinkers opposite. "Let's cut to the chase. I have the item you're looking for if you have secured the funds to purchase it."

There was a sharp tapping noise as Violet drummed her fingers on the polished lid of her attaché case.

Beeks squinted at Lucas and he drew breath, "Mr Price, your reputation has been questioned. How do you respond to these accusations?"

Lucas stood up and walked over to the filing cabinet. He pulled at the top drawer, which protested then juddered open with a metallic *clack-lack-lacklack*. Lucas took out a large, brown envelope which he handed to the two men.

Violet said nothing, watching Lucas in action from behind a coy smile.

"I don't respond to any such accusations," Lucas said, removing an X-ray from within the envelope. "I will simply state that sometimes when one is asked to procure certain obscure items then one must rely on individuals one would usually cross the road to avoid." Lucas accidentally looked over at Violet, who in turn raised an eyebrow in mock-shock.

"This," he continued, "is a chest X-ray of Marilyn Monroe. Or, as you'll see if you look in the corner there, Marilyn Di Maggio – which was her married name when the image was taken."

Redford had already plucked a mahogany-handled magnifying glass from his inside jacket pocket and was examining it closely and with some reverence.

"November 1954," said Redford to Beeks, nodding enthusiastically. "The date's correct... my goodness."

Lucas handed over the envelope to Beeks, who snatched it greedily and took out the rest of the contents.

"Careful," said Lucas with a laugh. "You break it, you bought it."

He had them where he wanted them now, it was time to close the deal. "So, gentlemen. Seventy five thousand pounds and we have ourselves an accord?" Lucas perched himself across the desk to Violet, clapped his hands and had to concentrate hard not to start rubbing them together.

"Oh, I don't think so," said Beeks, slipping the two X-rays back into the envelope and handing it to Redford.

"I'm sorry, what now?" said Lucas, thrown for a moment. "I thought these were going to be on display, the centrepiece to your restaurant?"

Beeks nodded patiently. This was a man accustomed to wielding his power to negotiate. "They may be real and, frankly, they may not. This is not a risk myself or Mr Redford are willing to take and certainly not one our employer would endorse. As such, the best offer we can make you is seven fifty."

"Seven fifty? I don't quite follow…"

"Seven *hundred* and fifty pounds."

Violet stood up, walked over to Redford and plucked the envelope from his hand. "Mr Price," she purred. "There are eighty five thousand pounds in that briefcase. You can count it if you like."

"There'll be no need for that, Lady Emsworth." Lucas not missing a beat. Whatever her play was he liked it and he was going with it.

"What?" said Beeks. "But–"

"Miss Monroe was my heroine, you see, I couldn't see these fall into the wrong hands." Violet opened the envelope and turned her naked back to the men whilst holding up the X-ray of Marilyn Monroe's chest to the window, letting the light stream through it. "And Mr Price and I have done business on many occasions before. You may have reasons to doubt him but I do not."

Violet slid the X-ray back into the envelope and turned on her heel, marching across to Lucas and cupping his chin with her hand. "Pop the receipt in the post darling."

"Now wait a bloody minute," Beeks screeched. "We were here first."

Violet turned to him, affronted.

"Mr Beeks," Lucas said calmly, "Lady Emsworth is a long standing customer of mine. I happened to mention that I had acquired these for you when we were dining together last week. She expressed an interest but I told her they were not available. My word is my bond."

"Then where's your bloody bond now, boy?" Redford blurted. "They're ours."

"Gentlemen, I would have been happy to sell them to you but to come to my place of business, my home from home, and to insinuate–"

"I don't think they insinuated anything, they said you were a liar, darling," said Violet, cocking her head to one side and raising an eyebrow.

"Shut up, you," said Beeks, holding up his fist and wagging an outstretched finger at her. "We *need* these," he whined. "He *promised...*"

Lucas held up two flat palms.

"Well," said Violet, putting the envelope down on Lucas' desk. "Perhaps."

Beeks panted slightly and stared at the envelope.

"But on two conditions," she added.

"Name them, Lady... err..." he stammered.

"Emsworth."

"Lady Emsworth."

"Very well, a deal is a deal. I will leave my money with Mr Price for the other item we discussed but I will allow him to sell you the X-Rays of Miss Monroe."

"Very gracious of you," said Redford, whose nervousness was now so pronounced that not only had he turned beetroot but had also been moved to actually look Violet in the eye.

"Condition number one – you must apologise to dear Mr Price here for your previous slurs."

Beeks and Redford mumbled and burbled something virtually inaudible.

Violet clapped her hands. "Pardon? Louder please."

"I apologise," Mr Beeks said. "Unreservedly."

Violet glanced across to Redford and nodded.

"Absolutely," said Redford. "I apologise for any and all implications."

"And I think it would only be right to match my offer," said Violet finally.

"What?" Beeks blurted but then, catching himself, he breathed in then out then took another pass at his response. "It would be the right thing to do. Of course."

Redford glared at Beeks but Beeks was unmoved. "Do you want to tell Terry we failed? Because I don't."

"Excellent," said Violet. "Job done, then." And with that she trounced out of the room.

"Lady Ems–" Lucas almost chased her but Beeks and Redford were picking up their bags from the floor. Follow the girl or follow the money?

Lucas watched the door close and walked, stunned, back behind his desk.

twelve

Lucas Vaughan ran his fingers through his hair and let out a manic giggle. From the pile on his desk he picked up a wad of twenty pound notes. It was maybe a centimetre thick and the cash strap that held the bundle together had a number printed on it. And the number was one thousand.

Flicking the notes under his nose, Lucas inhaled deeply. No matter how many times he did that he never could quite grasp why people did it. The money smelled like... well, it smelled like the inside of the bag it had been carried in. Lucas slid it across the desk, putting it back with its eighty four brothers and sisters and turned his attention to the attaché case the mystery woman had left. Pulling it across the desk it was clear that it didn't contain quite as much money as she had claimed, but she had left it and presumably that was for a reason.

He could have sealed that con without her. But, damn, she just stamped on the accelerator and sold that shit. And now Mr Beeks and Mr Redford were half way across town with... well they had an envelope full of X-rays at any rate.

The attaché case had two catches and next to each were three digits. A combination was required. Lucas spun the tiny wheels a few times, testing some obvious combinations, but nothing dislodged. There was time for that. But first there was the small matter of the death of Logan Price.

Lucas opened one of the large, lower drawers in his desk and pulled out a bag before scooping the money and the attaché case into it and zipping it closed. He held the handles tight in his fist for a moment and stared at the door to the outer office. After a moment his glance flicked to the seats previously occupied by Beeks and Redford and the tea cups that now lay discarded on the floor by the chair legs. He sighed and let the handles of the bag fall from his grip.

Picking up the phone Lucas pressed a single digit and heard the electronic buzz in the outer office.

In the earpiece the ringing stopped but no-one spoke at the other side.

"Miss Nicholson?" said Lucas, not really sure if he was even connected.

There was a faint sigh.

"Would you be so kind as to join me in my office?"

The line went dead.

Lucas stared at the door but, for a moment, nothing happened. No footsteps, nothing. And then, at the point he was about to give up and leave, the door burst open and Miss Nicholson stormed up to the desk with a scowl on her face.

"Miss Nicholson, I want to say something and please, please, please, let me finish before you respond."

Miss Nicholson pouted in silence.

"Miss Nicholson, I'm not an honest man. But, if you'll allow me, I will be honest with you."

She raised an eyebrow and glared.

Lucas reached up and pulled the blond hairpiece from his head, revealing the short, mousey-brown hair beneath. He threw it into his bag.

"My name is not Logan Price, I'm not a dealer in obscurities and I never had any intention of paying you," Lucas winced as the words dropped into the room.

Opening her mouth to respond, Lucas jumped in to stop her,

"Please!" he said. "Don't hit me yet. You have shown more loyalty in the face of an overwhelming bastard than I have any right to have deserved and..."

Lucas lifted the bag on to the desk and unzipped one corner.

"Today is the last day I'll be requiring your services, as I'm going to be closing down the business. I have something for you."

He reached in to the bag, took out a single bundle and placed it on the desk in front of Miss Nicholson.

"Your wages," he said and slid the cash across the desk. Miss Nicholson caught sight of the amount on the strap.

Lucas reached in to the bag again and took out another bundle. He hesitated for a moment, staring at the cash before eventually pushing it over the desk as well.

"Your severance package," he said and pushed the cash towards her.

Miss Nicholson stared at it as if he had showed her his internet browsing history.

Lucas' hand was still in the bag. He stared at Miss Nicholson and she stared back, actually speechless.

"Those two men. Beeks. Redford. If you ever see them again they are going to be very angry," he said, a rare seriousness creeping in to his voice. "I want you to get out of town for a while and when you come back maybe think about retraining. I've only known you for eight weeks but I'm pretty sure you're worth more than this."

Miss Nicholson looked like she might burst into tears as Lucas threw another bundle of twenties over the desk.

And another.

She picked up the money and stared at him for a moment, then flicked through the bundles, just to be sure. It didn't take her long to realise that he had just given her four thousand pounds.

"The woman who was here," she said. "She told me to give you something. If you paid me."

"Wha–?" Lucas' jaw dropped.

"She said that if you left without paying me I should rip it up and put it in a bin you didn't have access to," she continued. "I'll admit I nearly did it anyway but then I thought..."

It was Lucas' turn to stare in silence. Miss Nicholson leaned over the desk and pressed a small card of some sort into his hand, then quickly planted the lightest of kisses on his cheek.

"I hoped you would turn out better than you were and, well, I suppose you did." And with that she turned and left the office.

Lucas waited for the sound of the outer office door closing and then took the attaché case back out of his bag. There were six numbers scrawled in blue biro on the otherwise empty business card Miss Nicholson had given him. He spun the corresponding tumblers on either side of the handle of the attaché case. It only took a moment and then *pop* and *pop* the two catches opened and he was finally granted entry into the case.

He wasn't hugely surprised to find that there wasn't any money in there. Instead, inside was a small business card printed with a single mobile phone number. Lucas turned it over in his hand. The paper was of a heavy stock and the number itself appeared to be embossed upon it.

No words, he thought, just a number. He hated to admit it but this woman, whoever she was, had his attention. What was he going to do? Walk away and phone it later?

Hardly.

The telephone receiver was in his hand and his fingers were dialling.

And then it rang. Which also wasn't hugely surprising, given that he had dialled the number a second earlier. And then it rang some more. And then, perhaps to keep him guessing, it kept ringing. Lucas was about to hang up when the answerphone kicked in.

BEEEEEEP. "Hello Lucas."

The hairs on Lucas' neck stood on end as the woman's voice said his name.

"We just met and, if everything went to plan and you aren't a complete tool, you'll be listening to this with a bag of cash sitting next to you right now."

Lucas' eyes flashed to the bag, suddenly feeling like the mysterious woman might be able to make things disappear out of thin air.

"I'm putting together a crew and I could use a man of your talents. If you're interested meet me at the cafe on the corner of 4th Avenue. It's opposite the entrance to the park if you know the one I mean."

"Oh yeah, I know the one," Lucas said, and then suddenly felt foolish for talking back to an answerphone message.

"I'll be there until half past two. If you don't show I'll assume you have bigger fish to fry."

There was another beep, this time presumably the one that you were supposed to leave a message after. Lucas hung up. So she was putting a team together. And what happened earlier was, he supposed, some sort of job interview. Right then, time to get sorted out and... Lucas' train of thought was derailed as he caught sight of his watch. It was twenty past two and the cafe in question was half way across town.

Grabbing the bag containing the money and shoving attaché case and cards inside he sprinted out of his office, past Miss Nicholson's now vacant desk and out into the street, slamming the outer door closed and fumbling with the keys to lock the place up. He would come back later in the afternoon and remove all traces of the business because for now he had to catch a –

"TAXI!" he screamed as two black cabs drove off down the street. Lucas picked one and started tearing after it screaming, "TAXI! TAXI! TAXI!" It was almost as if when you were inside a car you couldn't actually hear what was being said outside. Fortunately for Lucas, the traffic lights up ahead were on his side and stopped the cab, allowing him to catch up. He tapped as politely as he could on the window and the taxi driver nodded. The lights changed from red to green but the taxi driver didn't budge.

Lucas clambered into the back and told the driver the destination. "And please, it's imperative I arrive before half past two."

The driver looked at the clock on the dashboard and shrugged. "I'll do my best mate, I'll go as fast as I can."

The traffic lights turned from green back to red. The taxi driver scratched at his beard. Lucas closed his eyes and tried not to swear.

thirteen

Thankfully for Lucas, it wasn't rush hour. So, after the initial false-start, the cabbie really did start to motor across the city centre. But between traffic lights, speed cameras and the general idiocy of other drivers, progress just wasn't as fast as he needed it to be.

The clock on the dashboard read twenty seven minutes past two. The clock on his mobile disagreed and insisted it was twenty eight minutes past two. Either way, he didn't have time to risk the long road that skirted around the edge of the park. There was only one thing left to do and so, with a grimace, he slid a twenty pound note out of one of the bundles in his bag and handed it to the driver.

"Keep the change, mate," Lucas said, the words sour on his lips.

Slamming the taxi door, Lucas started jogging towards the park gates. He wasn't exactly what you would call a gym rat, but he did stay in shape. He was pretty sure that if he kept a steady pace he could make it to the other side of the park in time.

After a half a dozen paces Lucas decided to revise that hypothesis. He certainly could have made it to the other side of the park in time if he hadn't been wearing a pair of leather loafers. For a moment he considered following the lead of so many Hollywood films where the lady takes off her heels to run in bare feet. But one glance down at the shit that littered the path here in the real world, and he was certain he would rather risk being late.

*

Violet took her phone out of her bag and checked the time. It was two thirty one. Well, he'd had his chance. He was good but he wasn't the only person on the list.

She clicked her tongue on the roof of her mouth absent-mindedly. Something had been playing on her mind since the encounter at Lucas' office. Something other than pulling a crew together or planning the job. She had recognised at least one of the men Lucas had been conning. And what had he said their boss was called? Terry? There was only one Terry in Kilchester. Big Terry. Interesting.

"Can I get you another cup of tea, madam?" A waiter slithered from somewhere unseen, apparently summoned by the clicking, and interrupted her train of thought.

"No, I didn't want anything, I was just..." she began and then, realising she didn't need to explain herself to him, stopped herself in her tracks. "The bill?"

"Customers usually pay at the counter," he started to say. "But it would be my pleasure to fetch the bill for madam."

The outfit was still working, still making her the centre of attention.

And that made her uncomfortable.

The waiter's urgency evaporated the further away from Violet he got. She watched him as he reached the counter. Instead of getting the bill he began flirting with a waitress.

She could storm out. Except that she'd been there for half an hour. A quick glance around and she could spot three customers who had been here as long as her. And two security cameras.

She took a deep breath and put all thoughts of leaving without paying out of her head. Three people and two security cameras that could identify her if she was unlucky enough to get pulled. It was too early in the job to do something stupid.

No, she would wait for the bill and—

"YES!" A voice echoed around the walls of the small cafe and a man fell through the door. Drenched in sweat and apparently struggling to breathe, he was barefoot but held a suit jacket and a pair of loafers in one hand and a black sports bag in the other. "YOUR LADYSHIP!"

Lucas lurched forward toward Violet, who didn't respond other than to smile back at him. Perhaps she wouldn't tell him her real name. Perhaps he could call her 'your ladyship' for the duration of the job.

The waiter finally gained some momentum, perhaps fearing that the cafe's latest addition would somehow remove his customer's ability to tip.

"I'm sorry, Sir," he said, putting a palm on Lucas' chest. "But there's a two-shoe minimum in this cafe." The waiter turned to smile at Violet and Lucas took the opportunity to hang his jacket on the waiter's outstretched hand.

He stood for a moment, panting, and then, from the inside pocket of the jacket, Lucas took first one and then two socks. Staring the waiter down the whole time he rolled the socks on to his feet and then slipped on the loafers.

The waiter stood and stared. Apparently in his world this was not the sort of thing that generally happened.

Lucas finally took his jacket and hung it over the back of the chair opposite Violet. "I'll have a cappuccino and..." Lucas looked over to Violet, who leaned back in her chair and gave him a little nod. "And the same again for the lady."

"There's no table service," the waiter sneered.

Lucas turned away from Violet and whispered something in the waiter's ear. The waiter ran off into the kitchen.

Once he was out of sight and the conversations of the other customers had started up again Violet asked quietly, "What did you say to him?"

"I told him that I was sweating like this because I had just murdered someone across the other side of the park and if he didn't produce the drinks very quickly indeed that I would tear his arms off and beat him with the wet ends," said Lucas.

Violet laughed her staccato laugh.

"Really?" she said.

"Well," Lucas smiled and mopped his brow with a couple of napkins. "Something like that."

"As nice as it would be to go on being called your ladyship, I should introduce myself." Violet held out her right hand. "Violet Winters."

Lucas took her hand and shook it warmly. "It's a pleasure to meet you at last."

Violet nodded, "And you. Do I need to explain my background?"

Lucas shook his head. "No. Well, probably not. Your name – well, I heard about the diamond job."

Violet nodded.

"So...everything that happened...all that...was it a test?" Lucas said sheepishly.

"It's always a test, Lucas."

Now it was Lucas' turn to laugh.

"And the X-rays. They were some nice fakes," Violet added. "I assume you didn't go to the trouble of stealing the originals?"

"Hardly," Lucas said. "I saw some pictures online and, well... I know people."

"Ghost norks though? Really?" Violet raised an eyebrow as the waiter returned and placed the drinks in front of them. Lucas gave him another of his hard-won twenty pound notes and the waiter left.

"I know," he said. "It wouldn't have been my first choice but these guys were desperate for something different. When I first hooked them I had a list of a few things I'd researched. 'Give me something original' they kept saying. 'That's so obvious'. 'Don't they have that in that place in London?' And in the end I said it, almost as a joke."

"And they went for it?"

"First time."

"But it didn't seem to be going too well when I crashed the party." Violet lifted the tea pot and poured some tea into her cup.

"I could have handled it." Lucas bristled for a moment, then noticed the smile playing at the corners of Violet's mouth. "You might have... sped things up a bit. Thing is, it's pretty hard to come by X-rays without robbing a hospital and... well... what if you steal one from somebody who's really sick?"

"A conscience?" Violet gasped in mock-surprise.

"No," Lucas blurted. "Well, yeah... sometimes. So in the end I bribed someone at the zoo. And then this forger guy I work with, he doctored them for me."

"So the X-ray of Marilyn Monroe is actually..."

"An orang-utan called Betsie. I believe."

The waiter returned with Lucas' change, placing it on the table by his elbow and scampering away.

Violet looked down at the new cup of tea and her mobile placed carefully alongside.

"Actually, shall we take a walk in the park instead of staying put?" she asked. "Lots of eyes and ears in here."

Lucas nodded and gathered up his belongings.

Violet led the way, striding forward in the ridiculously high heels she was still wearing, with Lucas skittering along beside her. The cars were moving along slowly on the road outside the park and Violet drew to a halt at the kerbside. She stared into the oncoming traffic, fixing her gaze on the male driver and giving him the full blaze of femme fatale. There was a screeching of brakes and a blaring of horns as the traffic parted for her.

Kilchester Park was quite sparsely populated at this time of day, the lunchtime crowds having dissipated back to their offices and the parents still waiting in the schoolyards to pick their children up and ruin the tranquillity of the park. A hundred metres into the park and Lucas was checking for eyes and ears. After another dozen or so metres he was satisfied no-one could overhear them.

"So what's the job then?" he said softly.

"I missed this place," said Violet, absently. "The park I mean. It's odd isn't it, the things you miss. It's not even a very good park in the grand scheme of things, is it?"

"What? I thought..." began Lucas.

"I mean, Central Park in New York. Now that's a park," Violet went on, increasingly distant. "And London is full of them. Sprawling, brilliant places you could get lost in."

"Well, you could get lost here too," Lucas admitted and Violet looked over at him as if suddenly remembering that he was there. "I did once. But then, I was pissed."

Violet laughed. "I like Kilchester. It's my town. Or it used to be."

Lucas walked along with her, swinging his bag.

"And, I think it will be again." Violet inhaled the park air. It was part greenery, part squirrel shit and part cars belching their toxins on the other side of the bushes that concealed the railings. "You see, there's a job."

Lucas' eyes lit up and he ran his spare hand through his hair which, by this time, was never going to be made presentable unless someone hosed him down in a yard with something industrial.

"I thought there might be," he said. "Tell me more."

"All in good time," said Violet, taking her phone out of her handbag for a moment and glancing at it. Another hundred metres in front of them was one of the smaller gates out of the park and Violet started to make her way towards it. Lucas realised this was his last chance to get her to spill before the crowds robbed them of what little privacy they had. This was no time for subtlety. Lucas tried not to panic.

"Now's a good time for me," he blurted, trying to remain as cool as he could. "I mean, I passed the tests, didn't I?"

Violet was striding forward, picking up her pace, looking over her shoulder towards the fence on the edge of the park.

Lucas recommenced his skittering. He was pretty sure that the damned loafers were giving him blisters. Panicking, he blurted, "I gave that girl four grand," and then, sensing that Violet's pace and proximity to the edge of the park were a sign that he was being ditched, "Do you want a cut? Is that what this is about?"

Lucas could hear the traffic now, tearing up and down the small road that ran parallel to this section of the park. Next to the gate he could see flowers tied to the railings.

Violet stood on the threshold of the park and looked Lucas straight in the eye. "It was never just about the money. Not this job, Lucas. All I want to know is... are you in?"

And with that she turned and walked straight into the path of a speeding car.

fourteen

For the second time that day Lucas sprinted towards one of the park gates. He heard the revving of engines. He heard the howl of rubber against road like an angry mechanical monkey. Skidding to a halt at the park gates, he realised that he had screwed his eyes tight shut.

Daring to open them a crack, he was elated to see the figure of Violet. Not, as his imagination had already painted her, broken and bloodied, but standing, feet apart. Standing tall like a Valkyrie, staring down...

...an Aston Martin.

Lucas darted forward, almost drawing level with the car as Violet moved around it herself. She tapped on the driver's side window. It slid down to reveal a man in a suit with blue eyes and a shaved head.

"Barry," said Violet with a nod.

"Violet," said the man in the car.

"You were supposed to steal the Lamborghini," Violet pouted. "We set it up especially."

"Not really my style," said Barry, straightening his tie. "A little ostentatious don't you think?"

"So you stole this because you thought I wouldn't be able to predict what you were going to nick?" she said. Lucas was now standing behind Violet, craning to get a view of the interior of the car.

"You were parading that bloody gaudy yellow thing around the city centre all day. Doesn't exactly blend, does it?" said Barry smugly.

"Knows his stuff, does Barry," Violet said, finally reintroducing Lucas to the conversation. "The finest wheelman I've ever worked with."

Barry grinned, all stubby teeth.

"Only thing is," said Violet, pretending to whisper behind her hand to Lucas, "so predictable."

"Pfffft," said Barry. "Like hell. There's no way you knew that–"

"We both knew," said Zoe, appearing from the back seat.

Barry made a noise like an emu being woken unexpectedly at 3.30am.

"Fuuuck me," he squealed. "Who the fucking fuck are you? How long have you been there?"

Zoe blew Barry a kiss. "Since before you nicked the car."

"How the shitting hell do you do that, Violet?" Barry panted. "You're like Derren Brown or some shit."

"Are you in, Barry?" said Violet.

"Course I fucking am. Get in."

Violet moved and opened the passenger door. "Lucas?"

Lucas nodded.

"In the back with Zoe," said Violet. "And no fighting, you crazy kids."

*

An industrial unit in the East End of Kilchester was hardly the most glamorous of headquarters, but Violet knew from experience that it was a hundred per cent more useful than hiring a city centre office. The comfort and convenience of a swanky office had to be balanced against the fact that the crew would be much more exposed to surveillance from rival gangs or even the authorities.

So that was where, with Violet's guidance, Barry had driven them. Outside there was a faded sign, half falling off the wall, announcing that the business was Brian Wade's Bubble Wrap. Unfortunately for Brian, like a lot of businesses in the East End, his business had gone to the wall when the country's recession had turned into a global financial apocalypse. His loss, however, was definitely Violet's gain.

She hopped out of the car and walked over to the single door. Fishing a key from her handbag, she opened it and disappeared inside.

Barry, Lucas and Zoe stared at the front of the factory unit, waiting. After a couple of minutes the roller shutters that constituted the majority of the rest of the unit began to rise. Barry eased the car inside and the three of them got out. The interior of the unit wasn't much more sexy than the outside. Barry parked the car in the loading area, which was probably large enough to accommodate three or four cars. Beyond that there were stacks of metal shelving, some filled with boxes spilling plastic bubble wrap onto the floor.

Lucas surveyed the scene with a vague sense of dismay. Even his cheap, plastic office had been nicer than this. Over by the car Barry began to clear the detritus, shifting anything that might fall away from his precious, stolen car.

"It's an Aston Martin Rapide," said Barry, noticing Lucas looking at him. "I figured we'd need a four-door and most don't have a usable space in the back."

"So you knew it was a trap?" asked Lucas.

"Trap? Nah," Barry stared at Lucas, the cogs turning in his head. "She doesn't do traps. I saw the yellow Lambo... figured she had a plan... wasn't a trap. It was more of a test I suppose."

"But you knew it was her?"

Barry stretched, pushing back his shoulders and causing his beer belly to extend. He dutifully scratched at it.

"You've worked together a lot, then?" Lucas ran his hand along the wing of the car but stopped when he saw Barry had started frowning.

Barry made a noncommittal noise at the back of his throat. Then took a clean rag from the inside of his jacket and started rubbing the spot Lucas had touched.

"You wait," he continued. "I just got a Mark One Ford Escort.

Fucking beautiful. I'll bring it down here and have a bit of a tinker while everything's coming together."

Lucas nodded. It seemed like the correct response.

Barry returned his attention to his new acquisition and Lucas nodded again, pretending to be interested in what Barry was doing. He wasn't what you would call a 'car person'. He was more of a 'call me a taxi, I'm pissed' person.

Right now, Lucas wasn't sure if being 'in' was the greatest decision he'd ever made. What exactly was he 'in'. Barry didn't seem concerned as he turned his attention back to clearing a space for the precious car, and Zoe, how old was she? She looked about twelve. She was glued to her mobile phone, standing in the corner. Probably texting, Lucas thought. He never did quite get the hang of texting, putting it down to the fact that his thumbs were too big to accomplish the task.

"Just updating your status?" Lucas asked Zoe. "'Just about to find out what criminal enterprise I'm about to get myself into. Lol.'" Lucas grinned like an idiot.

Zoe looked at him with pity in her eyes. "I was using my phone to see if there were any usable internet connections we can piggyback on."

Lucas dropped the grin on the floor. "And – erm – did you?"

Zoe shook her head and her fringe dropped in front of her eyes. "No," she said. "But it just means I'll have to run a spur off the junction box at the end of the street."

"I was going to pretend I understood that," said Lucas. "But then I thought, no, that will make me look like an idiot again."

Zoe laughed. "I guess we're all here for a reason."

"Speaking of being somewhere for a reason," Barry wandered toward her. "How did you know I would steal *that* car?" He pointed over to it.

Zoe dropped her arm to her side, her phone held tight in her hand, giving Barry her full attention.

"I'm not sure I should tell you," said Zoe.

Barry nodded and stared, waiting for the assistant to reveal the magician's trick.

"Oh, fuck it," Zoe went on, puncturing the suspense. "Violet reckoned that she knew you were following us."

"Were you?" Lucas said, a little too loudly.

"Yeah, mebbe I was." Barry scratched the back of his shaved head then ran his hand forward across what little stubble remained.

"Violet parked the car a few bays away then broke into the Aston. I hopped in the back and locked it from the inside."

"But *how* did she know," whined Barry. "*I* didn't know. Not until I got in there."

Finally, Violet re-emerged from whatever back office area she had been in, and strode back out amongst the three of them. She had changed out of the little black dress and instead wore simple black jeans and trainers and a black biker jacket.

"Oh, come on, Barry," she said. "It wasn't that hard to know which one you'd go for. You're a man of habit."

Barry raised his middle finger towards Violet and then pretended to scratch the corner of his eye with it. Violet stuck her tongue out at him.

"Anywaaaaaay," said Violet. "You'll be wanting to know why I've chosen you, I expect? Well, as clichéd as this undoubtedly sounds, this is a high-risk, high-reward job. I've done some initial planning and we'll need five people in our crew to pull it off efficiently."

Barry, Lucas and Zoe drew closer, nodding, a seriousness descending upon all of them.

And then Violet explained to the three of them what Fegan had proposed to her: the Dali, the fakes, the banker, the security, the bunker. All of it.

Afterwards they stared at her with the faintest of frowns decorating each of their brows.

"So," said Barry eventually. "And don't take this the wrong way..."

Violet arched her left eyebrow and stared at Barry.

"But," he continued, unperturbed. "You do have a plan?"

Violet continued to stare at him under the single raised eyebrow. "Nope," she said finally.

Lucas' mouth opened and closed a couple of times as he tried to process the enormity of doing this thing blind.

"Has today taught you nothing? Of course I've got a fucking

plan." Violet lowered her stray eyebrow and winked at Barry. "When have you ever known me not to have a plan? In fact the final details of the plan crystallised as I was leaving Lucas's office."

"Thank Christ for that," replied Barry. "Because Lucas here thought we were fucked, didn't you boy?" Barry playfully slapped Lucas in the stomach with the back of his hand.

Lucas tried not to give away the fact that he might be winded.

"Not only that," added Violet. "We've got a backer. Which means that all I need from you lot are your skills."

"And on the down side our cuts will be considerably reduced?" Lucas laughed at the shared joke. No-one else did.

And then Violet told them how much they were each in for. Zoe giggled. Lucas and Barry just stared.

"So, right up front I'm going to need you to get floor plans for the place, alright Barry?" Violet engaging them, drawing them all in.

Barry nodded. "Course."

"Everything. Gas, water, sewage, electric, phone. It's a bunker, so even the air has to get in there somehow and, if it does, then someone has drawn it and filed it somewhere and I want them all."

"I'm on it."

"Zoe," Violet continued. "Get this place set up and kitted out with whatever computer shit we're going to need."

"Computer shit?" Zoe put her hand on her chest as if wounded. "This is my art."

"And that's why you're here," said Violet. "We've got funding but it is *far* from unlimited. Also there's one thing I can't stress enough – I don't want any of you pulling any cons or robbing anyone while we're preparing. Not without my green light. And that goes double for you two gentlemen. Understood?"

"Understood," Lucas and Barry choroused.

"I'm not above conning or robbing the extras we need but anything that I don't specifically say yes to is strictly off limits. We can't afford to get drawn into anything extracurricular. This is going to be hard enough to pull off without third party interest. Once you're set up here, Zoe, I want you to collate everything Barry has pulled and I want you to take point on the security. Nothing needs to be cracked yet but we need to know what we're facing."

"Affirmative," said Zoe.

"Lucas," said Violet, and Lucas felt a swell of pride in his chest. "First thing I need you to do is introduce me to your forger."

"Oh," said Lucas, suddenly deflated. "Okay. He doesn't live far from here. We can probably walk."

"You'll have to," said Barry. "Cos that's not leaving here until the plates are changed."

"Oh yeah," said Violet. "Couple more cars and a van please Barry. Clean them up, get them ready and bring them here. Everything clear?"

Everyone nodded.

"Any questions?"

Lucas slowly raised his hand and asked, "Who's the fifth person?"

Violet tapped the side of her nose with her index finger. "All in good time, Lucas."

12th September

4 weeks to go…

12th September

4 weeks to go…

fifteen

"You see, that's why I work with Lucas. He always has something interesting for me, don't you son?"

"Son?" said Violet in mock-surprise. "You're Lucas' father?"

Damien ran his tattooed fingers through the grey mop of his hair. He stood in front of a half-finished painting, in streaked overalls and an equally decorated vest that had probably been white once upon a time. Through the gaps in the material Violet could see more tattoos. Full sleeve designs in bright colours, something that disappeared inside the vest and reappeared at the neck line, rising almost to his jawline. "Cheeky slag!" he said. "How old do you think I am?"

Violet began to respond but Damien cut her off. "It's just a phrase, isn't it? Like if I called you 'pet' doesn't mean you're a dog, does it?"

"Call me 'pet' and I'll show you just how vicious this dog can get," said Violet.

"Is this bitch serious?" Damien directed the question to a worried looking Lucas.

"She's very serious," said Violet calmly.

Damien put his brush down on a large table, then walked over to Violet, disregarding Lucas who had chosen instead to shrink away from the pair of them.

"I was asking him," Damien sneered. He wasn't much taller than Violet but this close she could see the muscles under the tats.

"And that was extremely rude of you," said Violet, stepping forward the last couple of paces to save Damien the bother. "Speak to me," she continued and then, saying the words slowly and letting them linger in Damien's face, "I'm. Right. Here."

"And what if I decide I don't want you here no more? What if I decide that whatever you want me to forge is beneath me?" said Damien, calling her bluff. He lifted his hand level with his chin. This close, Violet could see the detail in the tattoos. The individual spirals, where the hair grew out of the bright blue ink on the back of his hand. "What if I take this fist and beat you black and blue with it?"

"Not. Going. To. Happen," maintained Violet, unmoved.

Lucas looked like he might very well piss in his pants. He stood at the far side of the room, a look of complete panic on his face.

"Oh yeah, why's that then, Miss Cocky-pants?"

It took less than two seconds. Violet grabbed Damien by the wrist and moved around him, twisting it up his back. In one fluid movement she slammed him down on the table then jumped forward, landing her knee in the small of his back. Damien gasped for breath, winded by the force of his stomach hitting the table.

As he rasped and struggled for breath, Violet reached her left hand into her pocket and brought a small aerosol out before finally leaning forward and bringing it level with Damien's eyes.

"This is gunpowder-propelled pepper spray gel. If you try anything. ANYTHING," Violet hissed, "like that, I will empty the contents into your eyes. At this distance, that isn't going to be something that will just rinse away with a little eye bath. This will fracture your skull and pop your fucking eyeballs. You will be blind. You will have no eyeballs. Do you enjoy your eyesight?"

Damien nodded slowly, his breathing starting to return to normal.

"And I would imagine you need one or both of your eyes to do what you do here?"

Damien nodded again. He tried to flex slightly, seeing if there was any give in Violet's grip. But there was none.

"So how about we try this situation again, only this time you cut out the parts I don't like. How about this time you show me some respect?"

Damien didn't respond. Violet twitched her index finger and the tiniest bubble started to form on the nozzle of the pepper spray aerosol an inch from his open eye.

"Fuck me, NO! PLEASE!" Damien screamed. He tried to writhe free but Violet's whole weight was on his back so, although he moved her, the spray stayed firm in front of his face. After a couple of seconds he went limp again. "Alright, alright."

"You're sorry?" Violet asked politely.

"Yes. I'm sorry," he said. "Now let me go."

Violet hopped down and pocketed the pepper spray.

Damien stood up, shaking himself off like it was nothing. He turned to Lucas. "I like her. She's fucking crazy."

Lucas nodded and then, suddenly realising that might not have been the right response, looked over to Violet, who just rolled her eyes.

"You must be pretty good for people to put up with your shit," said Violet to Damien.

Damien nodded, "Right back at you."

"Really?" said Violet with a sigh. "You want to go again?" She reached into her pocket once more. "It'll still hospitalise you from across the room..."

Damien held his palms up in surrender. "Whoah, I'm just kidding. We're good."

"Right then, shall we get down to business?" said Lucas, his voice cracking only slightly. "What's this you're working on?"

Damien shrugged. "Personal project," he said.

Violet walked over to the canvas, which was daubed with bright streaks of paint. Behind it were prints of other pictures, some of them she recognised.

"Picasso?" she asked.

"The very same," Damien replied. "Had an idea that there might be an undiscovered work out there."

"Sounds like a decent con." Lucas began to feel more confident and tried to keep the conversation on safer ground. "Reckon you can pull it off?"

"I dunno." Damien stared intently at his partially completed work. "Not with this one. It's harder. Well, don't get me wrong, doing a copy ain't no fucking picnic but at least you've got something to work from. Trying to convince the art world that one of the most famous painters in the world did something and they didn't know about it…It's a pet project. Might take a bit longer."

"How long?" said Violet, picking up one of the photos from the table.

Damien shrugged. "Few more years maybe. So what exactly is it you want me to do for you?"

"A Dali," said Lucas, eager to continue this new and less threatening tack.

Damien nodded appreciatively.

"Will I have access to the original?"

Violet shook her head. "We'll get photographs. That a problem?"

"Shouldn't be," said Damien, putting down the Picasso pictures. "Is it a famous one?"

"Not really," said Violet. "It's blank. Almost."

"Blank? And you need a forger for that. Lady you must be–" Damien caught himself and stopped talking. When he started again it was with a slightly softer tone. "Tell me more."

And so Violet explained. Told a rapt Damien about Dali's greed and about how he had signed and signed and signed. She told him about the fakes and the originals and how in some cases even the experts didn't know which was which. And finally she told him about the canvas. The one that was different.

Damien took a packet of cigarettes out of his overalls. He offered the packet to Lucas and Violet, who both shook their heads. Taking one out, he shoved it between his lips and lit it.

"Does it need to pass close inspection?" he said, directing his question to Violet.

"Absolutely. No-one can know it's a forgery, inside or outside of the art world."

Damien exhaled smoke and laughed. "In that case we're going to need the right canvas. Get the paper wrong and we're fucked from the word go. I can get the paints, that's not a problem, but the canvas you'll need to source."

"Right," said Violet. "Not a problem. What do we need?"

Damien sucked on the cigarette and stared at her. "I'm good. But I ain't that good. Need to do a bit of research. Give me your number and I'll text you once I know."

Violet grabbed a pencil and a scrap of paper and scribbled down her number.

"I knew she liked me really," Damien pretended to whisper to Lucas. "And it'll cost you–" he began to say to Violet.

"–the same as you charge Lucas," Violet finished his sentence for him. "If you behave yourself and do a good job I might leave you a tip."

Damien laughed a cloud of grey smoke into the air. "Oh, it'll be a good job."

"What if you make a mistake?" Violet took a half a step back, away from the smoke Damien was exhaling.

"What do you mean?" Damien clenched his free hand into a fist once more.

"Cool your jets, cowboy." Violet smiled at him. "If I'm going to steal something I don't want to have to do it twice."

"What do you mean?" asked Lucas.

"I know what she means. If you're doing something bigger and you make a mistake you can cover it up. You can paint over it, blend it, you know, that sort of thing."

"Right," said Lucas.

"But for minimalist stuff like this, you know, Matisse, that sort of thing," he continued. "You get one chance. The brush hits the canvas and it's done. So in the unlikely event that I fuck it up..."

"But if I get you enough canvas..."

Damien ground the last of his cigarette into a nearby ashtray. "If you get me enough canvas I'll..."

"Do us two?"

"What? Piss off."

"Jesus," said Violet. "Are you sure you can actually do this?"

"Course I can fucking do it. And if you can nick enough canvas I'll do you two that are so fucking perfect you could use the signature to cash a cheque in a dead man's name. Okay?"

Violet nodded. "When will you text?"

Damien scratched his chin and stared at her. "Tomorrow afternoon."

Lucas thanked Damien profusely and, in an entirely obvious attempt to prevent further conflict, ushered Violet out of Damien's work space as fast as he could manage. When the door was closed, Damien drew two large bolts across it and stared at the back for a moment before wandering over to a set of small drawers and taking a mobile phone from one of them.

He stared at the phone for a second then started tapping at it. A few moments later he pressed a button to dial and raised the phone to his ear.

"Hello?" the voice at the other end echoed as if its owner was in a bathroom.

"Percy? It's Damien."

"Alright mate," said the voice. "How's tricks?"

"Not bad," said Damien. "Not bad at all. Fingers in pies. You know how it goes."

"Yeah. Course," said Percy. "Listen, I don't mean to be rude but I'm right in the middle of something. You after a favour?"

"Nah," said Damien. "Think you're going to owe me one though. Know that bitch you were looking for?"

The line went quiet for a second. "Violet?" Percy said eventually.

"Just left the studio. Looks like she's back in town. And she's doing a job with Lucas."

"And it was definitely her?" asked Percy.

"Crazy bitch nearly broke my arm and blinded me," said Damien.

"Sounds like her," Percy conceded. "Thanks, man. I owe you."

sixteen

Violet sat in the passenger seat of the van and touched the screen on the iPad in her lap. It blinked as she opened up the folder which held all the accumulated information about their target and the owner of the painting: Rollo Glass. The head of the Kilchester Bank, and here was his life laid out in front of her. When she could get the thing to work. Violet had been keen to go with paper folders. Traditional. Classic. But Zoe had had other ideas and had furnished them with iPads.

As Violet saw it, Glass was greed personified. A while ago she had been talking to a friend of hers who explained how the delicacy *foie gras* was made by force feeding corn to a goose. Rollo Glass' CV was the business equivalent. At fifty- four years old, Glass had gone into dozens of businesses and, in his financial capacity, force fed them until they were, at least from the outside, the very picture of a money making machine. And then? Sell it and move on.

It wasn't a perfect metaphor but it was what Glass' business style amounted to from Violet's perspective.

Outside of work... well, the initial research hadn't suggested there was a great deal to say about his social life and the weeks' worth of surveillance they had done backed that up. He was a man of routine and he was a man who worked long, long hours.

Out of the house at seven, into the office for around seven thirty. Lunch was at twelve sharp. From credit card records Zoe had already hacked they could see the small circle of eating establishments he preferred. All of them were high-end, high-price, ostentatious affairs.

An hour of troughing and quaffing either on his own or with one of the other executives and he was back to the bank until six thirty. The car would come to pick him up and take him to a restaurant to shovel more slops into his snout and then he would roll out, half-cut and belching, back into the car and home.

Rinse and repeat.

As a criminal, Violet didn't need a moral reason to steal from someone. It was just nice when someone as unpleasant as Glass was brought into view.

There were worse people in the world, of course there were. But most of them didn't collect obscenely expensive works of art and hang them on the sitting room wall.

Glancing at the clock on the dashboard, Violet noticed it was coming up to six twenty five. She fixed her gaze on the revolving door that was the primary entrance to the bank, and her mind started to drift. This was the worst part of the job. The watching. The waiting. It was so tedious but so necessary. Experience had taught her that if you left this surveillance to chance then you were storing up problems when you actually pulled the job. What you didn't want was the target turning up unexpectedly because you hadn't taken into account that they went to Karate classes every other Wednesday and not every Wednesday as you thought.

A thunderous metallic sound shook Violet back into the moment as the sliding side door of the van opened.

"Evening," said Zoe as she stepped out of the chill of the autumn night. Violet could hardly see her in her black jeans and bomber jacket.

"I was wondering when you'd be back. Did you bring some food?" asked Violet, before turning her attention back to the revolving doors.

"Nah, I forgot, sorry," Zoe replied with a shrug. "But I've got something better than food."

"At this stage," Violet sighed, "nothing is better than food."

Zoe rolled her eyes, closed the van door and started unzipping her backpack and removing items that Violet couldn't quite make out in the gloom.

"This," said Zoe to the back of Violet's head, "is a long range, directional microphone. Really it's two microphones. One at the pointy end you point at the person you are going to listen to and one at the – erm – arse end that sucks in all the extraneous noise and then cancels that out meaning that, more or less, all you get is the sound of the target.

"Which is whatever you point the pointy end at?" asked Violet without looking.

"Yup," said Zoe. "And I'm going to fit this up here just behind the driver's headrest so we should be able to wind the window down a crack, choose our direction and then..."

"Spies are us."

"Damn right," Zoe nodded. "But there's more."

"I was afraid there might be," Violet let out a huge sigh. "If only there were more food."

"Food's on me after this," Zoe replied and then, leaning over Violet, she clipped something small and blank to the corner of the windscreen on the driver's side. "That is a camera," she continued, taking the tablet from Violet and tapping the screen. It elicited responses Violet was hitherto unaware a tablet could produce. A live video feed of what was going on in front of them sprang up on the iPad's screen.

"See?" said Zoe, clearly very impressed. "Video and audio streams directly on here and there's a digital copy back at headquarters."

"Headquarters?"

"Well 'back at the factory unit' sounds much less glamorous."

"Fair point."

There was a *vrrrrrrm* noise and Violet reached forward and picked her mobile phone out of a cup holder.

She read the message on the screen then handed the phone to Zoe. "It's from Damien."

Zoe frowned.

"The forger?" said Violet.

"Oh yeah, him," Zoe looked down at the text then reached into her bag and took out a laptop. She quickly powered it up and the rattle of her rapid fire typing echoed around the interior of the van. "So this is the canvas we'll need, then?" she asked, pausing briefly to hand Violet's phone back before returning to hammering at the keyboard some more.

"Yeah, we'll have to see where we can source it." Violet sighed and stretched one of her arms, causing her shoulder to make an odd *pop* noise. "I think it can wait until the morning, though."

"You're alright," said Zoe, not bothering to make eye contact. "I'll see what I can find now."

Violet shrugged and went back to watching the revolving door.

"Oh, and there's more," said Zoe. "I've been digging around in the banker's finances. And there are discrepancies."

"Which is ironic."

"Quite." Zoe continued tapping away at the laptop as she spoke. "Amongst the myriad ways that he tries to avoid tax..."

"Why am I not surprised?" asked Violet.

"You don't get to be rich by giving your money away," Zoe replied, the light from her screen creating an unnatural pallor on her otherwise youthful face. "Anyway, we could probably use this one to our advantage."

"Tell me more." Violet looked from the tablet in her lap to the revolving door and back again.

"Well, Glass didn't want to pay tax on some of the paintings he owns. So through some complex accounting manoeuvre he actually *looks* like he didn't buy them. I won't go in to the details."

"Thank God for that," said Violet.

Zoe looked up from her search to smile a patronising smile back at her. "I wouldn't want to confuse your tiny brain with such complex machinations."

"Eh? What does that mean?" asked Violet, before turning to Zoe and going cross eyed.

"So instead of buying them he 'inherits' them," Zoe continued, unperturbed. "And to avoid paying tax on the inheritance he puts them to the tax man as what is known as 'conditionally exempt works of art'."

"Yes!" said Violet and pumped her fist in the air.

"You don't know what that is, do you?" asked Zoe.

Violet shook her head.

"Well, neither did I, but I did some research and it effectively means that if you are on that list and you don't pay the tax then you and me and the rest of the general public have the right to go and view the painting."

"That can't be right," Violet said, surprised.

"Honestly, I couldn't really believe it myself at first, but it's a thing. I phoned up the Inland Revenue and asked them and they said yeah, if we ask to see it then he is legally obliged to let us view the damn thing."

Violet stared at Zoe for a second. "You're winding me up, aren't you?"

"No, no, I swear and I've been in contact with his secretary," Zoe went on.

Violet laughed. "That's really bloody bizarre."

Zoe glanced upwards and pointed to the bank; Violet turned too. Rollo Glass was prising himself out of the revolving doors, his belly threatening for a moment to become stuck there, and then the doors ejected him onto the pavement. There was another man with him, tall and muscular. Probably some sort of security personnel. Zoe adjusted the microphone direction and suddenly the sound of the two men's conversation crackled out of the iPad's speakers.

"...to the opening of that new restaurant across town?"

"Probably head straight home to be perfectly honest." Glass spoke with a clipped, upper class accent.

"No problem, Sir." The other man was American. Or had been at some stage, Violet thought she could hear Cockney creeping in at the edges as he continued. "Would you like me to accompany you or–"

"No. No need. Not tonight," Glass replied before stepping into a waiting car. The other man closed the door and tapped on the roof of the car. It pulled away from the curb and into the evening.

Violet quickly sent a message to Barry to follow up at the other end.

"So, where were you?" asked Violet. "His secretary?"

Zoe nodded. "Yeah, she was a little confused at first but I explained it all to her, told her who to contact at the tax office and all that. Told her I was an art student studying at the university."

Violet shook her head in disbelief.

"Away she goes to check and she calls me back a couple of hours later to say 'no problem' and would I like to come and view the painting the day after tomorrow?"

"Not enough time to set ourselves up for a snatch, but a great little surveillance opportunity nonetheless." Violet's eyes were wide and she kept shaking her head in disbelief.

"My thoughts exactly," said Zoe. "With the damned place being underground it'll give us an unprecedented level of access. And, well, if I get the chance maybe I might be able to leave one or two little electronic devices behind. We'll just have to see how that goes. Oh, and while I'm doing that you might want to pay a little visit to Kilchester Museum."

"Any particular reason?" asked Violet, hopefully.

"Of course," said Zoe, pointing at her laptop screen. "Turns out they have the canvas you need in storage there. I just accessed their computer system and... you know..."

"And the information you needed just fell out of the internet into your computer? I'll wager that shit's illegal, young lady."

Zoe let her mouth fall open and placed a hand on her chin. "The very suggestion!"

"Well," said Violet, clapping her hands together. "I think that little coup means that dinner is, in fact, on me this evening."

"I'm not arguing with that," said Zoe before beginning to stash all the electronics she had distributed throughout the van since her arrival. Unzipping her bag she panicked for a moment, hunting for her purse, and then looked up to see Violet unzipping it and rifling through in an exaggerated manner. "How do you do that?"

Violet laughed and threw it back to her. "Misspent youth."

Zoe shook her head and shoved the purse into a deeper pocket of her backpack. Violet turned her attention back to her phone and began to text the final member of the crew.

Katie. I'm back. Did you miss me?

seventeen

The maitre d' of the as-yet-unopened Legends restaurant closed his eyes and took a deep, deep breath. The place would never again smell as new as it did at that moment. People talked about the 'new car smell' but that was so common, so... *vulgar*. So few people in the world could truly appreciate the 'new restaurant' smell. And certainly none of the people who had reservations for this evening. They were just restaurant tourists.

Changing his perspective, the maitre d' listened to the silence. There was nothing. He listened closer and could hear the sounds of his breathing, the slight squeak of his brand new, handmade shoes. If he really strained he could hear the faintest chinking noise, talking, and, most importantly, cooking drifting from the kitchen hidden far behind an unseen wall.

Eyes still tightly closed, he reached out his hand and touched the Egyptian cotton of the tablecloth next to him. Slowly his hand slid to the cutlery, the solid weight of the soup spoon, the fork, and, being careful not to damage his perfectly manicured finger on the serrated teeth, the brand new steak knife. He felt a thrill as he gently ran the pad of his index finger down the edge of the blade, each tooth so sharp it almost tore the flesh.

Finally, he opened his eyes to gaze upon the centrepiece. There, framed and backlit, were two X-rays of Marilyn Monroe. The fact that both bore her married name, DiMaggio, was a detail he would relish sharing with customer after customer.

Perfect. He thought.

"What time are we opening?" a voice with the texture of a pebble-dashed Rottweiler asked.

The maitre d' jumped and spun around.

"*We* are not yet open," he snapped and, pointing to the door, "I would politely ask *you* to leave, Sir." The maitre d' dropped his gaze from where he expected the person to be down to where he actually was. Before him stood a man, he could tell by the goatee and moustache that surrounded his mouth. But it was a man who was no more than four and a half feet tall. Making his first mistake, the maitre d' broke into a grin.

The man stared up at him and blinked slowly a couple of times. His eyes were dark brown, almost black, and he wore a light blue shirt and darker blue waistcoat and trousers with black, dress shoes. He ran his hand over his head; it was shaved bald to the extent that the lights glinted off it.

"I'm sure Sir doesn't have a reservation," the maitre d' smarmed, sliding around the small gentleman until he was standing on the other side of him. "Now I shouldn't like to cause a *big* problem out of such a *little* issue." Making his second mistake, the maitre d' stifled a giggle.

The midget didn't budge. Didn't turn. Just kept staring at the spot the maitre d' had previously occupied and sighed.

"Beeks. And Redford. Where are they?" he growled.

The maitre d' was slightly unsettled. Usually this level of patronising and mild unpleasantness was enough to convey the superiority of himself and the establishment. Usually the person would be blustering and making a scene. And making their way out.

"Mr Beeks and Mr Redford will be along in due course." The maitre d' was tired of the exchange now, he had a restaurant to open and this vertically challenged chap wasn't going to ruin his moment, even if he did know the names of the managers. "Listen," his third and final mistake beginning in earnest, "if you go on the website you can download a form to apply for a job as a waiter but I can't see a place like this employing a short arse like you. Now fuck off out of here before–"

The maitre d' closed his eyes as he began to speak, an affectation of superiority the midget took full advantage of. Turning his back, the small man plucked a steak knife from the table and, with a practised precision, spun around and slammed the serrated blade straight into the maitre d's thigh.

The amateurish insults which had been about to pour from the maitre d's mouth went unheard as he dropped, squealing, to his knees. Toppling still further forward, he almost fell on his face, but at the last moment the attacker placed his small hand on the maitre d's chest and held him in place. When the squealing dropped to a whimper, the small man began to speak.

"You have a knife in your thigh because you were rude to me you little fuck-puddle," he said. "I asked you a *very* simple question. I asked you what time *we* open."

The maitre d' had closed his eyes, so the man slapped him hard across the cheek.

"No!" he barked. "You don't get to pass out until I say you pass out you fucking cock snot."

The short bloke reached over to the table and picked up a second steak knife. The eyes of the maitre d' were wide and tears rolled down his cheeks; the blood from the wound on his thigh had soaked his trouser leg and was starting to pool by his knee on the polished, wooden floor.

"I want you to think about what I said. The question was what time do *we* open." The man touched the back of the maitre d's hand with the steak knife. "Now, you dirty little fuck-nozzle, why might I have chosen those particular words?"

The maitre d' shook his head and tried to say something, but it just came out as *whuwhuwhuwhuh*.

"I chose those words because my name is Big Terry," he said, walking in circles around the prone maitre d', whose gaze was now level with his own. "Have you heard of me?"

The maitre d' nodded twice.

"Elaborate please," said Big Terry.

The maitre d' whimpered. Big Terry took his right hand and wrenched it behind his back. Pushing his face into the floor, Big Terry hopped up on to his shoulders and held the maitre d's thumb apart from the rest of his hand. "I am going to cut this cunt off unless you tell me." And Big Terry ran the brand new blade across the pad of the maitre d's thumb, opening a valley and drawing blood immediately.

The maitre d' screamed again. There were other noises now. Noises from the kitchen. People were beginning to notice that something was going on that shouldn't be.

"I heard someone talking," the maitre d' panted into the carpet. "Someone said you were a gangster. That we should be careful."

"And what do you think, Mr I'm-so-much-fucking-taller-than-you?" Big Terry slowly dragged the teeth of the blade across the thin piece of skin that joined the maitre d's thumb to the rest of his hand. With each tooth a small notch of skin was sliced just a little deeper.

The maitre d' whimpered and then went limp.

Big Terry stepped off the man's back and surveyed what he had done, the passed-out face of the maitre d' pointing towards where he stood.

"Fucking piss-pot," he said after a moment and then launched himself forward, punting his foot into the maitre d's prone face.

The kitchen door burst open and a gaggle of staff spilled out amongst the pristine tables. Amongst the gasps and reticence, two figures emerged. Beeks and Redford.

As the pair walked across the restaurant, Big Terry stepped away from the body of the maitre d' and picked up a napkin. Looking down at his hands, he dabbed lightly at the blood spatter.

"Really? Terry?" Beeks said. "We only have one maitre d' and it's opening night."

Big Terry pointed a stubby index finger and Beeks recoiled as if the gesture had actually touched him.

"Sorry," he said. "*Big* Terry."

Big Terry nodded. "This man was far too rude to be working in one of my places," he said. "Get someone to clean him up, will you? There are customers waiting outside."

Redford was still silent, drinking in the details of what Big Terry had done; the colour drained from his face at the blood spreading toward the carpet. He glanced up at Big Terry and snapped back into the moment, signalling to the cowering staff to come and move the maitre d'.

"Is he..." Redford began.

"Dead?" asked Big Terry. "Shouldn't think so. Death's too good for that shit sack. Anyway, if I'd wanted to kill him I would have used this." From a holster inside his jacket Big Terry took a snub-nosed revolver and placed it on the table next to him. "Much quicker."

"Is there something we can do for you, Sir?" said Beeks, suddenly feeling very self-conscious about Big Terry's height. Was he supposed to comment on it? Was standing further away from him the right thing to do or would Big Terry prefer it if they were all huddled together. In the end, he decided grovelling from a distance was probably the right approach. Beeks nodded. And smiled.

"Yes, we were just briefing the staff in the kitchens when you–" Redford stumbled and recovered. "When you discovered our staffing issue out here on the floor."

Big Terry adjusted the position of the gun on the table, pointing the barrel in the general direction of the two men. He looked up above their heads and pointed at the X-rays of Marilyn Monroe.

"Those," said Big Terry. "Fucking monkey jugs."

"They're beautiful, aren't they?" Beeks gushed. "You can see the outline of her..." lowering his voice to a whisper "...breasts."

"I had a phonecall, a tip off. They're fakes, you toss rag," Big Terry bellowed. "You pissed my money against the wall for a centrepiece that's a fake. Do you have any idea how angry that makes me?"

eighteen

Two waiters scuttled in from the kitchen, darting over to the body of the maitre d'.

"What are you talking about?" said Beeks. "They're not fakes. Just look at them."

"What did you say?" Big Terry's words slammed around the room, echoing from every surface.

The waiters froze, not sure what the hell was going on.

Beeks didn't know what to say. He turned back around to look at the X-rays, squinting his eyes in concentration.

Redford held his hands up in surrender. "Big Terry, listen, I take complete responsibility for this." Redford's eyes flicked towards the gun laying cold and heavy on the rumpled tablecloth. "I took the lead on this, I thought I could trust the source." Redford fixed his gaze on Big Terry's eye but the midget maniac gave nothing away. "I'll personally–"

"How do you know they're fakes?" Beeks was still staring at the backlit X-rays with his back to Big Terry.

"What was that, cockass?" asked Big Terry, wrapping his hand around the gun.

Beeks held cupped hands in the air. "Because they look..."

Big Terry turned to Redford and the two waiters, who had managed to suspend the prone body of the maitre d' between them, held the short barrel of the pistol against his own lips and made a silent *shhhh*.

What little colour Redford had gained was drained from his face as Big Terry turned the gun towards Beeks.

"...they look..."

Big Terry pulled the trigger and Beeks' head exploded in a cloud of red mist, the bullet entering his head at the base of the skull and exiting through his forehead. Chunks of brain and skull were propelled toward the precious X-rays.

The accompanying sound was difficult to process for those unaccustomed to witnessing such events, but the combination of the wet brains and the clatter of skull against glass was enough to cause one of the waiters to lose control and vomit on himself, dropping the maitre d' in the process.

Redford closed his eyes and looked away, his ears still ringing from the shot.

"What?" said Big Terry, lowering the gun but turning to face Redford. "What's the matter. He your boyfriend or something?"

Redford didn't speak.

"Those X-rays sold in a California auction yesterday morning," Big Terry continued, punctuating what he was saying by waving the gun around carelessly. "Oi! You two," he shouted at the waiters. "I thought I told you to move him?"

The waiters stumbled back to life, trying without co-ordination to move the maitre d'.

"And when you're done, clean the mess up in here as well," he muttered, glancing to the semi-headless corpse of Beeks. Big Terry stepped towards the silent Redford. "Sold. Yesterday. California. Care to comment?"

Redford began to stammer but no words were forthcoming. Big Terry moved the gun forward and touched the back of Redford's hand with its barrel, which was still burning hot from the shot he'd fired a moment ago.

"Bugger!" Redford recoiled, clutching at his hand. "We... that is... I had no idea. We had a dealer, the whole thing seemed legit.

Lady Emsworth..." he trailed off.

"Lady who?" said Big Terry, suddenly interested. "Lady fucking who?"

"The dealer we got it from – there was a Lady Emsworth visited him. In an expensive car – a Lamborghini I think." Redford's words were distant but had a purpose. And that purpose was to stay alive outside of the next thirty seconds. "She said she did business with the dealer – Logan Price – all the time."

Big Terry nodded and lowered the gun once more. "Better. Now that's some progress. You–" Big Terry pointed at Redford with the gun and Redford winced but didn't break eye contact. "Get this mess tidied up and start making money from this fucking shitty restaurant. Look at this place," he said, looking around. "It's a fucking mess. I wouldn't bring my dogs here, you cunt."

Redford kept nodding.

"Get something to replace the X-ray out of your pocket," Big Terry continued. "Do all of that and do it fast, otherwise..." he nudged the leg of Beeks with his foot. "Otherwise you'll pray I killed you as quick as your bum-chum here."

"He was just my business partner." Redford began to speak but, when he saw the look it elicited on Big Terry's face, instantly regretted it.

"Yeah well, twice the share for you now if you last the week," said Big Terry and began to walk towards the kitchen entrance. He took a mobile phone from his pocket and tapped the screen a couple of times. "Back alley. Now. Make sure no-one sees me leave."

Redford heard the scuttling of feet and saw a brief glimpse of the staff scattering as the kitchen door burst open and then swung shut as Big Terry left. He closed his eyes and tried to take a deep breath, but all he could smell was gunpowder and death.

Opening his eyes once more, he looked down at Beeks, Big Terry's words still ringing in his ears. On the plus side, twice the share for him. Redford smiled. Not all bad then.

14th September

Just under 4 weeks to go…

nineteen

It had been twenty four hours since anybody had spoken to Violet. In that time Barry had filled the majority of the warehouse floor space with cars. One of those cars was a vintage Mark One Ford Escort and, in spite of the fact that Lucas considered himself to be the polar opposite of a 'car man', even he had to admit it was a thing of beauty.

Eyeing it up from the other side of the warehouse, Lucas was happy to admire the deep blue colour as Barry carefully applied coat after coat of wax, but was wary of getting too close in case Barry tried to engage him in conversation about the variety of extras he'd clearly installed. Lucas was pretty sure the wheels were different, there seemed to be some sort of cage inside of it and the seats looked like they might be out of a *Cannonball Run* film but he really didn't care to get into it any further than that. What he did want to get into a little further was the people he was working with. He fidgeted with the pack of cards he kept in his jacket pocket, occasionally glancing over and wondering how the hell Barry managed to find so many things to do on those damned cars when, at last, the door of the warehouse swung open and Zoe entered.

"Young lady," said Lucas with what he hoped was a winning

smile.

"Old man," said Zoe without hesitation. She looked serious, unsmiling.

"Successful day's surveillance?" he asked.

She shrugged. Lucas nodded in recognition and stood up, knocking over a large container of washers as he did so. His reflexes kicked in just in time, his hand darting to catch the toppling box. A few of the different sized silver rings spilled onto the floor. Lucas quickly collected them, then wandered up the metal stairs that ran up the back wall of the warehouse to the first floor. Behind a heavy fire door was a badly lit corridor with several other doors leading off into rooms he hadn't even bothered to explore until now. Poking his head into the first, he discovered that other than a few chairs, it was still full of rolls of enormous bubble wrap. And the light didn't work. So that was out.

The second door, however, was more promising. Opening that revealed a room that Zoe had partially kitted out with flashing computer-type equipment. He knew almost as much about computers as he did about cars, but at least this room had a table in the corner. Being careful not to touch any of Zoe's precious doodads he dragged the table into the centre of the room then wandered back to the first room and, after a couple of additional journeys, had moved five chairs around the table.

He stood back, nodding his head at what he'd created, when Zoe wandered in. Seemingly oblivious to him, she pulled her phone out of her pocket and plugged it in to one of the dangling wires, then picked up a keyboard and started tapping away.

"Are you actually doing something there or just pretending so you can see what I'm up to?" he asked, sitting down at the table.

"Six of one, half a dozen of the other," Zoe said, finally allowing a half-smile to dance momentarily across her lips.

"D'you know why Violet's been missing in action?"

Zoe shook her head. "She isn't, she's in the office."

"Has anyone actually spoken to her recently?"

Zoe shook her head again, her smile gone.

"Fancy a game?" Lucas placed the well-worn pack of cards on the table. She nodded her head and sat down opposite him.

Lucas pretended he was about to deal the cards, then stopped. "Hang on," he said. "I'll see if Barry wants in. Will you get Violet?"

Zoe nodded and wandered off out of the room with Lucas a few steps behind. If he played this right he could stand to win back three or four times more than he'd generously given to his secretary. A move that he still wasn't sure whether or not he regretted.

"Barry!" Lucas shouted from the top of the stairs. "We're playing cards, you in?"

Barry was half way up the stairs before Lucas had even realised he'd stopped working on the car. "Damn straight," he said as he reached the top. "Violet in?"

Lucas shrugged. He wanted to know what was going on with Violet, with all of them in fact, and he knew from experience that poker was a great leveller and a great loosener of lips. "Two seconds, I just needed to grab those washers."

Lucas galloped down the stairs to collect the container of washers he had knocked over earlier and, as he returned to the table, heard footsteps coming down the hallway. Moments later Zoe and Violet walked through the door, Zoe looking relaxed, Violet scowling and pensive.

"Everyone know the rules?" asked Lucas.

"Of what?" Violet snapped.

"Poker. I'm sure you're familiar with it," said Barry, taking his place at the table. "You never know, you might actually enjoy it. Straighten that miserable face of yours."

Lucas shuffled the cards, but his eyes didn't stray from Violet's face. Barry's words made Violet wince. Only for a millisecond, not something that most people would notice, but Lucas was getting in the zone, looking for tells. The thing was, he didn't want her to be pissed off. He wanted her to be relaxed, he wanted to know more. More about the plan, more about what they had found out. He wanted to know more about the people he was working with, but above all he wanted to win their money.

"So, are you going to tell us?" Barry asked Violet.

Violet kept staring at Lucas shuffling the cards. Zoe looked nervous, she was trying to hide it, but it wasn't working. Her eyes danced around the room from Violet to Barry, Barry to Lucas and back to Violet. Lucas was pretty sure she was going to be the easiest mark.

Barry reached past Zoe and prodded Violet in the elbow. Zoe gave a half-laugh as Violet slowly turned to Barry and let out a long sigh.

"I made a mistake," said Violet.

Lucas tried to distract everyone from the seriousness of what Violet was saying by beginning to deal out the cards. Zoe picked her cards up to look at them, Barry just lifted the corner of each card to check what his hand was. Violet left the cards where they were.

"We all make mistakes," said Barry and then, breaking into a smile, he added, "but not all of us mope around like a miserable bitch for days afterwards."

Zoe slowly put her cards back down on the table, staring at Barry slightly wide-eyed, waiting for a reaction from Violet.

Violet glared at Barry and then burst out laughing. "Miserable bitch?"

Barry sat back in his chair nonchalantly and shrugged his shoulder. "Seemed appropriate. Seemed it would get a rise out of you at least."

"The plan..." began Violet.

"The plan that you haven't told any of us?" interrupted Lucas.

Violet nodded, still smiling. "That's the one."

"So..." began Zoe, tentatively. "What exactly went wrong?"

"It's complicated," replied Violet. "I'll tell you, I promise. It's just that, right now, there are a lot of balls in the air."

The others stared at Violet, waiting for her to go on.

"One of the balls... It fell."

"Plenty more balls where that one came from," said Lucas, sensing it would do them more harm than good to push Violet to tell them any more yet. She wasn't pretending to be infallible and he liked that. There was nothing more scary than someone out of control who didn't realise it. "I haven't got any chips, I'm afraid. But I've got these washers. Small ones are worth five quid, medium ones ten and the large ones a whopping twenty pounds. Shall we start with, say, a thousand apiece?"

There were murmurs and grumbling around the table but everyone seemed happy enough with the arrangement. Lucas picked up the remainder of the deck and began shuffling the cards and Barry began dishing out the washers.

Putting the deck back down, Lucas slid a large pile of washers into the centre of the table and everyone else began arranging their own washers into neat piles in front of them.

"Now, how about we cheer everybody up a little bit. That was the whole point of this game after all," said Lucas. He looked over to Zoe. "So…tell us a story."

Zoe frowned.

"What was your worst job?" asked Lucas. "Or your first job? Whichever is funnier." He grinned at her.

Zoe shook her head. "No no no no no. You first."

He scratched his chin, the stubble there a couple of days old. "Okay then. Suppose I could go first."

As the game began Lucas started to tell a tale. The story, not of his first job, but the first time he was in charge. By the time Barry had lost his first hundred pounds Lucas had described all of the other players involved in the job.

"We were a bit further down the line than we are on this job," he said, winning another hand and scraping the chips towards him. "But we were no less planned."

"What the fuck were you actually stealing?" asked Barry, a hint of irritation creeping into his voice. Lucas smiled. Irritation was good. Barry was already proving easy to read but that made it even easier.

"A Fabergé egg," said Lucas as he dealt another hand.

With that statement Violet burst out laughing. "Starting small then, were we?"

Lucas put down the pack of cards. "I'm ambitious, that's all."

Zoe tapped the table in appreciation, shooting a wide grin in Lucas' direction.

"She knows," Lucas pointed at Zoe.

"So, what exactly went wrong?" asked Barry.

"I was getting to that," said Lucas. "I'd done a ton of research. And, like you, I knew exactly what a Fabergé egg looked like. What *does* a Fabergé egg look like, Barry?"

Barry threw a couple of ten pound washers into the centre of the table. "About the size of a fist, pretty bloody gaudy."

Lucas nodded. "Precisely. So in all likelihood, you would have made exactly the same mistake I made. It was the night of the robbery, the egg was being held in this big house on the outskirts of Kilchester. We'd been posing as carpet cleaners, so we had access to the house. I walked into the room where the egg was supposed to be. You expect the alarms to go off, don't you?"

"They usually bloody do," laughed Barry.

"Except they didn't. I just waltzed into the room and it was almost empty. The most prominent thing I remember was a pedestal right in the middle. On top of the pedestal should have been the egg, but instead of the big, gaudy, expensive thing we were supposed to be stealing was a smaller, plain, white egg."

Zoe's hand went to cover her mouth and she started laughing behind it.

Lucas nodded. "I told you - she knows."

Zoe nodded.

"Anyway, I searched the room. Then I searched the adjoining room. Then I searched all the other rooms on that floor and I still didn't find anything. An hour and a half of searching later and I had all of the rest of the team screaming in my ear to get out. Eventually, even I gave up. I locked the place up and left."

Lucas instinctively noted the different expressions on everyone's faces. There was a good chance they would have the same expression on their faces if they had a good hand later.

"Did it ever turn up?" asked Barry.

"It was there the whole time," said Lucas with a sigh. "Unfortunately, I hadn't quite done enough research. Turns out that the very first Fabergé eggs were white."

Zoe placed her cards on the table, laughing. "I fold. So it was there the whole time?"

Lucas nodded and, anticipating a win for Violet, said, "I fold too."

He looked over to Violet and was relieved to see that she seemed to relax a little as she took the chips and won the hand. She caught his eye and he gave her a smile as he gathered in the cards. It wasn't that he was trying to reassure her, it was more to do with fact that he was stacking the deck and he didn't want her to glance at what he was doing with his hands. Once he was happy that he knew which cards were where he began to shuffle, the practised shuffle of a man who had been taking money from card players since his early teens.

"So…" He began tossing cards across the table to each of the players. "Zoe, you going to regale us with your story?"

"Well…" Zoe's eyes darted around the room, looking for someone else to go next.

"Or maybe Violet?" Lucas was treated to the full beam of her dead-eyed stare. She reached down to the pile of washers in front of her, selected a few and threw them into the centre of the table.

"I'll tell you a story," she said and Lucas felt compelled to look away.

"Okay, yeah," he said.

"I was six years old." Violet carefully placed her cards face down on the table. "And I went to that big shopping centre on the outskirts of Kilchester with my mum and dad. It was new at the time and it felt like a treat, but something wasn't quite right. When you're that age I think you believe every trip is about you. Somehow, though, I knew this one wasn't."

Zoe fidgeted with her washers, obviously uncomfortable with where this was going. She raised by a couple of hundred, confident in her hand, perhaps, but showing no signs outside of the stakes.

"I remember at school that week all the children had to draw pictures of their mummy and daddy at work and I got into trouble because I wouldn't draw anything. I told the teacher I wasn't allowed to talk about their jobs."

Barry had been staring conspicuously at his own cards, refusing to make eye contact, for some time but he finally gave in, placed his cards in front of him and stared at Violet, rapt.

"I wasn't allowed to talk about their jobs because they were like us. I didn't know what that meant at the time, not really. No matter how you grow up, you think that's how it is for everyone. Except you can't really understand, at six you're just too young, you've got no moral compass. And on *that* day I'd been pestering them incessantly, demanding to go to work with one of them. This story is about that day."

Everyone's cards were on the table now. Everyone stared. Nobody spoke.

"So we parked the car, walked into the shopping centre. The next part I only really know from what I read in newspapers afterwards, when I was a teenager. The pair of them were pulling some sort of confidence trick on the jewellers that had just opened. They used me as bait, sent me into the store pretending to be lost, told me after ten minutes to tell the people in the shop that I had seen my mummy and daddy outside. So I did. Only, when I got outside they weren't there. They'd been arrested and I didn't see them again for two years.

"The part I do remember, the part that doesn't go away, is standing just down the mall, just far enough that the jewellers couldn't see me, waiting for my mother and father to turn up. And of course they didn't."

The room was silent save for the hum of the computer equipment that surrounded them.

"Well, aren't you a barrel of fucking laughs?" Barry clapped his hands, breaking the mood Violet had created.

Lucas reached instinctively for his cards. "Is that even true?" he asked. "Half the time I'm not even sure if you're just spinning us some line of bullshit." He laughed nervously, but to his relief Violet seemed to have relaxed and a smile crept onto her face.

"Well, I could have told you about the time me and Katie got deliberately arrested and then broke out of prison, but you would have to buy me a hell of a lot more drinks to get me to tell you that story."

"No? Who's Katie?" Zoe asked.

A smile broke over Violet's face, she raised her eyebrows and nodded.

"Police cars?" Barry interrupted. "I've got a good one for you. Some prick I was working for... not you Violet..."

Violet rolled her eyes.

"Well, some bright spark came up with the idea that, after we nicked whatever it was we were nicking… I forget what it was now… But anyway, the idea was that the getaway car would be a police car."

Violet nodded in appreciation.

"That's a pretty bloody good idea, actually," said Lucas.

Barry shook his head. "It's a shit idea. I spent two days taking photographs of police cars. Once I had those I went out and stole a car. Same make. Same model. Resprayed it white, got decals cut, made a passable lighting rig for the roof. Is there any beer in this place?"

"No!" Zoe shouted. "There isn't any beer. Finish the damn story."

Barry pretended to look incredulous. "Fine. I'll skip to the good bit. To try and be as authentic as possible, I had some number plates made. The same number plates from one of the police cars in the photos."

Lucas groaned. "I know where this story is going."

Barry laughed. "I even had a uniform. And a hat. So I was sitting outside, in the car, just like always and I see a police car go past. The adrenaline is pumping and I'm watching like a hawk but it gets to the end of the street and turns left so I just, kind of, mentally cross my fingers. But then I clock him in the rearview mirror, he's gone around the block, so I take the handbrake off, foot hovering over the accelerator. Are you sure we don't have anything to drink in this place?"

"FINISH THE DAMN STORY!" Zoe barked.

Barry sighed. "I thought you could fill in the rest yourself… My mates poured out of the place they were knocking off and piled in to the car just as the police car drew level. The driver wound his window down and waggled his hand, you know, to tell me to do the same thing. So I did. Wound my window down and he says 'Do you know your car has the same number plate as mine?'"

Everyone was laughing, no one interested in the game.

"That's one awkward situation," said Lucas through the laughter. "What the hell did you do?"

"What could I do?" replied Barry. "I started to answer, then accelerated away. Of course, he lit up his lights, turned on the siren, all that flashy shit. I waited until we hit sixty, he was riding our bumper, I slammed on the brakes."

"Were you not hurt?" asked Zoe.

Barry shrugged. "A bit, but the main thing was that it totally fucked up the front of their car. Set the airbags off, stopped them in their tracks."

"Why didn't it set your airbags off?" asked Lucas after another round of laughter had died down.

"I'd been arsing around with the car. Accidentally turned them off. Just as well really."

The cards lay on the table and every single one of the chips lay in front of Lucas.

"I'm glad we're not playing for real money," said Zoe, glancing at the washers.

"What the fuck?" Lucas wore a wounded look upon his face.

"You didn't actually believe that we would play a real cardsharp for actual money, did you?" asked Violet.

"Well, yes, I did actually." Lucas gathered up the remainder of the cards and shuffled them irritatedly. "Come on then, Zoe. You might as well tell us your story before we all call it a day."

"My most embarrassing job? The one that went the most wrong? That's easy. Not that long ago, I was sitting in the library dressed as a schoolgirl, minding my own business."

Barry and Lucas both leaned forward.

"Not like that, you perverts," said Zoe. "I was in disguise. It was… when was it Violet?"

"End of August, I guess," came the reply.

"End of August. I was running a scam at the bank, surveillance thing where I use the…" Zoe trailed off, realising that no-one apart from her was interested in the details of how she did it. "That part's not important. The point is, I was using all this stuff," she waved her hand above her shoulder, indicating the computer equipment behind her, "to steal money from people. Only, as I was watching the people in the bank, something unexpected popped up on my screen. My own bankcard was being used by someone else. Some cheeky cow had stolen my purse with my card inside."

Everyone stared at Zoe, waiting for her to finish the story. Everyone except Violet.

"What?" Violet affected a faux-innocent voice. "I had to get your attention somehow."

"I realise that now," Zoe began laughing.

As the others drifted out of the room and about their business, Lucas reflected on what he had learned. Violet had realised what he was up to, that much was true, but none of the rest of them had any idea until she told them.

And *that* was very interesting indeed.

19th September

3 weeks to go…

twenty

"I really don't understand why you are so desperate for my hair to be blonde." Zoe almost stamped her foot in annoyance at Lucas, who had been fussing around her at the crew's warehouse for longer than she felt comfortable.

Lucas sighed and stood back. "I thought I told you," he said, distractedly going back to the pile of women's clothes that were lumped on a nearby desk.

"No," said Zoe, her hand going to her hip petulantly. "You didn't. And quite frankly this whole thing is getting a bit creepy. I'm perfectly capable of dressing myself to go and see the painting."

Lucas stopped what he was doing and stared at her, his brows knotting in confusion.

"What?" he said after too long a pause. "No! Did you think? Hang on..."

Now it was Zoe's turn to look confused. She had had men perv on her in the past, of course, but when you confronted them they rarely had the look of stunned disbelief that Lucas was currently sporting.

Lucas caught himself and regrouped. "When you pull jobs," he said, trying to adopt a slightly more avuncular style by leaning back on the desk, "how often do you come face to face with the mark?"

"What's that got to do with anything?" asked Zoe defensively.

"With all the computer stuff, I'm sure it's important and all but—"

"Important? Of course it's important," Zoe snapped. "We're hardly going to be able to walk in and take out a painting simply because we persuaded them with the sheer force of our personalities. Well, you certainly won't."

"For the sake of making my point and the fact that I was trying to pay you a compliment I'll pretend I didn't hear that last bit," said Lucas. He folded his hands together and placed them in his lap and then, realising he might look like he was stroking his cock, placed them instead on his knees. "The point is that's where I am on every job I pull and you need to look a certain way. To act a certain way."

Zoe stared at Lucas. Leaning back on the desk behind him, hands on his knees, creating a kind of hunched-back frame that drew all attention to his crotch.

"You really aren't comfortable around women, are you?" she said eventually, relaxing slightly.

Lucas unknotted himself and stood upright once more. "It's not that. It's just that... this stuff is important. I'm not perving on you or whatever, I don't think of you that way, it's just..."

"So you're saying I'm unattractive then?" Zoe looked wounded.

"What-uh-well, that's erm, no... But..." Lucas babbled.

Zoe grinned at him. "Only teasing," she said. "So it's important is it?"

The tension dropped from Lucas' frame and a smile crept into the corners of his mouth. "Yes. It's really important."

Zoe had noticed a change in Lucas since a few days after the poker game, like he had relaxed into his role and was beginning to enjoy it. Either that or he was getting ready to stab them all in the back.

"I understand undercover... I can blend," she said.

"Perhaps you have a certain...natural talent... but this isn't blending in with a crowd. This is one-on-one, real-face-to-real-face.

"Okay then," said Zoe, relaxing a little. "But why blonde?"

"Well, when people meet you for the first time," said Lucas, becoming animated, "and you aren't, you know, like their wife's best friend or something like that. When you're more transient in their lives then their memory of you is less accurate. People tend to use more broad brush-strokes to define who you are."

"Like a placeholder?" said Zoe, looking through the clothes on the table and choosing a pair of baggy jeans and a purple hoodie that bore the logo of some American sports team. She proffered them to Lucas, who nodded at the jeans but removed the hoodie and replaced it with a dark, purple checked shirt.

"Exactly like a placeholder," said Lucas. "Now put them on."

Zoe raised an eyebrow and Lucas turned around to face the wall. Zoe examined the wall in front of him for reflective surfaces and then began to remove her clothes.

"So, there's a reason I want to be a placeholder and not a person today then?" asked Zoe as she pulled on the baggy jeans.

"Certainly there is," replied Lucas. "If the banker ever realises that the painting has been stolen."

"You mean if we fail," said Zoe.

Lucas nodded and stared at his feet, bored of looking at the wall.

"Eyes front, soldier," Zoe snapped, pulling a black vest over her head. Lucas' head shot back upright.

"Sorry, I wasn't..." Lucas mumbled. "But yeah that's what I meant. If the police get involved the first person they're going to look at is the art student who happened to come and look at the painting a few weeks before it was stolen. And when they look into the student..."

"Point taken," said Zoe. "They find the student doesn't exist, so they get a description from whoever I'm seen by today. You can turn around."

Lucas turned. "Good start," he said. "Trainers are a nice touch."

Zoe did a little curtsey, dipping her right leg slightly to show off the two-inch platform soles. "I'm a quick learner," she said.

"Yes, you are," said Lucas. "Now we need false tan, a beauty spot, big eye make-up, blond wig and glasses."

"Glasses?"

"Glasses."

"Sweet," said Zoe. "I've got some that look like Ray-Bans but they've got a camera in them."

"Like James Bond and shit," grinned Lucas.

"Jane Bond," replied Zoe, pulling the blonde wig over her head and tucking some of her own stray brown hairs inside. "You're loving this, aren't you? Having your very own dolly to dress up."

"Honestly?" Lucas wandered over to a pile of computers and wires Zoe had brought with her. "I really am. As a man I'm much more limited as to what I can do before I start to look like..."

"A cross dresser?" Zoe suggested.

"Although would that be so bad?" said Lucas, picking up a dress from the pile.

"You'd make a beautiful princess." Zoe laughed, picking up a make-up bag and wandering off toward the bathroom.

Lucas put down the dress and watched her leave. Zoe reached the door and turned around. "Well," she said. "Are you coming?"

Lucas jogged to catch up with her. "Oh yeah," he said. "But I have to warn you, I'm going to be a back-seat driver."

"You go, girlfriend."

When Zoe stepped out of the bathroom ten minutes later, the transformation was complete. Heavy, bright blue eyeshadow framed eyes decorated with long false eyelashes. The rouged cheeks framed the neon red of her lips and all on a canvas of deep, fake, orange tan.

Fishing around in the cases of tech that littered the room Zoe eventually located the glasses and carefully slipped them on.

"What do you think?" she said, giving Lucas a twirl.

"Wonderfully memorable." Lucas clapped his hands, giving her a mini round of applause.

"Memorably unmemorable," added Zoe. "Of course, now I need to trick it out."

"What do you mean?" asked Lucas. "Do the glasses not send the signal back here?"

"Maybe in the movies," Zoe sighed, grabbing a small tablet computer and wandering up the stairs toward the back room she had repurposed as the tech-zone.

Lucas followed her, stepping over wires and plug extensions as he entered the room.

"Bloody hell, it's hotter in here than before," he said.

"Yeah," said Zoe, plugging the tablet into one of the desktop computers and tapping on the keyboard in front of her. "Once you start to get a few running they kick out a fair bit of heat."

"So why can't you wander around and beam everything here then?" asked Lucas.

"You know when you're in a department store or somewhere like that?" she replied.

"Yeah."

"And you can't get a mobile signal?"

"Oh right."

"Yeah, it's a bit like that, only with the banker's flat it's underground." Zoe turned back to her programming. The tablet burst to life with reams of text flying across the screen quicker than either of them could have taken it in. "So it's a right pain in the arse to get anything in or out of there. I'm going to relay everything from the glasses to this tablet, then I'll download the lot once I'm back here. Plus I'm putting some software on the tablet that'll work with the GPS so the two things will create a kind of three dimensional map. I'd like to say it all happened automatically but actually it's a fucking lot of work."

"Sounds complicated," said Lucas.

Zoe nodded and, apparently satisfied with what she'd done to the tablet, unplugged it. "It is what it is. Tablet will also be harvesting anything digital that might be useful too, it'll pick up a bunch of stuff like networks, security stuff..." Zoe trailed off, sensing she was losing Lucas. "And I need a coat of some description, oh fashion captain, Sir."

"Right then," said Lucas, glancing at his watch. "I know the perfect one. And it's got lots of pockets so you can put all your... all your shit in them. Then we gotta go, time's ticking."

twenty one

The door to the headquarters burst open and Violet strode in, followed a moment later by Katie, who was moving a little more slowly so she could duck to get under the frame.

"Who the fuck is that?" Violet pointed at Zoe.

"Who the fuck is that?" Lucas pointed at Katie.

"It's me, you dipshit," said Zoe.

"You're not going out of the house dressed like that, young lady," said Violet, relaxing a little. "What have you done to yourself?"

Zoe stepped forward into the middle of the room and gave them a twirl. The army surplus jacket Lucas had selected for her billowed out and, for a second, the tablet computer strapped under her checked shirt could be seen, attached to Zoe's body with a modified gun holster.

"Lucas was helping me, making me look like someone else so I can't be identified after the fact," said Zoe.

"He did make you look like somebody else," said Violet. "And that somebody was clearly very drunk indeed before she got dressed and put her make-up on."

"Who the fuck's that?" Lucas repeated, pointing to Katie.

Violet ignored him, deliberately refusing to make eye contact.

"Barry? Are you busy?" she shouted.

Over in the corner Barry put down the spray gun he was wielding and took off his protective mask. "I need to finish the wing or it'll look shit but, yeah, I've got a minute."

Violet smiled in appreciation. "Barry, this is Katie," she said. "Katie, this is Barry."

"Fuck me. You're a big one aren't you?" said Barry.

"And strong with it, Barry," Violet retorted. "So watch your mouth or you'll end up carrying your teeth home with broken fingers."

"Pleasure to meet you m'lady." Barry bowed with a flourish and Katie silently laughed, her hand shooting up to cover her mouth.

"Over there, dressed like the vomit of a unicorn, is Miss Zoe Zimmerman," said Violet and Zoe waved then pushed her glasses up her nose. "She's about to go and case the flat where the painting currently resides and give us all sorts of technical advantages in the process."

"Damn right," said Zoe.

"I think that's it," said Violet and clapped her hands.

"Well, fuck you," said Lucas angrily. "I'm as much a part of this crew as anyone else, you know?" He stormed over to Katie, who raised her eyebrows and looked down at him. "Lucas Vaughan," he said and looked to Katie for a reply. Katie just smiled and shrugged. "You as well? Really?" Lucas began turning red, raising his voice to a shout. "You know, you could say something. Anything really. 'Hi Lucas' or 'Pleased to meet you' but–"

Katie reached forward and put her hand over Lucas' mouth and nose. He tried instinctively to step back but Katie extended her arm. Unable to breathe, Lucas grunted, but Violet quickly stepped in.

"Katie can't speak, Lucas," she explained.

Katie removed her hand and Lucas stared down at those big feet of hers.

"Sorry, it's – it's..." he stammered. Katie placed her index finger under his chin and lifted his head. He could feel her strength even in that one finger. Their eyes met and Katie gave him a smile, then her eyes flicked to Violet and back before going into a roll.

"Yeah, I suppose she is a bit," he said, and exhaled, not really sure what had just happened.

"Anyway, people," said Violet, holding aloft a black courier's tube. "We have in here something a little special."

Katie reached forward and plucked the tube out of Violet's hands, replacing it with one of the parts from Barry's car engine, which was significantly heavier. Violet wobbled slightly as she struggled not to drop it on her own head.

"You robbed the museum?" said Zoe excitedly.

"We came. We saw. We set up a little dead end. We smashed some things up. We scarpered." Violet laughed her machine gun laugh and carefully lowered the engine part down to waist height.

Barry, Zoe and Lucas all gathered around, eager to hear the first real triumph of the job. Violet told them about meeting Katie, getting in and finding everything, and about how they had set all the alarms off in order to leave in a hurry.

"So what did you steal as a decoy in the end?" asked Zoe.

Violet produced something quite small and flat covered with a sheet. She placed it on the floor in front of them all and unwrapped the object carefully before putting the sheet to one side. The five of them were looking at what appeared to be a slab of marble, the size of a small laptop. There were some words etched on it:

"The bad artists imitate, the great artists steal." *Pablo Picasso*

Except the name 'Pablo Picasso' had been crudely scrawled out and the name 'Banksy' etched underneath.

"Is it supposed to look like that or have you been fucking with it?" asked Barry, not quite sure what to make of the plaque Violet had delivered.

"It's a Banksy," said Zoe, knowingly. "You know Banksy, don't you, Barry?"

Barry shrugged. "Name rings a bell like but, nah. Not really."

"He's a famous graffiti artist," explained Zoe. "Only he usually sprays stencils on walls. Sort of anti-establishment, political statements, you know?"

"Oh," said Barry and wandered back off to finish respraying the car.

"Only he doesn't usually do stuff like this, does he?" Zoe directed the question to Violet.

"Not sure really, I'm not a huge expert. It seemed... appropriate," said Violet with a wicked grin. "After the amount of money the museum paid for this piece to simply put it into storage... It seemed like the artist would probably appreciate what we were doing."

"He wouldn't mind you nicking his stuff?" asked Lucas, a little confused.

"Not if we donate it to a charity shop and they get the proceeds," said Violet. "I think he'd like that very much indeed."

Katie nodded, satisfied with the explanation.

"I spotted it on the inventory you gave me, Zoe, so cheers for that," Violet continued. "And the floor plans, alarms, everything were spot on. Good job."

Zoe blushed and was about to say something. "So you got the canvas too, I take it?" Lucas butted in.

Katie launched the courier tube like a javelin through the air but instead of throwing it high and far she ducked and hurled it straight at waist height. At Lucas' waist height.

Lucas wasn't expecting it and took the full force of the blow in his solar plexus, knocking the wind out of him. Katie shrugged as Lucas doubled over, horrible rasping noises parping from his mouth as he tried to breathe normally.

"Katie," Violet hissed. It was too late. Katie was already stalking off to explore the further reaches of the warehouse. Violet and Zoe fussed around Lucas, helping him sit down. Violet tried to calm the situation, explaining that Katie had a bit of a temper, that perhaps he should be a bit more careful as to what he said around her because, like a Wookiee, Katie had a tendency to tear people's arms off if she lost.

"If she loses what?" Lucas wheezed, cracking a smile that no-one believed.

Violet smacked him on the back. "Good man," she said. "That's the spirit."

"So," said Zoe, rapidly losing interest in Lucas and turning back to Violet. "You got the canvas, you got a decoy that you're going to give to a charity shop... We didn't have a plan for how you would get out."

"Oh, I suppose we didn't, did we?" said Violet and began to wander off after Katie. "And it's canvases. In the plural."

"Violet!" Zoe snapped. "Tell me!"

"If anyone's interested," said Barry from the other side of the room. "I couldn't give a shit."

"No-one is," shouted Violet and then, turning around to Zoe and Lucas once more, "Well, we lifted the canvases no problem at all. There should be enough there for two attempts at the Dali signature according to the measurements Damien gave us."

Lucas winced and smiled, which gave him the look of someone suffering the after effects of an unexpectedly hot curry.

"Then I thought the best bet would be to smash our way in to where they were keeping that." Violet gestured towards the Banksy plaque. "And once we'd got hold of it I set the alarms off."

"What?" asked Zoe.

"What?" echoed Lucas.

Violet grinned.

"You do realise I could quite easily have disabled them?" Zoe began, but then paused for a second, raising her index finger and wagging it soundlessly at Violet as she calculated something in her head. "So..." she said a moment later. "So...if you set the alarms off then the security guards would know where you were and you wouldn't be able to pick the locks because the alarm triggers the magnetic seals."

"Correct!" exclaimed Violet.

"Wait!" said Lucas. "So how *did* you escape?"

"What?" said Violet, pretending to look confused. "Ohhhhhh... well that was easy. I bumped into a security guard out front before we broke in. Stole his identity card and used it to open the doors we needed to open and then walked straight out the front door with the canvases and the Banksy."

Violet blew Zoe and Lucas a kiss and then flounced off after Katie.

"She's good," said Zoe when Violet was out of earshot.

"She's a fucking maniac," whispered Lucas as he popped open the courier tube.

twenty two

It was starting to rain. Although, given that this was Kilchester, that was hardly any great surprise. It was always starting to rain in Kilchester, Zoe thought as she stared across the road. She had to get to the banker's flat before a downpour came, if for no other reason than she had no idea how her ridiculous make-up would react to a soaking.

She wasn't usually nervous like this, but then she wasn't usually out of her comfort zone to this degree.

Zoe touched the glasses on her face. Unused to having them there, she found herself unable to stop fidgeting with them. But there was no need to be nervous, she told herself. Rollo Glass wasn't expecting to be robbed and, today at least, he wasn't going to be robbed. She took a deep breath and crossed the road, approaching the entrance lobby to the flats.

It was an odd sort of building and not really what Zoe had expected, although it had to be said that she didn't really have any experiences of underground bunkers. The piece of land that the building sat in was fenced off from the rest of the street, although there was no gate; the gap in the fence was easily big enough to fit two cars side by side and led into a car parking area. Anyone unaware of what lay beneath could have been forgiven for thinking that this was nothing more than a car park and that the person in the building was the attendant. As Zoe walked over she scanned the perimeter and saw the first round of cameras pointing down towards the two or three expensive cars left there.

The building itself looked like an overpaid architect had been asked to design a greenhouse and had then been furnished with too much money to build it. Although only a single storey and perhaps five metres wide, the front of the building was made entirely of glass, so the security guard behind the desk inside could easily see whoever was approaching. As Zoe got closer she could see the tops of a couple of computer monitors on the desk in front of him. "A secure feed from all the cameras which are monitored at an external location and attended by a security guard twenty four hours a day." That's what it had said on the website of the security firm. She certainly hoped so, because that was exactly what she was going to attempt to intercept. Behind the guard was a single wooden door and over to the other side, away from the desk, were a pair of brushed metal doors.

The guard's gaze flicked from the monitors to Zoe as she reached the outer door and pushed the handle. It didn't budge.

Panic rose inside of her as the guard raised his index finger and pointed at her once, twice, three times. Then she realised that he wasn't pointing at her but at the intercom to the right of the door. She tried to stop her finger from shaking as she pressed the button.

"Can I help you, Miss?" he said politely, his voice crisp and electronic from the intercom's speaker.

"Yes – uh – I have an appointment to see Mr Glass's assistant," she said, pushing the nerves down inside.

"Oh, the student." Zoe could see the guard smile, and there was a buzz as he unlocked the door. "Come in."

Before the door was even half way open the guard was by her side, ushering her through and carefully ensuring it was fully closed behind her.

"Wow this place is..." Zoe pretended to look around in wonder, taking in the lack of alternate escape routes and three more internal security cameras.

"I know, it takes a little getting used to." The guard smiled and gestured to a small leather sofa over by a potted plant away from his desk. "Would you like to take a seat? I'll call down and let them know you're here."

"I don't suppose…" Zoe bit her thumb and gave the guard big eyes over the top of the glasses. "Is there a toilet I could use?"

"I'm not really—" the guard began.

"I've just been on the bus so long." Zoe gave the guard a couple of slow blinks.

The guard glanced at the locked door and almost empty car park. "Can't do any harm, can it?" he said. "Follow me."

He walked towards the wooden door and Zoe followed. The guard reached down and grabbed a security card on a retracting cord and swiped it on a card reader by the door. A little light went green and he opened the door to a stark utility corridor which led to two further rooms.

"I'll have to stay out here," he said, gesturing to his desk. "It's the second on your left there."

Zoe thanked him and he closed the door to reception. Surveying the small corridor, she was certain there were no cameras back here; she moved quickly down to the second door. It was, indeed, a small toilet with a washbasin and paper towels. Nothing very exciting. Ducking into the other room only revealed a kitchenette. There were a couple of cupboards, a kettle, a sink and – bingo! Behind the door was a junction box. Zoe pulled a cable out of one pocket and a device smaller than a thumb from another pocket. She plugged the cable into the device and then into the network junction box.

Tucking the device in amongst a cluster of other wires, Zoe pulled a cable tie from her jacket pocket to secure it then ducked out of the kitchen and into the toilet. She burst through the door but, as she turned her head, there was someone watching her. A woman – she must have been watching the whole time and…

Zoe looked at the woman again. Blonde hair. Glasses.

It was her own reflection.

She stared at the unfamiliar person staring back at her and resisted the urge to splash water on her face, knowing that it would destroy the layers of carefully-applied make-up.

On with the show, she thought, and flushed the toilet. Ran the tap into the sink for a moment and then headed for the door back into the foyer. Reaching the connecting door Zoe pulled at the handle. Locked. Her heart was pounding in her chest as she knocked firmly on the door. A moment later the smiling security guard opened it and led her back into the light.

As she walked out she noted more closely the layout of the guard's desk, the computer's base unit underneath, the two monitors each divided into four squares with alternating footage from... well, it didn't matter right now. As long as the camera in her glasses could see, she would be able to piece together the details once she was out of this place.

"I took the liberty of calling Miss Lester," said the security guard. "She'll be up in a–"

There was a *bong* noise as the lift signalled its arrival. The woman inside was middle aged with a severe perm perched above a face so made up it made Zoe look positively naturalistic. She wore a trouser-suit and a harassed look on her face and kept stabbing at her mobile phone. She made a frustrated growl and shoved the device in her pocket.

"Are you Miss... er...?" Miss Lester said. "I was trying to check on my phone but I can't get a damned signal in this place."

"Call me Sally," said Zoe and held out her hand to shake.

Miss Lester looked at it as if it were a dead cat. "You can call me Miss Lester," she said sharply. "Get in the lift, let's get this over with."

Zoe stepped inside the lift. The interior was mirrored and, once again, there was a security camera in the corner, this time housed in a spherical protector. Miss Lester reached over and jabbed the button on the lift marked '-1'.

The lift's lights blinked and it began slowly to descend.

twenty three

Lucas pulled the car Barry had given him up to the curb and cut the engine, glancing at the tube on the passenger seat. With everything that was going on with the crew, *in* the crew, he still hadn't made the time to dismantle the office from his last job. The job Violet had helped him with. He tried not to think about it. The X-ray payday was a tiny fraction of what this job was worth so he would get to that when he had time, but it kept bubbling to the surface. He wasn't happy.

Another member of the crew potentially meant another share that had to be paid which, in turn, meant less money for him. After that bloody giant woman had embarrassed him in front of everyone he wasn't sure how he felt about that. And yet, Violet had handed the tube containing the canvases to him. She had given him a special assignment, so he might be prepared to give this interloper the benefit of the doubt.

Barry seemed alright. Reliable, a manly man's man. And Zoe, she was off the scale clever. But this Katie. Katie who didn't speak.

Didn't speak, he wondered? Or couldn't speak?

What was the point of her being part of the crew?

But Violet had asked him to go back to see his forger contact, to deliver the canvases. So here he was once again at Damien's studio.

"Come in, brother," Damien said, opening the door

The smell of weed wafted out and Lucas glanced over his shoulder to the outside world, looking to see who might notice. Damien couldn't give a shit, Lucas knew that. In fact, as he stepped inside and quickly closed the door, he realised that Damien had answered the door with a spliff in his hand.

"So you didn't bring the bitch with you this time then?" Damien dumped himself on a sofa in front of a large, flat screen television. The sound was turned off and a movie was playing that Lucas recognised but couldn't remember the name of.

"No, I–" Lucas began to reply.

"You look stressed, man," Damien interrupted. "Have a seat." He shoved the joint into his mouth, grabbed a lighter and puffed it back to light. "Have a smoke."

Taking a long pull on the joint, Damien closed his eyes for a second then offered it to Lucas, who shook his head. Damien was holding his breath, holding the potent smoke in his lungs, and held the spliff between his thumb and forefinger, waving it at Lucas.

"Fuck it," said Lucas and plucked it from Damien's grasp. Putting it to his lips he took a tiny toke, not sure whether the thing would knock him on his arse. "Cheers," he said, letting the smoke waft out as he spoke.

"No worries," said Damien in a rasp, his exhale practically filling the room with smoke. "She got the canvas then?"

"Yeah." Lucas took a longer drag this time then passed the joint back to Damien.

"Where'd she get them from?" asked Damien.

Lucas shrugged, still holding the smoke back, but it caught and he started coughing, hacking away.

"Amateur," Damien grinned. "This shit'll put hairs on your chest, you pussy."

"Arsehole," Lucas retorted.

"Shitbag," Damien laughed.

"Cock womble." Lucas shook his head, a smile beginning to invade his face.

"Cock womble?" said Damien. "What the fuck are you talking about? Is that even a thing?"

"It is now," said Lucas and threw the courier tube over to Damien. It bounced to rest on the cushion of the sofa next to him.

"So this is you now then, is it?" Damien squinted, concentrating on the silent screen of the television. "You're just going to be that bitch's bitch from now on are you? I remember when Lucas Vaughan was his own man..." He took another pull on the joint and handed it back to Lucas.

Lucas took a drag. The smoke was hot but it didn't feel like he needed to cough this time. He could feel his eyelids getting that heavy, stoned feeling already. This was some strong shit.

"I'm a man, man." Lucas caught himself not making sense and decided to take another pass at that sentence. "I am a man. My own man." That was it, he nailed it second time around. "This is just a... what's the word?"

Damien shrugged.

"Well," said Lucas, getting back on track. "Point is, she thinks she's in charge. She is in charge. But when the time comes and we've got the real painting things might change, mightn't they?"

Damien slapped his legs and jumped into the air making whooping noises. Lucas squinted at him and offered the joint. Somehow he'd let it go out. Had he had it that long? He didn't think so.

"So dark horse Lucas joins the team," Damien giggled, tiptoeing around the room. "He pulls the job and then..."

"That's the plan," said Lucas, running his fingers through his hair and leaning way back in the chair. "Just wait until we've got the painting and then–"

"Then whip it out from under her nosey-nose!" Damien's hysteria seemed to be subsiding slightly. "Well, it's good to see you're branching out, brother. Probably just as well, the cats she's got on her tail."

Lucas was dimly aware of the conversation getting away from him, but this was something important. He tried to shake the fog from his head but just ended up shaking his head. "On her tail?" he managed. "What do you mean?"

"We've been in business a long time now, am I right?" Damien pressed a button on a nearby remote control and the television went dark.

Lucas nodded, slightly worried about the serious tone Damien was taking. They had been in business together for a long time. Since Lucas' first jobs he'd used Damien's skills to produce all kinds of forgeries, but also he was a man who knew people. A man to whom people told things.

Damien held up his index finger. "Percy Parker," he said. "You know him?"

"The fence?" Lucas asked, the adrenaline starting to create an equilibrium in his system. "Yeah, I was gonna talk to him about shifting the painting once I..." Lucas shifted uneasily in his seat. "Haven't seen him in a while though. He's still around?"

"Around and very interested in your boss's return to Kilchester." With extreme effort Lucas pulled himself up from the cushions that were now engulfing him and leaned forward as Damien continued. "Seems that he has unfinished business with Lady Violet. Wanted to know the moment she turned up."

Lucas rested his head in his hands, elbows propped on his knees. "Is he still independent?" asked Lucas.

"Yes and no," replied Damien. "I branched out into passports, driving licenses, that sort of thing. We stay independent on that but his day job these days..." Damien held up a second finger. "He works for Big Terry."

"Big Terry?"

"Big. Terry."

"Fuck."

"Fuck indeed," said Damien, looking at the burnt out roach of the joint left in his hand. "Takes some balls to work with that crazy little bastard."

"And Percy wanted to know she was back?" asked Lucas.

"The very second her pretty little face peeped back into our city," replied Damien. "Ask around, he's been... eager, shall we say?"

"And you think Big Terry's interested?"

Damien shrugged. "Not sure. But if he isn't now, how long before he is?"

"Well, you could say the same thing about your little passport sideline, couldn't you?" Lucas added, before realising he sounded a bit petulant and trying to paste a smile on his face.

"It is what it is," said Damien. "Make hay while the sun shines then when the tractor comes..."

"Give him the fucking money?"

"Yeah," Damien sighed. "Something like that."

"I want you to do two forgeries. Not just one," Lucas said.

"She get enough canvas?"

Lucas nodded.

"Tell her I fucked one of them up? That sort of thing?" Damien asked.

Lucas nodded again. "Something like that. That's why she got more canvas. In case you make a mistake."

Damien's mouth twisted into a snarl but Lucas interrupted before he could respond. "You want more money? For the second one?"

Damien scratched at his stubble as he thought.

"Nah," he said eventually. "We go way back. Besides, when she was – erm – rude to me I doubled my price so we're all good."

Damien pulled some more rolling papers out of his pocket.

"So how long before you'll have our Dali fakes sorted then?" asked Lucas. He stood up slowly, but his head still believed that it was too fast, and promptly made him feel dizzy and nauseous.

"Well, that depends," said Damien. "The money–"

"Is in the bag."

"Paint will be touch dry in three days," said Damien. "Wouldn't recommend moving it before then."

Lucas nodded.

"And did you get me a copy of the original?" Damien stretched, rolling his shoulders backwards and causing them to make a *pop* sound. "Because, you don't get this sort of picture on prints in the gift shop."

"We're on the case," said Lucas. "I'll email it over to you later today. One of the crew is casing the place as we speak."

"I'd love to see that slag's face when you leave her standing," said Damien. "All the work, all the planning, all up in smoke when

Mister Lucas Vaughan waltzes off with the prize."

Lucas winced and took a deep breath. "Alright, man, you've got to keep quiet about this."

Damien put his finger over his lips then gestured to the blank passports spread over one of the coffee tables.

"We both need to keep quiet about something, eh?" Damien said.

Lucas nodded. "Right, I've got to go. I'll email you later. And Damien..."

"Yeah?"

"Thanks for the head's up, man, I appreciate it."

"All part of the service for my friends."

twenty four

Inside the lift, Zoe was trying to run through the things Lucas had told her about blending in. Unfortunately she kept getting it confused with things she had read in books or seen in movies. Was she supposed to make conversation or not make conversation? Be memorable or forgettable? Those parts of the plan were a bit of a blur, but the parts she'd worked on herself, those things were almost instinctive.

Get inside the foyer? Check.

Piggyback on the security system? Check.

Find a way to get underground and to the front door of the flat while remaining undiscovered by the other residents? Well, she was in a metal box which was the only means of getting in or getting out so she supposed that counted.

"Does the lift take long?" Zoe decided to venture. She caught a glimpse of the beginnings of a disdainful look manifesting itself in the corners of Miss Lester's eyes.

"Too long," Miss Lester replied. She took her phone from her pocket once again. "And nothing works down here." She prodded at it a couple more times. "And I have work I should be doing instead of–"

"I really appreciate you taking the time to let me look at Mr Glass's collection." Zoe tried sounding sincere. She wasn't sure if it worked as she didn't have a great deal of practice.

Miss Lester allowed the rest of the suppressed hatred to spread across her face.

Zoe knew she had to try a different tack, so jumped in with the one thing she knew better than anything else. Technology.

"I'm pretty good with phones," she said, pasting a big, dumb smile on her face. "I can probably get it working for you. If you like."

Miss Lester eyed her suspiciously, then it was as if someone had flicked a switch on her back and the fight went out of her. "Bugger it," she said, handing the phone to Zoe. "If you can get this thing working then I'll give you an extra five minutes with the painting."

"Oh, erm–" Zoe paused, showing Miss Lester the screen. "I need the PIN number."

"Fifteen - oh - nine," she replied.

"Birthday?" asked Zoe.

Miss Lester nodded.

"Mine too," Zoe lied. Once she was inside the phone, Zoe tapped to the settings and began to give herself access to all sorts of interesting titbits. "I don't suppose Mr Glass gave you the password for the network?" she continued, partially so that Miss Lester would feel involved, but mostly to try and save her the task of hacking the network from last year's phone model.

"Oh yes," Miss Lester said. "There's an email with it in but I tried it. It doesn't work."

"Would you be able to find the email for me?" asked Zoe.

Miss Lester took the phone from her and flipped around for a while, sighing and huffing. After about thirty seconds she handed the phone back. Zoe grabbed the password and went about reconfiguring the phone to work off the back of the building's built-in wireless network. Another thirty seconds and the phone was back in Miss Lester's hand and chiming repeatedly to signify new messages, new emails, new voicemails.

"Well done, that girl," said Miss Lester, beaming from ear to ear. "What was the matter with it?"

"Oh, the settings were wrong," Zoe shrugged. The settings were right, now. Miss Lester could go about her business. And the tablet that Zoe had concealed about her person was also given a lovely little back door to the phone and the network. It was more than she could have hoped for.

At last the lift shuddered to a halt, shaking the mirrored walls and creating an odd funhouse feel to the proceedings. Nothing else happened. Zoe turned to Miss Lester, unsure of how to proceed.

"Oh, don't worry," Miss Lester said. "The doors will open in a—"

They slid open to reveal a brightly lit hallway with a deep, plush carpet that Zoe could feel even through her shoes the moment she stepped on it. It was bright down there. In fact, given the state of the British weather it was brighter down under the ground than it was up in the foyer with the security guard. Zoe turned her attention to the walls, trying to locate the source of the light.

Apparently spotting what she was trying to do, Miss Lester looked away from her phone and said, "It's odd, isn't it? Almost too bright for a lightbulb."

Zoe nodded and used the moment to turn around in a full circle, letting the camera in her glasses drink in as much of the detail of the hallways as possible.

"Apparently it's some sort of natural light bulb, they use them in light therapy," Miss Lester said.

"That's a thing, is it?" Zoe asked.

Miss Lester laughed a little bubble of a laugh, "Yes, dear, that's a thing."

The two women moved down the corridor, Miss Lester leading and Zoe following in silence for a moment until, once again, Miss Lester took her gaze away from her phone to address Zoe. "So how the hell did you manage to find out that Mr Glass," Miss Lester nodded her head, an almost imperceptible bow at the mention of his name, "had this painting. Which one was it again?"

"The Dali," said Zoe, as matter-of-factly as she could manage. "Oh, there's a website. Government website. It's got a list of all the ones that are available in the whole country."

Zoe and Miss Lester passed a door, presumably the door to the first flat. It was large. Larger than a normal front door and there were no distinguishing marks on it to signify who lived there. There was no handle, just a card-swipe to the right of the frame.

"I was surprised when I heard from you," Miss Lester continued. "You're the first to have come out of the woodwork."

"Really?" Zoe tried to sound genuinely surprised. "They told us about the website in the first semester."

Miss Lester shrugged and they continued in silence past another door, this time on the opposite side, and on further still until they reached a final door, facing them at the end of the hallway.

"I didn't know – I mean – who lives in a place like this?" asked Zoe, who had, much to her own surprise, finally begun to relax into the role of Sally the student. "He isn't a–"

"He's a banker," said Miss Lester, swiping her keycard and rolling her eyes.

"Oh, right!" said Zoe injecting a hint of surprise. *And the winner of the Oscar for best performance in a hallway goes to...* "So he's just security minded. I suppose the paintings he's got are worth a couple of quid, aren't they? Is that why it's all keycards and security guards."

"This door," said Miss Lester as she stepped inside the flat, "is not simply locked, it also carries an additional security system that will silently call the authorities if it is triggered. There's no 'picking the lock'. There's no getting in and no getting out without this." Miss Lester brandished the keycard.

"Wow," said Zoe and then, after entering the flat, "this place is amazing!"

The flat that she had imagined was simple; spacious enough but compact. This was quite the opposite, looking more like someone had taken a Norse feasting hall and handed it to a reality television makeover show. The high ceilings, the huge rooms.

Zoe had been concerned when donning the surveillance spectacles that she would look out of place trying to scan every corner. But, here in reality, craning her head to drink in every detail of this opulent underground abode seemed exactly the right thing to do. The central area was open plan but doorways and archways led off in different directions around the edges. She craned to see into room after room as she was led through the place. There was no way she was getting every detail but she was getting a good layout of the place, and she could extrapolate the rest when she got back to her desktop.

"Okay then," said Miss Lester, pointing to an archway off to the right. "Here we are."

Zoe walked through, and it was as if the designer of the house had had a taste bypass. The room was what fathers in 1980s American movies call a 'den'. Except it appeared that instead of moving on to whatever the hell the twenty-first century equivalent of that was, Mr Glass had decided that he wanted to be rooted in that 80s timewarp. From the huge oak desk to the stuffed, dead creatures hanging from plaques on the wall and the ash trays with half-smoked Cuban cigars, this was a paean not to bad taste but to a complete absence of taste.

Of course, there was the small matter that, as the head of a bank, he was able to afford something slightly more expensive than the classic 'dogs playing poker'. And so, between the stuffed, dead animals were Rembrandts, Turners and there, in the corner, was the Dali.

"You remember that security system we spoke about?" asked Miss Lester.

Zoe nodded and tried to do doe-eyes.

"Well, there is a further independent security system covering the paintings. Remove any of them from the wall and the place will lock down and the police will be called. And if you were thinking about having a root around in any of the drawers, please remember," she pointed to the corner of the room where another camera surveyed the place, "someone is *always* watching."

Zoe laughed like it was a big joke and then reached into her pocket and took out a notepad and pencil. "This is all I need," she lied.

"I'll leave you to it," said Miss Lester. "You have six minutes."

"But I thought you said I could have an extra five?" Zoe smiled and gestured towards the phone in Miss Lester's hand.

"That includes the extra five."

twenty five

In the eight weeks Miss Nicholson had worked for Lucas, or Logan as she had known him, she was sure she had the measure of him. As a result, she felt quite confident to fly in the face of his advice to get out of the city for a while. In spite of the money he had given her he was, on balance, a bloody idiot. And she wasn't going to get anywhere in her life by listening to bloody idiots.

Although she certainly wouldn't admit it to anyone, she had taken a small amount of his advice and had gone on a little city-break. A trip to London to the British Museum she had always promised herself. She'd had an enormous amount of fun but all of her friends were still at work and it was short notice, so she'd had to go on her own and as a result had only booked the hotel for two nights.

Besides that, now that she was effectively unemployed, she thought that the money would be better spent as the bloody idiot had suggested: training for a new career. Of course, she had no intention of going back to the office — there was no point. But then, on that crisp autumn morning she had reached into her bag for her compact and it wasn't there.

That event, in itself, was not that unusual. She was always

putting it down somewhere or leaving it in her other bag, but this time she had exhausted all the usual places. Had it been her glasses case, her lighter or even her phone she could have come to terms with the loss and replaced the item. The compact, however, was different. It had been left to her by her grandmother after she died and, although now it contained no actual make-up, she carried it for the mirror. The mirror and the connection to her family.

After days of intermittent searching she had finally remembered. She had left the compact at the office and, much as it pained her, she was now rounding the corner of the street and heading back there hoping that Logan Price wasn't in.

Trying the handle of the outside office she was pleased to find it locked. She fished around inside her bag until she found the keys her boss had given her. He wasn't in the habit of turning up to the office on time, in fact most days he hadn't turned up at all. She liked to think she had more integrity. When she was paid to do a job, she wanted to be as professional about it as possible, and in this case that had meant turning up on time. Whether or not that lazy article of a boss bothered to or not.

Letting herself inside, Miss Nicholson walked quickly over to her desk. Nothing had been moved since she had left, in fact a fine layer of dust had begun to form on the exposed surfaces. She wasn't surprised. Sitting down at her desk, she opened the right hand drawer and a little buzz ran through her as she spotted the compact nestled between a box of pens and a stack of unused envelopes. She quickly picked it up and slipped it into her handbag.

"Is Mr Price in the office today?" A voice came from the outer hallway, causing Miss Nicholson to jump.

"Err, no," Miss Nicholson blurted, then, regaining a little composure. "At least, he's not here now. He might be in later. I don't work for him any more so I wouldn't know."

"And yet you have keys to let yourself in to the office, do you not?" said the voice as it turned from the hallway into the office.

"Well yes, but..." Miss Nicholson began.

"Which would lead me to believe that you are still in his employ." The voice sounded like glass being ground in a pestle, but Miss Nicholson was surprised to find that its owner was extremely small

151

in stature.

"Well..." Miss Nicholson tried to speak again.

"My name is Terry," said the man. "You can call me Big Terry. Can I trouble you for your name?"

"Alison. Alison Nicholson," she said, not quite sure what to make of the man. "'Big' Terry? I don't mean to be rude but, well, do you have an act or something?"

Big Terry laughed a hollow, deep laugh with manic edges. It sounded like a big dog being beaten with an angry otter and it made Alison deeply uncomfortable.

"No, my dear," said Big Terry. "I am not in the entertainment business. Although I do find the business I deal in entertains me. My name is in reference to my standing within certain fraternities."

Alison nodded, not really sure what he was talking about. "I see," she lied. "And you have business with Mr Price?"

Big Terry had reached Alison's desk and proceeded to clamber awkwardly onto the chair facing her desk.

"That I do," said Big Terry. "He has placed himself in a position where my undivided attention has been focused upon his actions."

Alison shifted in her seat.

"I was just leaving," she said, not really liking where this conversation was going.

Big Terry shook his head. "You don't know me, do you?" he growled.

"I'm sorry, no, should I know you?" she asked.

"You don't know me, but you are a polite young lady." Big Terry leaned forward. "I like people who are polite. People who help me. Are you going to help me?"

"I'm not going to sleep with you if that's what you're implying," Alison said sharply. With the expanse of desk between them she felt a spark of bravery within her, in spite of the man's cold eyes and oddly intimidating demeanour.

Big Terry held his palms up towards her, his stubby digits outstretched. "You misunderstand me..."

"I don't think I do, Sir," Alison said, standing up. "I don't know what business you have with that – that – arsehole. But it's nothing to do with me. I no longer work here."

"You really have no idea who I am, do you?" said Big Terry. "Please, Miss Nicholson. Alison. Sit down and I'll explain. We can help each other. And then, when we're done helping one another, you can go."

Alison stared at him. This man was the reason Mr Price had told her to leave town. That prick was the problem here. Not the midget. She sat down.

"I am a businessman, Alison," said Big Terry. "I'm really not keen on any other definition beyond that."

"You're a gangster, aren't you?" Alison sighed.

Big Terry shrugged. "I wouldn't call it that exactly."

"You're threatening me though?" she asked.

"Threatening?" Big Terry frowned. "Certainly not. At present there is no need for that. Right now we are just two people having a polite conversation about a mutual acquaintance."

"Right then," said Alison, preferring the conversation when it was on the subject of manners. "How can I help you then, Sir?"

Big Terry smiled and nodded. "I wish to make contact with Mr Price. Do you have a means of contacting him?"

"No," Alison blurted and then, realising that probably wasn't the right answer, let her mouth hang open for a second while she tried to come up with something a bit more useful. "Although," she scraped the depths of her memory and finally found something worthwhile. "He called me from his mobile. A week or two ago. I didn't put it in my phone book but it'll be in my call history."

"Miss Nicholson, I'd be most grateful if you could find that for me," Big Terry said.

"So," said Alison, flushed with the modicum of success she'd managed to wring from this awful situation. "What's he done? I mean, has he double crossed you or something?"

Big Terry laughed his grinding laugh again. "Double crossed? Sounds like something from an American cop show. He tricked an employee of mine into giving him a large sum of money under false pretences."

Alison was staring at her phone, flicking the screen through the days of calls, finger-travelling backwards on her personal timeline. "Are you going to hurt him?"

"You don't sound like you care," said Big Terry. "If I were to say yes, would that bother you?"

Alison looked up at him, giving the question some thought.

"How would you feel if I told you that one of the gentlemen who Mr Price took advantage of was no longer on this mortal coil?"

Alison stared at him, not sure how she felt about that.

"How would you feel if I told you I shot him in the back of the head?"

"I have to say," said Alison slowly, "I don't know. I mean, with the greatest respect, sir, a gentleman of restricted height walked into my old office five minutes ago, I found out he's a – for want of a better word – gangster and that if I don't help him that something horrible might happen to me. How would you feel?"

"Helpful?" offered Big Terry.

"I feel helpful," Alison nodded. "I suppose a part of me realised that Mr Price was into something a little 'off' but do I want you to harm him? I don't know."

"It's a tough decision." Big Terry nodded sympathetically.

Alison looked back down at her phone. Her hand was shaking slightly.

"I just want to go home," she said softly. "I only came back to get my grandma's compact, I left it in the drawer. Please, can I just go home?"

"Alison," said Big Terry. It came out as a growl and her eyes flicked back up to look at him but, oddly, he was still wearing what passed for a sympathetic smile. "You aren't a part of this world. You'll give me the number on the phone, if you have a picture of him..."

"I have, I have one I took, I can–"

"Excellent," Big Terry interrupted. "You'll give me that too. And then you'll go away from here and your world and my world won't ever come together again. And if anyone ever asks about any of this then you just tell them the truth."

"The truth?" asked Alison, a tear welling in the corner of her eye.

"That you never met me. That, to the best of your knowledge, I never came to the office. That the name 'Big Terry' means nothing

154

to you."

"Right," said Alison. "That truth."

Big Terry nodded.

"And..."

"I'll find Mr Price and I won't kill him."

"You won't?"

Big Terry shook his head. "I will ask him politely to pay me the money he owes me. I'll give him a reasonable timeframe to do it."

"And if he doesn't manage it?" said Alison, thinking of how hard he had found it to pay her.

"Then I'll cut off his hands and shove them down his fucking throat."

"I found the number," said Alison.

Big Terry reached into his jacket pocket and removed a business card. On it was written 'Big Terry Enterprises' and an email address and a mobile number.

"Text me the number," he said. "Email the pic."

Alison did as she was told.

"It's been a pleasure meeting you, Miss Nicholson," said Big Terry. "If you leave the keys I'll lock up when I'm done."

Alison grabbed her bag and bolted for the door. "Thank you," she managed to shout as she ran.

twenty six

Someone is always watching. The words echoed in Zoe's ears and she had to stifle a grin as she adjusted the glasses. The glasses that were recording everything she saw and relaying it to the tablet computer in the holster strapped to her body. At that moment they were recording Miss Lester as she left the room and entered a different part of the underground mansion. It seemed odd that, until now, they had referred to this sprawling underground abode as Rollo Glass' 'flat'.

She waited until Miss Lester was out of her line of sight and then finally had the opportunity to do her single most important task. Zoe took a deep breath and moved towards the painting. Taking pride of place between the stuffed and mounted head of a confused looking gorilla and another more elaborate painting was a plain, silver frame containing the canvas. Even in her own head she struggled to call it a painting, and that was doubly true now.

Salvador Dali, the great surrealist, had produced this...

Blank canvas.

Except down in the bottom right hand corner where he had signed it. The signature reminded Zoe of a picture she had seen of the artist, his moustache crazily long. Surreally so, you might say.

His signature looked like that, she thought.

It was disconcerting, though oddly compelling. A complete absence of art in the middle of this room of collectible crap. Zoe leaned in close, making sure the camera glasses captured every brush stroke of his signature. The canvas was a lot smaller than she had imagined.

She didn't have long, but she didn't need long. She moved in close, scanning the canvas inch by inch, looking for any other obvious marks or imperfection but there were none. It was, simply put, a blank canvas with a signature in the corner.

Once she was satisfied that she had captured enough additional images she turned her attention to the frame. Or, more importantly, how the frame was attached to the wall. With her head pressed against the cold wall and the smell of stuffed and dusty gorilla in her nostrils, Zoe made a careful inspection of how the painting connected to the security system. Her gaze followed the wiring around up the wall and into a junction box in the corner.

Happy that she had what she needed, Zoe looked at her watch. Three minutes left. Time to get herself lost.

Treading softly, Zoe made her way to the archway that led out of the room containing the painting. She stood for a moment, listening, and could hear Miss Lester had taken Zoe's gift of communication and was currently using it to abuse one of her fellow employees.

"Do you have any idea how much a mistake like that could cost us?" she shouted into the telephone.

Zoe stepped into the main hallway. The place was positively palatial. Would she be able to map the whole thing in three minutes? She wasn't sure, but she had to start somewhere and moved quickly off in the opposite direction to Miss Lester.

The next room down from the main atrium seemed to be some sort of closet, holding coats, umbrellas and shoes. She darted inside, turned slowly, allowing the camera to drink in as much as possible and then quickly stepped out into the atrium again.

And so it continued through room after room, all the while keeping her ears pricked up for Miss Lester's pacing and shouting. Zoe visited the rooms in turn: the kitchen, the bathroom, guest rooms, a game room and even a bathroom with a baffling abundance of bidets. Finally she found herself entering the room directly next to the one which contained Miss Lester. Zoe was in the master bedroom.

It was dark when she entered, so Zoe flicked the light switch and the room lit up. It was, in keeping with the rest of the place, absolutely massive. In the centre of the far wall was a queen size bed, she could see a walk-in wardrobe, a desk, en-suite bathroom; she was pretty sure that this room was bigger than her last flat. Looking at her watch once more, Zoe realised that her six minutes were up, but she could still hear the irate ranting of Miss Lester, so figured she could map the rest of this room before...

There was an unfamiliar noise out in the hallway. Footsteps. And they weren't Miss Lester's, they were too heavy. Zoe panicked and stumbled into the en-suite bathroom, the heavy footsteps getting nearer by the second. She glanced around, her eyes quickly becoming accustomed to the half-darkness. This was a room in which she definitely didn't want to be discovered.

"Mr Glass," Miss Lester's voice, calm, polite and just a little slimy.

There was a grunt of acknowledgement but the footsteps did not slow.

"I'll be with you in a moment," Miss Lester continued. "I just need to send a couple of quick emails to resolve an issue I've been dealing with."

Another grunt. Closer to Zoe this time. And then the footsteps stopped as they hit the carpet of the master bedroom. Zoe moved away from the bathroom door and pressed her back against the wall. On the opposite wall was a mirror and she could see the banker in the bedroom. And in his hand was a gun.

Zoe clamped her hand over her mouth. It had all been going so smoothly and now she was going to end up shot. She stared at the mirror, watching him stalk across the room towards the bathroom door. How could he see her there, in the darkness? The cameras? Perhaps.

Taking her hand from her mouth, Zoe prepared herself to round on him as soon as he entered the bathroom. What would she do?

Wrestle the gun from him? Grab his wrist?

Rollo Glass took two more steps toward the bathroom then turned and walked up to the side of the bed. He sat down on the corner with his back to the bathroom. Zoe stared, mentally plotting where the door to the bedroom was. She had to make a move. He didn't know she was there. She had to get back to the relative safety of the hall, otherwise...

Otherwise he might actually use the damn gun.

Zoe held her breath and padded out of the bathroom and towards the door of the bedroom. There was a metallic click and Zoe froze, imagining the hammer being cocked on the weapon. But a glance over her shoulder revealed nothing more than the banker unlocking an ornate box. As he placed the pistol inside, Zoe left the room and, hardly caring about the exact location of Miss Lester, darted straight back to the painting. She stood, staring, her back to the door and her heart in her mouth.

Zoe stared at the painting and waited. Waited for the hand on her shoulder, for Rollo Glass to come in and confront her about her little trip off-piste in his underground lair. She waited for Miss Lester to come in and whisk her outside with a *never darken our doorstep, you're lucky we don't call the police.*

Zoe kept staring at the painting. She kept waiting. After a while she shuffled her feet a little to ward off pins and needles, as standing so still was starting to make her uncomfortable. God, that painting was boring. How long had she been staring at it now? Had they forgotten about her?

She kept... oh fuck it... she was bored. Where was that bitch Lester?

Zoe slowly wandered out into the main hallway.

"Hello?" said Zoe.

Nothing.

Her eyes flashed left and right. Some of the lights were out in a couple of the rooms she had been in. In fact it was as if...

Everything went dark.

Zoe screamed.

It was a scream of *I'm still here* as much as a scream of fear. It wasn't fear. Was it? Or was it the fact that it was so dark down there that it didn't feel like night, it felt more like a suffocating death?

Zoe put her hands out in front of herself and swung around in the direction she remembered the front door had been. Taking the smallest, shuffling steps she edged herself forward. What the fuck was going on? Was this a trap? A punishment? A pre-emptive strike?

Stumbling into the void, Zoe suddenly remembered the tablet she was carrying. A tablet that had a camera... that had a flash... that she could...

The front door of the flat opened and light spilled into the cavern like luminous milk.

"Oh God," Miss Lester's voice echoed around Zoe's temporary subterranean prison. "I'm so sorry. I got caught up with Mr Glass' business."

Zoe blinked her eyes, trying to get them to remember how to focus again.

"Please don't sue us," said Miss Lester sheepishly.

22nd September

2 ½ weeks to go…

twenty seven

Two days had passed since Zoe pulled the surveillance job on the banker's flat. Given all the possible things that could have gone wrong, Violet knew that so far the plan had held. The players were playing their parts, the game was, as the saying goes, was on.

Except something had become apparent from the moment Violet had stepped out of the meeting with Fegan and taken on the job for the first time. Violet knew that there was someone she was going to have to deal with. The more the plan for the Dali job had come together in her head, the more she had known that she would stay in Kilchester and the more necessary it would become to deal with her ex.

Percy Parkin, the slippery fuck, was a boil on the arse of Kilchester and Violet had come to the conclusion pretty early on that he would need to be lanced if she were ever going to stay. And she wanted to stay. She had missed this, the hunt, the chase, the thrill of the job. Violet wondered whether Fegan had really realised the gauntlet he had thrown down. In all probability, a challenge like this was the one thing likely to suck her back into the game and back into the city.

The city her ex-boyfriend had tried to kill her in.

Eighteen months was a long time to dwell on how to respond to something like that. And Violet had run through most possibilities. Killing him had remained top of the list for a very long time. She would daydream ways: new, inventive, painful ways of offing him and newer, even more inventive ways of disposing of his worthless corpse.

But after a while even that had lost its appeal.

Mostly.

These days she veered more towards wanting what she'd read in various horrendous lifestyle magazines was called 'closure'. And whether that closure was achieved with or without the use of violence, well, she was less concerned about that.

For Violet, before any plans regarding Percy came to fruition, she needed to confront him, to hear if there was anything that he might be able to offer by way of explanation. For him to look her in the eye and tell her why. And so she'd organised to meet him. Katie thought it was a bad idea. And had said so. Or rather, she hadn't said so, but Violet could tell. Katie oozed disapproval of the whole idea.

And, of course, there was the fact that he had tried to, at best, get her arrested or, at worst, have her killed. Some very real reasons to be wary of Percy.

After lifting the canvases from the museum Violet had bought a burner phone and texted Percy from it.

This is V. I'm in town and we need to talk.

He got the text, she knew that because she had been following him surreptitiously and watched him check his phone. She was surprised at how unmoved she was, seeing him for the first time since the last time.

When she left the house to do the job that day, how had she felt? Had she loved him? She couldn't remember any more. When she thought back to their time together it was... foggy. Unclear. Certainly she remembered him saying it.

But now he was a loose end. And to stay she had to know that loose end wasn't going to wrap around her legs and drag her under.

He responded to the text the next day.

Nothing to talk about. See you around I expect.

She made a point of not over-analysing that. Left it a few hours and texted again.

2pm tomorrow. Cafe in the Park. Unless you'd prefer I find you?

A threat. Whatever aspects of Percy's personality Violet had liked back when they were together, she had always known that he was a coward. Twenty minutes later and she had her response.

Fine. I'll be there.

Violet had chosen the Cafe in the Park for one simple reason. People.

It was always packed and that meant protection for both of them, because neither would risk pulling anything in such a crowded place. Of course, the fact that it was in the park also meant that, should escape be required, there was also plenty of cover. A win-win.

*

Eleven days had passed since Percy Parkin had received the phonecall from Damien telling him that Violet was back in Kilchester. Given all the possible things that could have happened to him at that moment in time, her return was a minor irritation – but an irritation nonetheless. How long had it been? A year and a half since he got rid of her?

Except he hadn't got rid of her. As plans went it had been, he thought, a pretty well thought out one. He had met that girl. What was she called again? He couldn't remember but at the time he'd been with Violet and that bitch had become such a fucking downer, sucking the fun out of his life.

Patricia? Was that her name? She was young, she liked to fuck and, at the time, it'd seemed that was enough. All he had to do was get rid of his current girlfriend. Only Violet could be difficult. Really fucking difficult. That was what had pushed him towards the other woman.

Paula? No. That wasn't it.

But Violet was back in his city. The city he'd tried to have her locked up in.

Even after eighteen months she'd be pissed off about that. And Percy had seen her pretty pissed off in his time. He wasn't entirely convinced that she would rule out trying to kill him. But it had been so long since he thought about any of it. It was like a daydream of another life. At the time he was still working freelance, before he really got in the game and started working for Big Terry.

Pippa? Maybe that was her name. She was the one who came up with the idea. Percy had wanted to stay with Violet, wait until she got the cash from the diamond heist then get it spent and kick her out on her arse. But Poppy... was that her name? She had insisted that this was a better idea. That was just like a woman, Percy thought. Blackmailed him with sex and then threw the competition in jail.

It seemed to make some kind of sense at the time.

Paige? Whatever her name was. She was new, without the baggage that Violet came with. At the time. And Percy had been trying to decide how to react to Violet's return for nearly a fortnight when *beep*.

This is V. I'm in town and we need to talk.

He got the text when he was coming back from the pub. Didn't want to text back pissed because if she was contacting him Violet was most likely a fucking powder keg. By the time he sobered up he'd forgotten he'd got the damn message. Then opened his phone and just couldn't be arsed with her shit.

Nothing to talk about. See you around I expect.

That was it, he thought at the time. Problem dealt with. Showed her who was boss, kept the door open if they ever ended up doing business in the future. Now back to bed.

He was jolted from sleep a couple of hours later when she texted again.

2pm tomorrow. Cafe in the Park. Unless you'd prefer I find you?

Fuuuuuuuuuuuuuuuck. Had Phyllis ever been this high maintenance? He couldn't remember. Wasn't even sure if her name was Phyllis. All Violet ever wanted to do was talk. That was half the problem. What was there to talk about?

For all he knew she had spent the last year and a half at fucking ninja school. Well, it looked like it was time to clear the air. And at least she had chosen somewhere public. He'd have to case the place first, of course, but it showed a degree of reconciliation on her part. Maybe she didn't even realise he'd called the police.

No, that wasn't going to wash.

Fine. I'll be there.

This was going to be a fucking nightmare. However he came out of it, all he could see was him losing. Looking like an idiot, getting jumped by someone on some stupid fucking crew she'd assembled. Well, he'd be ready. And armed. Because... ninjas.

23rd September

Still 2 ½ weeks to go…

twenty eight

Percy had done his due diligence inasmuch as he had done a couple of laps of the pathways surrounding the Cafe in the Park. He wasn't usually this careful but had a sense that this time he might need to be. Anyway, he hadn't found anything unusual. No ninjas. No ambush to speak of.

He shoved his hands in his pockets to ward off the chill that had begun to descend. The weather was supposed to be sunny. But this was autumn and, well... it was bastard freezing. In the left hand pocket of his jacket was his protection, a flick-knife that made him feel like he was in a mafia movie.

In spite of the relatively short distance, Percy's breathing was heavy. He was out of shape. Not 'so fat you need a wall taken out to leave your house' out of shape. More 'too many pies' out of shape. As he came into view of the cafe he immediately saw her at the table in the window. She certainly wasn't out of shape. In fact she was in better shape than a year and a half ago. Maybe this could be the start of something new between them. He put on his most alluring smile and walked through the door and towards the table.

"You can wipe that stupid look off your face for a start," Violet stated matter-of-factly. "Because that ship has sailed."

Percy sat down, pretended she hadn't said anything. "Violet," he said. "What do you want? Why have you dragged me to this fucking awful place?"

"Sit down," said Violet. A command, not an invitation. "I ordered you black coffee. That still how you take it?"

Percy nodded. "You looking to come back?"

"I am back."

"You back to work?"

Violet nodded.

A waitress arrived with their drinks, Violet's espresso cup dwarfed by Percy's large coffee.

"Better be careful who you choose for your crew," said Percy as the waitress picked her way through the tightly packed tables, back towards the counter. "Make sure you don't get some guy who's only looking to fuck up, get busted back to prison."

Violet stared at him, her palms flat on the table, the fury rising inside her. She knew what he was getting at, making out it was her fault the diamond heist had fucked up.

"You've worked with some small-time mindwrongs in your time," said Violet.

Percy opened his mouth to speak, but Violet shot right in there.

"You ever see me knocking off an off-license for a laugh with a 'Born To Lose' tattoo on my chest?" Violet spat the words at him like bullets.

"Might improve those saggy tits of yours," Percy sneered and then he shouted, "Prunella!"

"What!?" Violet simultaneously incandescent with rage and completely blindsided by his outburst.

"I've been trying to remember her name since you texted me, sorry," Percy laughed and lounged back in his chair, apparently oblivious to the trouble he was stirring.

"Who?" was all Violet said.

"Oh, er," Percy stumbled over how to describe her. "Your replacement."

Violet's mind raced back to the heist, the phonecall, the woman's voice in the background.

"Percy." Violet took a deep breath. "Listen to me, you prick."

Percy lost just a little of his bravado.

"I'm coming back to Kilchester. I'm going to do what I do best here, and if you want to continue doing what you do best then we need to resolve this."

"This what?" Percy could hear it in his own voice: the swagger was evaporating. Violet was different. She was cold. Driven.

"I need you to listen. And I need you to think before you speak. I know this does not come naturally to you but I am *this* close to putting you through *that* window right now."

Percy squirmed in his seat but, unfortunately, he believed her, so figured he would listen. Curse those potential ninja skills.

"That night. You called the police."

Percy lifted the coffee to his lips and blew on it.

"It doesn't surprise me in the slightest that you had neither the spine to break it off with me in person nor the intelligence to get me arrested." Violet could feel herself losing it. "It surprises me even less that you had forgotten the name of the girl that was my *replacement*." She needed to keep a lid on. At least for now. "I mean what sort of person tries to have his girlfriend arrested rather than break up with her... No... don't answer that. It's a rhetorical question."

Violet stared. Percy stared back. He wasn't grinning any more.

Looking at him now, doughy, his hair visibly thinner, the attitude, Violet felt... like it had happened to someone else. But it hadn't. She had been with him.

"I have a real question," said Violet eventually. "What Will did to Jenny. Was that meant for me? The nightstick to the head. Was that part of your master plan?"

"Planning and thinking, that's all you ever did." Percy didn't want to take this lying down. "I heard about what Will did and *no* it wasn't what I wanted to happen. That Will's a fucking psycho is all."

Violet finally picked up her espresso and took a sip. It was already cold. She sipped anyway, letting the bitter goodness wash across her tongue.

She carefully placed the tiny cup in its equally tiny saucer.

"That's all?" she asked slowly.

Percy grinned and shrugged.

"That's all?" Violet was getting quieter with each word and yet people at the surrounding tables were still beginning to turn around and stare. Percy instantly regretted grinning. "That is pretty fucking far from all," she hissed. "This was never about how you broke up with me. It was about the fact that you put Will into that crew whether or not you told him to beat someone to death."

Percy's face dropped. "What the hell are you talking about? Why would I–"

"So that's all Jenny was… collateral? A bad judgement call on your part? Is that what you're saying?"

Regaining his composure, Percy rounded on Violet. "These things happen. You do what you have to do."

"That's precisely the point, Percy. You didn't have to do any of it. You didn't have to try to get me arrested, you didn't have to put someone in the crew who you knew was… was…" Violet faltered, the image of Jenny's battered head still raw in her memory. "Was that the plan? Take care of her then take care of me? Two dead birds then throw Will to the wolves?"

Percy picked up his coffee and blew on the surface.

"Was that your plan, Percy?"

Percy shrugged as he put the coffee back down. "I forget."

"I want to know," said Violet, her voice thin and quiet, the hatred from her eyes boring into him. "I want to know whether you intended to hand me over to the police or kill me. Is that such a hard thing for you to talk about?"

"Is that why we're here? Because I'm sick of talking. That was always your problem, all you wanted to do was talk, talk, talk." Percy leaned over the table towards Violet. "You want to talk about your feelings?" he said in a whiny voice. "You want to hug it out? Piss off. It would be easier if you were banged up because if I came to talk to you at least there'd be a sheet of glass between the two of us, and if you were dead I would still be in bed right now."

Violet jerked her head forward as if she were going to head-butt him. Percy flinched away from her, knocking his almost full and very hot coffee off the table and onto the floor. The whole cafe went quiet.

The waitress scampered over with a cloth and began mopping at the mess Percy had created. The background mutter of conversation began again but Percy and Violet just stared each other down.

"Would you like me to get you another one?" the waitress asked.

Percy looked over to hear. "No, I won't be staying."

"You need to make amends. What you did had consequences. For you. For Jenny," Violet said as the waitress made her way back to the counter. "He beat her half to death. And that's on you."

Percy didn't sit down. "It's been a year and a half, Violet. And I get it, you're bitter about it all and now you roll into Kilchester and want your revenge. Well, I'm going to tell you now, it is not going to happen." Percy's phone vibrated in his jeans pocket but he ignored it. He was on a roll and he wasn't going to stop. "You want the truth? You want closure? I told Will to put Jenny down. I told him to put you down and I called the police on all of you. You know what else? I did it because a woman whose name I can barely remember suggested it to me."

Violet stared. The other twenty people in the cafe stared. The waitress stared.

Percy glanced around and became suddenly self-conscious, dropping his voice to a whisper and leaning towards her again. "I'm not some rinky dink fence now, I've moved on too. I work for Big Terry these days, so if you're staying in town, stay out of my way. I'll certainly be staying out of yours."

Violet didn't speak. Left the silence to hang and then slammed her palms on the table.

Percy flinched again and jumped back.

Violet stood up and walked out of the cafe.

twenty nine

Percy waited what he considered an appropriate amount of time before leaving the Cafe in the Park. It wasn't that he was embarrassed; he didn't give a fuck what the other people in the cafe thought of him, it was simply that he didn't want to end up bumping into Violet.

Who the hell did she think she was, trying to tell him what to do? Percy glowered out of the window for a moment and then remembered he'd received a message on his phone. Fishing it out of his jeans' pocket wasn't the easiest thing in a sitting position but he wrestled it out.

Are you around? Need to speak to you about shifting something. Lucas.

This Lucas bloke was keen to get Percy to shift some painting or other. And he hadn't even stolen it yet. Cocky little bastard. But Damien vouched for him and had put them in touch, so...

If you couldn't trust your friends, who could you trust?

I'm in the city centre. Can meet you there if you like.

Percy texted then pulled his coat tight to ward off the cold and began to walk the path through the trees that led out of the park.

Yeah, inside or out?

This Lucas bloke was keen. But respectful. Letting Percy choose the venue. He liked that. Not like Violet and her bloody threats and demands. He thought about it for a second then began texting back.

War memorial on Fawcett Street. 5 minutes.

*

Violet had to move quickly to get away from the Cafe in the Park to ensure Percy wasn't following her. She couldn't risk him seeing the van they were using. His was a flapping mouth and if she was going to make sure he got what was coming to him then she needed to stay out of his direct line of sight.

How did she feel now that she had confronted him? She had anticipated that her worst suspicions would be proved right and there they were – confirmed. The chill wind had taken her temper off the boil enough that she felt clear headed, but Percy's admission and, well, his whole goddamn attitude towards her was enough to confirm that revenge would be dealt.

Taking her phone from her pocket she sent a quick text to Lucas. *Time to pick up the package.*

Leaving the park, Violet pressed the fob on the van's keyring and it *chirruped* its acknowledgement. Lucas' reply came back as Violet climbed into the driver's seat. As she pulled the car into the traffic and turned up the heater, she wondered if Damien had finished the forgeries.

Trying her best to multitask, Violet whipped off her jacket as soon as she hit a set of traffic lights, managing to pull on a black cap and matching hoodie before the lights turned green. It was time to do some surveillance. Her phone vibrated again. This time it was Katie.

East exit

Violet was already en route and by the time Percy exited the park she was parked way up the street at the east exit of the park where it met Fawcett Street. As soon as Violet had eyes on Percy she cut the engine. Still not sure whether he would stop around here or move on, Violet climbed out of the driver's seat and started setting up some of the monitoring gear as Zoe had shown her. The camera feed was live and the red circle on the computer meant that it was recording but the audio wasn't up and running.

Staring at the feed of Percy crossing towards the war memorial, the fury began bubbling inside of her and peaked as she saw a familiar face approaching from the other direction.

Lucas.

Trying to remember how to position the directional microphone, Violet wound the passenger window down and adjusted it, pointing it where she thought it should go. Violet watched as Percy approached the war memorial and sat down on the bench in front of it. She watched as Lucas approached the war memorial and sat down beside Percy.

The two men started talking.

She put on the headphones. Nothing. It wasn't picking anything up.

"Fuck," Violet hissed under her breath. "What the fuck is going on?" She fumbled with another wire and with a *pop* that nearly deafened her voices started coming through. The wrong voices.

Violet stared at the screen in a panic. She had to know what they were saying.

"Fuckshitfuckshitfuckshitfuck," she spat, trying and failing to move soundlessly within the van. Reaching forward, she got hold of the microphone and adjusted the direction. Adjusted it again. And again. And finally she had it.

"...Damien for years," It was Lucas' voice. Coming through the headphones.

Zoe had said that if it was coming through the headphones it was recording.

Violet stared at the computer screen, transfixed. She was amazed, too, at the quality the microphone could pick up. Admittedly it had a swirling, crackled, quality, like some sort of cyber-demon, but you could clearly hear what was being said.

"Yeah, he mentioned you but right now you've got nothing for me to shift. So why the fuck are we here?" Percy, playing the big man, Violet thought. Trying to impress Lucas with piss and wind.

There was some interference in the signal as two young girls walked through the field of the microphone.

Violet winced as their posh accents and inane babble invaded her headspace.

And then they were gone and Lucas was speaking again. "–that you work for Big Terry but, because of how this painting is coming into my possession... I want to keep as few people in the loop as possible."

"What do you mean?" asked Percy. There was a metallic *ching* as he flicked open a Zippo and touched the flame to a cigarette. "If you want me to do this off the books I need to know the score."

"It's a painting. It's worth–" Lucas cut out again, this time it was absolute silence. Violet returned to swearing profusely and plugging and unplugging wires.

"How fucking much?!" Percy started coughing, apparently in surprise. "Mate, you have some big balls to be talking those numbers."

"Damien said you could shift it though. Can you?" Lucas sounded desperate.

Violet stared, a frown plastered across her brow, watching intently at how the meeting was playing out.

"Who's running the crew?" Percy took another drag on his cigarette and pulled his coat in tighter.

"Does it matter?"

"It matters."

"Woman called Violet Winters. You know her?" asked Lucas.

"Do I know Violet Winters?" repeated Percy. He laughed a thin laugh through his nose. Violet stared at the image on the computer and had to resist the urge to push his head through a window for the second time in as many hours. "I am aware of her, yes."

"Well?" said Lucas. "Can you shift the painting without involving anyone else?"

"So Violet has put together a crew to rob a painting. Which painting was it?" Percy was fishing. Violet adjusted the headphones and shook her head. What was Lucas thinking?

"Ah, no," said Lucas. "I'm not having you jumping in there and grabbing it first."

Violet's phone started buzzing. It was Zoe. She ignored it. Whatever it was could wait.

Percy shrugged. "So you're going to help her to steal this

mystery artwork and then you're going to… what? Walk off with it, leaving the stupid cow standing there with nothing?"

Violet went back to her mental list of 'most painful ways to kill a man' and started picturing the outcomes. It was either that or scream so loudly they would see her.

Lucas nodded. "That's the plan."

"My friend," said Percy. "I think we have ourselves an agreement, in principle. I'll take thirty per cent."

"Thirty? Can you do any better?" Lucas sounded like an amateur.

"No," said Percy. "No I can't."

"Okay then," said Lucas. "But one thing I want to ask."

"Fire away," said Percy, flicking his cigarette butt in an arc toward the gutter.

"How can you make sure Big Terry doesn't find out."

"Listen to me," said Percy, and leaned in closer to Lucas. "Big Terry is a big fucking moron. He wouldn't notice a turd if you smeared it on his top lip. I've been skimming off the top of practically every deal I've ever been involved in for him and he doesn't notice any of it."

"Really? How the hell do you manage that?" asked Lucas, awed.

"Well," Percy replied. "Maybe it's because I'm skimming off the top. So he can't see it!" Percy laughed his reedy laugh.

"I don't get it," said Lucas, smiling politely. "What do you mean?"

"Have you met Big Terry?" asked Percy.

Lucas shook his head.

"He's a dwarf. A midget. Whatever the fuck. He's a short arse. So if I'm skimming off the top then he can't see it because he's too fucking short. Geddit?"

"Oh, I see." Lucas nodded but didn't laugh.

Violet took off the headphones and laid them down. So there it was. Betrayal. Only thing was to decide what to do with the information. Could Lucas–

The phone in Violet's pocket had not stopped vibrating through the whole exchange. She couldn't ignore it any more. It was Zoe. Violet opened the most recent text.

Call me as soon as you get this. Have found out they are moving the painting from the banker's house. We now only have four days or the painting is in the wind.

Violet screamed.

thirty

An uncomfortable silence had fallen on the warehouse as Zoe, Barry, Lucas and Katie waited for Violet to return. Usually Barry would be tinkering with the cars, and Zoe doing things to the computer equipment that no-one else understood, but even they were just sitting around. Waiting.

Zoe had told them all that the painting was to be moved and now they were waiting for their leader to return. To tell them it was all going to be alright. To inspire them.

Eventually Lucas had gotten bored of staring at their faces, staring at the walls, and had whipped a pack of cards from his pocket.

"Not after the last time," Zoe said with a sigh. "So don't give me any of your over and under Texas Pokering, alright?"

"I could teach you," said Lucas, trying to put on his game face and not look like he was about to empty the purses and wallets of everyone there. "Show you how to cheat."

"Fuck it," said Barry, pulling a table between them. "Show me your magic finger, sir."

Katie pulled up a chair, tapped the table and nodded.

"Come over here with me." Lucas patted the chair next to him.

"You can *teach* me," said Zoe as she moved to Lucas' side. "But tap a chair like I'm a dog again and I'll snap off your fingers."

Lucas nodded and shuffled the cards.

Twenty minutes later and Zoe was none the wiser as to how to keep track of the position of each card in the deck, Katie's enormous hands weren't coping well with false shuffles and Barry was pretty sure that he was down thirty quid.

"What the fuck happened to you morose motherfuckers?" was Violet's opening gambit when she eventually did step through the door.

There were various mumblings from the collected crew but nothing concrete.

Violet closed the door and walked towards them, frowning as she saw the pile of money in front of Lucas.

"Cheating," said Zoe. "Lucas was teaching us how he does it. He's—"

"A fucking card-counting cunt," Barry interjected.

Lucas held up his palms. "It's a fair cop," he said with a grin.

Barry shook his head in frustration. He and Katie reached over to Lucas and grabbed their money back from the pile. Lucas pushed the remaining notes away from himself then picked up the cards and carefully put them back in the the box and into his pocket.

Violet put down a bag containing computer equipment from the van on the table in front of him, but when Zoe instinctively went to collect it, Violet stopped her.

"Tell me the whole story," she said to Zoe. "Everything."

"When I was down in the flat the secretary couldn't get her phone to connect to the network," said Zoe, and ran her hand through her hair, moving it out of her eyes. "I mentioned in passing that I might be able to get it working. I may even have implied that I was a bit of an expert..."

Lucas laughed, "Did you mislead that poor, unsuspecting woman?"

"I may have." Zoe gave an exaggerated flutter of her eyelashes, the picture of innocence. "So anyway, I cloned her phone. Then I connected it to the network, of course. Took about thirty seconds. All I did was—"

"You cloned her phone?" Barry interrupted. "What the fuck does that mean?"

Zoe looked at him for a second, weighing up the question. Trying to work out whether he was trying to undermine her or actually didn't know. She decided to go for the latter.

"Essentially what you do is you make a kind of digital copy of her phone," said Zoe. "A clone. And once you've done that, any call that phone makes, any it receives, any data that goes in and out... You can access it all."

"And you can do this with any phone?" asked Barry, taking his own phone out of his pocket and eyeing it suspiciously.

"Sure can," said Zoe with a grin. "Don't worry though, you lot are far too dull to warrant additional attention. It's bad enough having to spend time with you in person without being forced to listen to your tawdry babbling on the phone. Especially Katie, she never shuts up."

Everyone laughed, the tension in the room falling away slightly.

"So you intercepted a phonecall?" asked Violet, still smiling but wanting to get things back on track.

"A text," Zoe corrected. "From Rollo Glass. Apparently the painting is being put into storage."

"Because of your visit?" asked Violet, and then, realising the implication, "I don't mean you blew it, I just mean in case anyone else wants to jump on the bandwagon."

"It's okay," said Zoe. "No, it seems pretty routine. I think he just has so many paintings that he rotates them."

"Same as me," said Barry. "Only mine are done by my niece. And she's four."

"No need to jump to her defence, Barry," Violet smiled. "If it wasn't for Zoe's smarts we'd be busting in to find our target gone."

"So what now?" asked Lucas pointedly. "We change the plan? Hit it on the way out?"

"Not enough time to plan," said Violet. "They'll use a security firm and we'd need a man on the inside." Violet stared at Barry, making the calculations in her head. "No. No time."

Violet clicked her tongue on the roof of her mouth and began pacing.

"No," she said, weighing up the case for and against in her head. "But if we kick it up a notch. With a couple of minor alterations we could pull this off. Especially with all the extra data Zoe managed to pull from her little undercover operation."

Zoe did a miniature salute with her index finger.

"Right then," said Barry. "Then what the fuck are we waiting for. Let's do what you say, boss. I've been twiddling my thumbs for too long anyway. Might as well get in gear before I get bored and start blowing shit up."

"Wha–" Zoe began.

"How long did Damien say the painting would take?" Violet interrupted, aiming the question at Lucas.

"What day is it?" Lucas asked and then, before anyone could answer, "today was the earliest he said it might be ready. I can give him a ring if you like and ask–"

"No," Violet stopped pacing and pointed at Barry. "You. Go and be... oh fuck it, Barry, go and be rude to him, he's a waste of blood and organs anyway and if he's not finished give him some sort of incentive."

Barry nodded.

"And take Zoe," said Violet, glancing at the bag of surveillance tech from the van. "Good experience for you Zoe. Making sure the dog doesn't slip his leash."

Zoe shrugged.

"What about us?" asked Lucas, gesturing towards Katie.

"Mr Vaughan," Violet sighed. "Do you imagine I keep you around for your good looks?"

Lucas began to verbalise something but Violet cut him down. "I need your brains." She turned to Katie and gave her a wink. *And your looks.*

*

"So is this all you do then?" asked Zoe, finally breaking the silence between herself and Barry after an awkward first five minutes. "Drive fast and paint cars?"

Barry was staring petulantly out of the windscreen, concentrating unrelentingly on the rush-hour traffic. He glanced occasionally in the rearview mirror and frowned slightly. They had moved around two hundred metres in five minutes and things were showing no sign of getting any better. Zoe had a feeling that Barry was also smarting because she'd wanted to take the Aston Martin. He told her no and took the old car instead, the Mark One Escort. His pride and joy.

Not that this vintage bucket of bolts was a bad car. It just wasn't an Aston Martin.

"I'm good with my hands," said Barry. "All sorts of ways."

"I bet you are, big boy," Zoe smirked, watching Barry's face drop in embarrassment.

"I'm a dab hand with explosives too," said Barry, trying to steer her away from making him feel like a pervert. "And how old are you. You look..."

"About twelve years old, yes I'm aware of that..." Zoe snapped.

"Glove compartment," Barry said matter-of-factly, before turning the handle that wound down the driver's side window. He reached out and adjusted the side mirror.

Zoe popped the glove compartment and reached inside. There was a block of something in a grey wrapper. Maybe twenty centimetres long, maybe ten centimetres wide and the same in height.

"Plastic explosive," said Barry and then scratched his nose and yawned.

"Jesus Christ, are you insane? What's it doing in the glove compartment?" said Zoe, holding on to the block as if it were a baby bird, touching it with only her fingertips.

Barry laughed and moved the car forward another couple of metres. "Don't worry, without a detonator it's practically impossible to set it off."

"Practically?" said Zoe, carefully placing the block back in the glove compartment and slowly closing it. "Meaning that there is a chance?"

Barry checked his mirrors again, his brow furrowed. "Fuck this," he said, slammed the car into gear and pulled out into the oncoming lane, flashing his lights and honking the horn as he began accelerating towards the cars coming in the other direction.

Zoe winced and pushed herself back into the passenger seat,

checking her seatbelt.

"Don't worry," said Barry, calmly. "They'll move out of the way."

"And if they don't and we crash. How likely is it the plastic explosive right in front of me will go off?"

"Not going to happen," said Barry, continuing to slowly accelerate into the oncoming traffic, which was, miraculously, veering out of the way.

"I'm going to close my eyes and when I open them can we be in a slightly less life threatening situation?"

"Spoilsport," said Barry, turning off the main road onto a quieter, more suburban one. "We're almost there anyway."

Barry guided the car down a couple more streets and pulled in to the side of the road. He and Zoe unclipped their seatbelts.

"Wait," said Barry, frowning again.

"I'm not sitting in the car like a kid."

"Don't turn around," Barry continued. "But someone's been following us."

"Even after your trick with the wrong side of the road?" asked Zoe with a smirk.

Barry sighed. "Unfortunately, yes."

Zoe dropped the smirk and flipped down the sun visor. She adjusted it and stared into the vanity-mirror. "White car?"

"Yeah," Barry replied. "Amateurs. But persistent. I was thinking if you had any of those magic gadgets of yours you might get a photo while I'm in there."

Zoe nodded and reached into her shoulder holster, pulled out her tablet. "Reckon I can get something usable."

Barry opened the door and stepped out of the car, shutting it firmly behind him. Zoe watched as he walked to the front of the forger's house. It was a big, old terraced house, the green paint on the bay window frame peeling to reveal the white of the previous colour underneath. Barry picked his way up the overgrown garden path and pressed the doorbell. Zoe wound down her window and edged the tablet out just far enough that the camera cleared the door frame; took a couple of test shots.

Glancing back over to Damien's house, Barry had vanished. Gone inside.

She pulled the tablet back inside and checked the results.

Not good. Two men had left the car.

Zoe had a moment's panic, hunkered down into the footwell and twisted around. The men weren't coming for the car, they were heading for the house. She had to warn Barry.

Her hand darted into her pocket, whipped out her mobile and dialled Barry. There was a pause as the call connected. The men were crossing the road.

"Comeoncomeon connect, you shit!" Zoe cursed.

The call connected. Barry's phone began to ring. In the glove compartment.

"Bastard!" Zoe shouted. The two men were entering the garden. They were seconds away.

She had no choice, Zoe reached over and slammed her palm on the centre of the steering wheel. The horn blared. Zoe kept her hand pressed on the horn, the two figures turning around to see what the commotion was.

And they started to move towards her. That wasn't good. That wasn't good at all. Zoe took her hand from the horn and snapped a picture of the two men. They started running. That was really, really bad.

And then it struck her – lock the car doors! And then something struck one of the men. And that something was a cricket bat. And wielding it was... Barry! Where the hell had he come from?

Zoe's hand hovered over the button which controlled the door lock, not quite sure that was the right move. The second man turned around to face Barry but Barry was already on top of him, the cricket bat swung high in the air. The man held up his hands to protect his face but Barry's swing wasn't aimed at his head. The apex of the swing was much lower, aimed at the ankles and swung with such force that the man was swept from his feet. Barry rode the momentum and ran to the car, jumping inside and turning over the engine.

"Nice distraction," he said to Zoe and slipped the courier tube over his head, dropping it into her lap along with the cricket bat. "I'd put that seatbelt on if I were you."

thirty one

Barry stamped the accelerator flat to the floor and the car took off down the street, the modified exhaust so loud that Zoe could feel the reverberations in her stomach. She fastened her seatbelt and looked over her shoulder out of the rear window. The two men were getting to their feet and running to their car.

"I got a picture of them," said Zoe, nervously.

"I know who they are," Barry replied, his eyes glued to the road ahead. He twisted the wheel, sending the car into a slide. They almost seemed to come to a stop; Zoe was pinned back in her seat as it jumped forward.

"What do you mean you know who they are?" Zoe held the courier tube tight in one hand and her tablet in the other. "Who are they?"

Barry touched the brakes as they loomed up on a smaller family car. He honked the horn and flashed his lights at them. They ignored him.

"Oh, just some people I owe money to," he said and then revved the engine.

The oncoming traffic cleared. Barry heaved the car into the other lane and darted forward once more. The houses were thinning out as they headed into an empty commercial district, and with rush hour over, the road ahead was almost clear.

"How much money do you have to owe to warrant sending people to do you harm?" asked Zoe.

"I was on a losing streak at the casino." Barry glanced in the mirror. The white car careered out of a side street and into their slipstream. "I was losing for, like, thirty two hours straight."

"How is that even possible?" Zoe asked, her eyes darting to the speedometer as it moved up and up and up.

"Trust me," said Barry. "It's possible. You know the Princess Casino?"

"That car ferry that sits in the river?" Zoe craned around in time to see their pursuers ram their rear end.

They lurched unpleasantly forward. There was a tearing noise. The car swerved, but Barry corrected its course.

"They converted it to be a casino. Unfortunately I don't have Lucas' super-human ability to win at cards," Barry said.

"I thought you were supposed to be some sort of genius driver?" Zoe snapped, panicking. "Should I throw the explosives out the window? We could..."

The road began to widen into dual carriageway. Four lanes of fun for them to play with.

"What?" said Barry, watching the white car gaining on them. "Blow them up?" He shook his head. "I've got no detonators and besides, it's too imprecise."

There was another crunch; this time they had pulled alongside and were trying to ram Zoe and Barry off the road sideways. Looking ahead, Barry slammed the brakes and dropped behind the white Mercedes in the outside lane.

"My beautiful car..." Barry grumbled. He tried to gain on them but the white car accelerated out of the way easily.

"Never mind the car," said Zoe. "You can fix the damn car, just get us out of this alive, okay?"

"Don't worry," said Barry, giving her a wink. "I've got a plan."

He started accelerating towards the white Mercedes once again. This time they slipped into the inside lane, allowing Barry to overtake. He grinned as Zoe stared past him to the passenger in the other car. She could see a trickle of blood on the man's brow from where Barry had hit him.

The Mercedes lunged sideways again and smashed into them, almost sending them into the central reservation.

"Barry," said Zoe quietly. "What's the plan?"

Barry nodded up ahead. There was a car in the inside lane in the path of the Mercedes. But in front of them, nothing.

The Mercedes tried to speed up, to undertake, but Barry had a little held back. He gunned the engine and they jumped forward, matching the Mercedes' speed. The car up ahead was a hundred metres away.

Ninety metres.

The Mercedes dropped back, thinking he could slip behind Barry and Zoe.

Eighty metres.

One thing he could definitely do was slow down. The two cars remained side by side.

Seventy metres to impact.

Zoe stared at the two men. The passenger in their car was panicking. For some reason that made her more relaxed.

Sixty metres.

Fifty.

The Mercedes accelerated, thinking they could slip in front of Barry and Zoe, but Barry's plan, whatever it was, had anticipated their ruse.

Forty.

Slowing down had given Barry a little extra kick to match the Merc's acceleration.

Thirty metres.

Twenty.

As Zoe stared out of the window she could see the driver of the Mercedes; he had two options: slow down, or crash into the car in the inside lane.

Ten metres.

Zoe had read on the internet that in certain circumstances someone's perception of time could be drastically altered. Like right then, with the adrenaline being overloaded in her system, she could see those two men and she could see the concentration on Barry's face. The same concentration she experienced when she got lost in her work.

Zoe smiled as she stared at the two men in the Mercedes. Smiled as they crossed the ninth and eighth metre from the approaching car.

Smiled as the Mercedes slammed into Barry's side of the car, forcing them into the central reservation. Smiled as the Mercedes took their place in the outside lane. And even smiled as the world outside the window flipped upside down and flipped and flipped and flipped.

Such an odd thing for the world to do.

Of course, the world doesn't do that for long before the whole thing comes crashing down and turns...

Black.

thirty two

The first thing Zoe could hear was coughing. It was loud.

She opened her eyes and the black went away.

There was smoke or maybe powder in the air. It smelled dusty. Not like talcum powder. It looked like talcum powder though.

Something was wrong.

Well, Barry had crashed the car. That was something. But something else was wrong. Was she injured? It felt like there was a weight — rather than pushing her down it was as if it was pulling her upwards.

Zoe moved her left arm and immediately regretted it. Pain shot from her shoulder where the seatbelt had held her in place.

Pain. That wasn't so bad. She could deal with pain. Dying in a car crash or being blown up with plastic explosives, on the other hand, were two things she would have been significantly more cross about.

She tried to speak, but her voice was too hoarse to make much impact on her environment.

Blinking her eyes woozily, Zoe focused on the motes of dust in the air. She should get out of the car. Yes. She needed to make sure she had no major injuries.

Okay then, here we go. Zoe moved her right hand and clicked the seatbelt release.

Gravity, which until that point had simply been irritated by her, pinned upside down in the car seat, decided to make an example of her and dropped her to the ground — which, from Zoe's perspective, was the roof of the car.

Momentarily disorientated at seemingly falling upwards Zoe's brain quickly adjusted as she opened the passenger door and got to her feet. Looking over toward the road, there was no longer any sign of the white Mercedes. They were alone.

They.

Barry. Where was Barry? Zoe limped around to the driver's side of the car. Barry was lying half in and half out of the car. How had she not noticed that sooner?

"Barry?" Zoe managed to say, her voice cracking as she spoke. "Are you alright?"

Barry groaned and began to move, dragging himself out of the wreck of the car.

He got to his feet; his face was a bloody mess, his left eye closed up, blood streaming from his nose and a gash in his lip. Moving quickly, he came towards Zoe. She flinched slightly as he reached for her head. "You're cut," he said.

Zoe reached up and touched her brow. There was a small graze. "What?" she asked. "I'm fine, I think. You're a mess."

"I'm sorry," he said, his hand still held over her ear, cupping her head gently. "I'm sorry."

Zoe reached up and took his hand, gave it a little squeeze. "I'll live," she said. "The seatbelt, maybe the roll cage saved me. Can't say the same for you."

Looking inside the car, Zoe grabbed a hoodie from the wreck and tore a couple of strips off it. Taking one, she started to dab at Barry's nose.

"The seatbelt didn't break," said Barry. "I was fine. I was conscious."

"So what happened?" Zoe asked.

"The blokes from the Mercedes." He winced as Zoe dabbed at his lip then took the rags from her to finish the job. "Dragged me far enough out that they could start kicking me. Then kicked me until I passed out. But not before they took the courier tube and your tablet thing."

"They've got the painting?" Zoe sighed. "Fuckers."

*

Zoe had managed to salvage Barry's mobile phone from the wreckage of the car. She called Violet.

Violet, in turn, did not react well to the news.

Zoe and Barry walked the half a mile down the road to the meeting point in relative silence, each contemplating the problem alone. By the time they got there both had the beginnings of ideas forming.

Like many roadside cafes, the Kilchester Travel Chef was not a place of rest, nor was it a place of recuperation for the weary traveller. The franchise appeared to have been excreted onto the world by a deranged giant. Its awful architecture jutted menacingly out and appeared to put you in danger of actual physical harm if you were brave enough to stare it down. As if this wasn't bad enough, the chef of this particular franchise was a man possessed with mediocrity. Not for him the extremes of good or bad, his unconscious directed him only to the middle road.

The mediocre.

Violet was already inside, sipping mediocre coffee that had been served to her in an untimely fashion. It wasn't that it had taken too long. It hadn't arrived immediately. It had arrived just before the moment when, as a customer, you could legitimately become slightly irritated at the beverage's absence.

On the journey over to the cafe Violet had regretted her outburst to Zoe. All she could think about was the fact that they had four days. Lose the forgeries now and they were out of the game. But Violet's mind didn't work like that. Not for long. She was 75% optimist. If they were lucky, the men who had stolen the forgeries thought they had two autographs. It wasn't exactly easy to identify what the paintings were and if you Googled them you would most likely find what she herself had found: a plethora of pages dedicated to the majority of Dali signatures which were, comparatively speaking, worthless.

197

There were options. There were always options. She just needed all the facts first.

Violet's regret at her reaction turned to horror when they finally appeared at the cafe. Zoe limping slightly in her left leg, her shoulders drooping. And Barry... his face was... a bloody mess.

Feeling like a monster, Violet stood up so the pair of them could see where she was and come over. She watched as Zoe's gaze flipped around the cafe looking for her, then saw her, and then...

Zoe burst into tears.

Barry tried to put his arm around her as they walked towards the table but Zoe shrugged it off. Trying to claw back her composure, she grabbed a handful of napkins from an empty table and blew her nose with a rasping *parp* that echoed throughout the small establishment.

They sat down at the table, Violet on one side, Barry and Zoe on the other.

"I don't even know why I'm crying," said Zoe blowing her nose again. "He was the one who was hurt, not me."

"It's shock," said Violet, trying to sound as understanding as possible. "Your whole system's in shock. Barry's just..."

"This isn't my first car crash." Sensing that he should comfort Zoe, Barry finished Violet's sentence. "Or the first time I've had a kicking."

"Well that's not very reassuring," Zoe snapped. She stared at him for a second, big tears welling in her eyes, and burst out laughing.

Violet and Barry joined in and Zoe seemed to calm again.

A silence descended on the table and, for a moment, all that could be heard was the murmur of customers and the chink of metal on plate.

"It's my fault," said Barry eventually.

Violet lifted her hands and rubbed her brow, her palms covering the whole of her face. She ran her fingers through her hair and levelled her gaze at the pair of them.

"I overreacted," she said slowly. "On the phone. I'm supposed to be in charge of you lot and what with being the leader *and* making the plans *and* making sure we steal priceless works of art..."

Barry and Zoe nodded. Violet was picking up speed as she

spoke and, although she was looking at them, there was a sense that she was looking slightly past them.

"Well, we need to be a team," she continued. "And as a team, to be perfectly frank, we could have done without this little fuckup, Barry."

Barry shifted in his seat uncomfortably but didn't interrupt. He was trying to work out if Violet was staring past him. He had begun to suspect that she was, in fact, staring two minutes into the future.

"But shit like this crops up from time to time and while I was driving over here I got to thinking about jobs we've pulled in the past. We would usually do a dry run, go in there a week or two before and test the plan, make sure it would all just go like clockwork. But on this job we can't do that."

Zoe opened her mouth to speak, but Violet just kept talking. "We've been chipping away with our eyes too focused on the horizon and I've been forgetting about certain human elements. There have been some things going on which have made me doubt certain people..." Violet trailed off, her gaze going completely glassy for a second before she snapped back into the moment. "But that's exactly why I think we need to deal with this little hitch quickly and fucking fiercely."

Zoe smiled, her eyes dry, her confidence returning. "Sounds like fun. What do you mean?"

"We take the casino," said Violet.

"We take the casino?" Barry asked in disbelief.

"Tomorrow night," added Violet.

Zoe laughed. "Are you absolutely sure about that?" she asked. "A casino? With twenty four hours to prep?"

Violet grinned. "Course I'm sure. It'll be a fucking blast. Be like being twenty two again, won't it Barry?"

Barry smiled. Pain shot from his busted lip and he tried to hide the wince. "Yeah, I'm not that old you know?"

"Take down a lot of casinos when you were twenty two, did you?" Zoe asked.

"One or two," Violet cackled. "Rumour has it. You'll love it."

"I remember those heady days," said Zoe. "Oh... no, wait... I don't because I've only been twenty two for about three months."

Barry groaned. "Now I feel old," he said. "So... how?"

"Well, first we need to establish that the forgeries are definitely stashed there," said Violet.

"Shouldn't be too hard," said Zoe. "They took my tablet, so I'll be able to get a trace on that. Plus we should be able to tap into their security feeds remotely. Those places think they're banks but..."

"Excellent," interrupted Violet. "So once we're sure... this is the plan..."

Violet laid it out very simply. Zoe would work surveillance, acting electronically as their eyes in the sky and co-ordinating in case anything unexpected happened. Lucas would be on the floor of the casino. He had a certain talent for the cards and could be relied upon to stay on the tables indefinitely. Also, it wouldn't break the bank for them and whilst he played he could feed information from the belly of the beast. Violet and Katie would penetrate covertly, make their way to wherever the painting was being held, and lift it before the four of them made their way quietly back to base.

"And where am I during all this?" asked Barry with a sigh. He knew the answer.

"Outside. Out of the way."

"But why?" asked Zoe.

"Because," Barry replied, "if they see me then they'll know it was me who took the paintings and they might come after us again."

"At the very least they would increase security and vigilance, which is the last thing we want for a quick in-and-out," said Violet.

"Just one other thing," said Zoe. "We'll need to get my tablet back because it's got the access codes for the bug I planted at the banker's flat."

"Oh," said Violet, nodding. "Has it now? Well, that's just grand. Looks like that'll be on the shopping list too."

Zoe looked sheepish. "Sorry," she whispered. "I would have backed them up but... I never have the thing out of my hands..."

Violet shrugged. "Right then, do you want a lift back to civilisation or what?"

24th September

~~2 ½ weeks to go…~~

48 hours to go...

thirty three

There was a low mumbling across the five earpieces.

"Violet receiving, over." Zoe saw Barry jump, not expecting the voice in his earpiece. Violet continued. "And you lazy shits better get checking in given the price we paid for this tech."

"Lucas standing by."

"Red four standing by." Barry smirked. Zoe glared. Barry continued. "So why don't we have nicknames? Shouldn't we have nicknames? It's Barry. Standing by."

"We don't have nicknames because you're too thick to remember who's who when we have nicknames." Violet remained stern and in command.

"Who was that aimed at?" Lucas asked, his voice more muffled than the rest.

"Take your pick," said Violet then, relaxing slightly, she cackled down the line. "Not Katie, she's right next to me."

"Katie, can you acknowledge? Over." Zoe ploughed on in the face of the overwhelming stupidity that stood in her way.

A panel lit up on the laptop screen in front of her. Katie's transmitter was working.

"So, what's the point in Katie having one of these when she

doesn't talk?" Barry squinted in concentration.

The screen blinked red in front of Zoe; Barry could see the colour reflecting off Zoe's face.

"Sorry Katie," he said, a little quieter.

The screen blinked green.

"We're all in this together, Barry," said Zoe. "Except you. You get to sit on your arse and shut up."

There was laughter in the earpieces. Barry chewed lightly on his busted lip. The swelling in his face had subsided but the cuts and the black eye were still evident.

"The reason we can use our own names is because we're about twenty five times more high tech and more secure than the most high tech secure things you can imagine," said Zoe with a smile. "And here we go…"

Something was happening on Zoe's laptop that Barry couldn't make out, but he could see from the flurry of activity that it was something important. He toyed momentarily with the idea of going over to have a look but decided against it. The last time he had tried, it had been a jumble of text and code that he didn't understand.

"Ladies and gentlemen, this is your captain speaking," said Zoe, affecting a mid-Atlantic drawl. "On behalf of the flight crew let me welcome you aboard flight twenty one forty two to the Princess Casino. Lucas will be touching down on the floor of the casino in the next couple of minutes and will need to maintain almost radio silence, so if he has anything interesting or useful to say then now would be a good time to say it."

"Over and out," said Lucas. He was walking along the Kilchester riverside approaching the floating cash vortex that was the Princess Casino.

Kilchester was an odd sort of a city. Like many towns around Europe, it had grown from a Roman settlement that expanded from the river docks, and had then spread like an infection over the surrounding lands on both sides of the river for the subsequent two thousand years. Travel far enough downstream and you would wind up in the sea. As a result, occasionally, a huge ship would drift into town.

One such ship was the Princess Casino. Originally a car ferry, some bright spark had thought that converting it into a floating casino would be a hugely profitable idea. The north of England's very own slice of Las Vegas. On a boat. Permanently moored in a permanently cold dock in the shitpipe of Kilchester.

Against the odds it had remained afloat. On the water if not financially. After the original owners had jumped ship, a string of respectable national casino chains had fallen over themselves to try their hand at panning for gold. But the river was particularly unforgiving to those not of its city.

That was until the Baldoni Brothers took over. The Baldoni brothers managed to sail on the right side of the law — and their customers — while simultaneously perfecting as many different ways to extort money from their patrons as was humanly possible.

And it turned out there were quite a number of ways to do exactly that. As Barry had found out to his cost.

Lucas stepped from the docks up some gaudily-decorated steps leading to a covered walkway and on, past the bouncers into the belly of the ship. Once you were inside the ship, the it's-neither-day-nor-night feeling kicked in immediately: all the usual tricks, banks of slot machines on the way in; flashing neon; and, of course, no clocks.

Passing the rows of slot machines, Lucas headed through crowds of people clustered around roulette tables and towards the window in the wall to get some chips.

"Security pretty lax on the floor," said Lucas, not sure if there would be any signal for the transmitter inside the boat.

There was no response on the communicator and he was about to give up on the update when Zoe's voice came through in his ear. "Excellent," she said, as clear as if she were walking along beside him. "Sorry I didn't come back straight away there, I'm multi-tasking."

Lucas nodded and began to wonder if Zoe could tell if he was nodding. "No cameras to speak of. A few on the tables, but…" he trailed off as he reached the cashier. He handed over a thousand pounds.

"Yeah, seems as though they're mainly for show," said Zoe. "I've hacked their feed and half of them are turned off. If I had to guess

I'd say they've maybe got one guy half-heartedly monitoring what's going on. More than likely they are relying on the dealers spotting anything untoward and then escalating it from there."

Lucas nodded again. The cashier handed him over his chips. "Thanks," he said and smiled at her. She stared back, unblinking.

"You're welcome," said Zoe's voice. "I'm going to hook everyone else in. One second."

There was a crackle in his ear. "Right, everyone," Zoe continued. "Using Lucas' signal, I've triangulated where my tablet is and, roughly speaking, it would be in what would have been the captain's quarters. I mean… I couldn't get the floor plans of the ship at such short notice but–"

"Zoe," Violet shut Zoe down. "Stop apologising. We are all doing our best. Stay focused."

Stay focused, thought Lucas. It was time to focus. Scanning the tables, he spotted one that was crowded and whose female dealer looked a little weary around the eyes. Perfect. He sat down at the blackjack table and created a neat stack of chips to his right. The dealer smiled and Lucas smiled back. Judging by the size of the card shoe they were playing with four decks rather than the usual six, which made Lucas' task a little easier.

Lucas threw down a couple of low value chips and started counting the cards.

*

"So Lucas is just going to sit there and win money," said Violet. Katie raised an eyebrow.

They were dressed head to toe in black and had just climbed the fire escape of the ship. With Zoe's guidance they had successfully avoided any entanglements with the casino's security staff and Violet was presently working her magic on the emergency exit's deadlock.

"What?" Violet asked quietly. "It's a plan."

Katie lowered her eyebrow, looked away, then looked back and raised it again. Violet sighed and went back to teasing the lock with her lockpicks.

"Well, he reckons he's been banned from all the major casino chains. He's quite touchy about it, actually."

Katie frowned.

"Because it means he's been caught," said Violet. "Shows weakness, doesn't it?"

Katie's eyebrows arched upwards in acknowledgement. She nodded, then turned her gaze outwards, scanning the area for anything unusual. There really wasn't likely to be any intrusions at this point but you could never be too careful.

"All we need him to do is get on a decent winning streak. With the security they've got here, that should be enough to get them to look in the wrong direction," Violet said. "Of course, there is a chance that they'll take badly to it and beat him to a bloody pulp. But that's a risk I'm willing to take."

Violet closed her eyes, feeling the inside of the lock with the delicate tools, picturing the tumblers, feeling for the sweet spot.

Katie tapped her foot twice sharply on the metal of the fire escape. Violet's eyes snapped open. Katie grinned down at her.

"I'm not falling asleep," Violet hissed. "I'm concentrating. This isn't as easy is it looks, you know?"

Katie flexed her left bicep and the tight, black, long-sleeved top she wore struggled under the strain, stretching comically.

"Yes, yes." Violet rolled her eyes. "I'm sure that repeatedly lifting increasingly heavier weights is just as difficult as becoming as dexterous as a motherfucking ninja. Some of us aspire to more than simply having thicker arms."

There was a loud clunk and Violet pulled the door towards them.

"Motherfucking finger ninja," Violet whispered, nodding in self-approval.

Katie flexed harder, pointing the index finger of her flexed arm, and snarled, pulling a ridiculous bodybuilder pose. Violet stifled a laugh and poked her head into the dark bowels of the boat. They were in.

thirty four

"So..." said Violet with a sigh. "I'm not too proud to admit that we've probably walked past that sign three times."

It seemed that it wasn't as easy to navigate the bowels of an unknown sea vessel as you would imagine. Without the blueprints, without the preparation, Violet and Katie were becoming more than a little lost.

"It was easier at the museum," Violet continued. They were at a junction, with the main corridor continuing ahead of them and a side corridor shooting off to the left. Violet pointed down the corridor to the left.

Katie shrugged.

Violet put her finger in her ear and tried to activate her earpiece.

"Zoe, can you hear me?" Violet asked. She waited for a few seconds. "Zoe? Zoe are you there? Waste of bloody money these earpieces are…"

Katie looked expectantly but Violet shook her head. "Nothing," she said. "Inside all this metal must be blocking the signal."

Suddenly Katie went stiff. Drawing herself up to her full height, she stood stock still, eyes wide. Violet was about to move forward when Katie slowly lifted her hand and placed it on her shoulder.

They stood in silence, each of them staring in a different direction, each of them waiting for something.

'Something' arrived in the form of the barrel of a sawn-off shotgun as the cabin door directly behind Katie burst open.

"Good afternoon, ladies," said a voice with as much charm as roadkill.

Violet and Katie turned around, slowly raising their hands. The owner of the voice held the shotgun high, aiming it in the general vicinity of their heads. Glancing past their muscle-bound speaker, Violet counted four – no, five – other security guards. All big, all muscled and all dressed in ill-fitting tuxedos.

Scanning the threats, Katie could see that the man closest to the door was the only one with a firearm. So it wasn't all bad news. Given the lack of bulges in their jackets and around their ankles she was fairly convinced she was right about that. Just as convinced that two of the other four had plain knuckle-dusters, one had a knuckle-duster with some sort of moulded knife attachment and the last of them wielded a dull machete.

Something of an ill-advised choice given the surroundings — but everyone had their weapon of choice. Katie was pretty sure she could take them, and looked to Violet for confirmation. But as she turned her head the barrels of the shotgun had been placed against Violet's temple.

"–repeat... Five security guards waiting for you in room 512." Zoe's voice suddenly echoed in Katie and Violet's earpieces. "Please acknowledge."

Katie made a move as if scratching her right wrist and pressed one of the sensors Zoe had given her.

"Shitbags," came the response. Zoe's end went dead once again.

"We've been watching you since you came in," the shotgun security guard said.

"We're just lost," said Violet, her eyes focused on the trigger of the shotgun that was pressed against her head. "Can you tell us the way back to the gaming floor? We were looking for the toilet and–"

The shotgun-wielding security shoved the rough ends of the sawn-off against Violet's brow. She rocked back on her heel, ready for the shove, not letting it catch her off guard.

"Hear that lads?" sawn-off said. "These ladies are lost."

Loud, derisive laughter poured out of the cabin.

"We've been watching you since you broke in through the emergency exit, you dumb bitch." Sawn-off shoved her again but didn't step out of the cabin.

Katie was waiting. If he stepped in front of her she could disarm him before he blew Violet's head off, then swing around and take the other four down with two shells before they knew what...

"You, short stuff, start walking," sawn-off continued. "Long, tall, Sally..."

More laughter from the audience in the cabin.

"Get your enormous arse walking too." He made a snorting noise, as if he had a cold and was trying to clear his sinuses down the back of his throat. "Try anything and I'll cut the pair of you down before you can take three steps. Understand?"

"Yes," said Violet.

Katie nodded.

"Say it!" Sawn-off spat the words, tiny globs of saliva flying in a cloud in front of his angular face.

Katie took half a step away from him, her hands still held in surrender.

"She doesn't talk," said Violet.

Sawn-off turned the barrels toward Katie, stepping out of the room. The knife-wielding security guard came into the corridor too, stepping behind Katie, out of her line of sight. Sawn-off moved closer, he was six foot two, six foot three maybe, with a buzz-cut that looked like the head of a hammer.

"She'll speak if I tell her to speak," sawn-off said, having to look up to address Katie. In spite of his own height she still had a good six inches on him.

The knife-wielding security reached up and touched the tip of the blade against the nape of Katie's neck, drawing it across and scraping the skin a little. Not enough to draw blood but enough to make Violet want to say something.

"She won't. Can't," Violet said, a pleading tone entering her voice as her eyes flicked from the knife to the shotgun to Katie's face. Katie was unmoved.

"I've never had one as big as this before, boss," knife-boy said. "Maybe we can give her something to talk about."

Knife-boy cut a piece of material from the corner of the top Katie was wearing.

Sawn-off laughed. "Yeah boys, what do you think...I once fucked a bird that was this big..." He threw his arms wide to illustrate his point.

Katie didn't miss a beat. Her hands — still held in the surrender position — clenched into fists and she threw first one then the other straight into the side of sawn-off's head.

When it came to inflicting injuries, Katie was a surgeon, and the literal double-whammy hadn't just been an opportunistic attack. Far from it.

The first punch, thrown with her dominant right hand, impacted on sawn-off's jaw. Choosing the jaw rather than, for example, the ear caused the head to begin to suddenly twist around. As Katie knew only too well, this would cause a force of acceleration which, after the briefest of moments, is countered by rapid deceleration.

That is, unless you've hit someone so hard their head has come off, but that only usually happens in video games.

At this point, the brain smacks against the inside of the skull and bounces back. Next it would smash into the opposite side of the skull and, if you'd been hit as hard as sawn-off had, then this might continue a number of times before the brain came to rest

The second blow, also to the jaw, was for two purposes. Firstly to accentuate the fast-slow internal beating being doled out to the victim's brain and secondly to slam sawn-off into the wall in an attempt to disarm him.

Squalls of panic filled the room as sawn-off hit the wall and slid down. Katie spun around to take out knife-boy, but as she lunged forward into the cabin one of the knuckle-dusters produced another gun.

Katie hesitated, then held her hands up in surrender once more.

It was small and snub-nosed, but it was a gun, and as skilled as she was, Katie knew she wasn't bullet-proof. As snub-nose stumbled forward, barrel-first, Katie's ear crackled into life. It was Zoe.

"Katie, Violet, if you can hear me, hold tight." She sounded panicked, but it was a controlled panic. "We have your location. If you can stay alive for five minutes we can give you a distraction. A big one."

As snub-nose exited the cabin, knife-boy scrambled down to check on his colleague. Sawn-off was conscious but was like a wiped blackboard. His broken jaw hung at an unpleasant angle from his face.

"Can you last five minutes?" Zoe's voice again, just for Violet and Katie.

Snub-nose moved forward and shoved the barrel of his gun into Katie's mouth. He was shorter than his colleague, and as a result had to almost fully extend his arm to do so.

"I bet I could get you to talk," he said. "I can get any woman to talk. All it takes it a lit cigarette and a bit of imagination. Then you can't shut them up, can you lads?"

The rumbles of agreement were still there, but they were less confident.

"Then the only way to shut them up is to shove a cock in their mouth. Bet you'd like that, wouldn't you, you big, dumb, broad?"

Katie raised her head a little so that snub-nose could no longer reach her mouth, then carefully tapped her wrist to indicate to Zoe that five minutes would be absolutely fine, thank you very much.

thirty five

Lucas had spent the past fifteen minutes wishing he could turn off his earpiece. Or at least get Zoe to shut the fuck up when she was trying to contact Violet and not him.

He was trying to concentrate and she kept buzzing around inside his head like a goddamned mind-fly. Whatever the fuck that was. What was that?

"Split, sir?" the dealer was pointing at his cards, glancing at the other players.

Lucas stared at the cards he had been dealt, snapped his consciousness back to the table and began apologising, saying how maybe he might take a break but then feeding them the inveterate gambler's line of 'just one more hand' and that yes, he would split.

There were a host of possible winning hands, depending on the choices his fellow players made. Lucas had now been counting the deck for over an hour and, thanks to a combination of factors, he was now fairly certain of the position of the majority of cards within it. Of course, the main reason for the ease of counting was that the dealer was fucking incompetent.

Three times she should have shuffled or replaced the decks and three times she singularly failed to do so. Every time she didn't bother shuffling Lucas threw a few hands. He didn't want her to lose her job. At least, at the beginning he didn't.

But the more he won, the less he cared. He'd been pretty sure, when his winning had passed the twenty thousand pound mark, that she would call security, and she *had* appeared to make some sort of call to management.

A call that remained unanswered. And now, with Zoe babbling in his ear, Lucas had found out that this was because the security staff were otherwise engaged. And so he went for it. Winning hands, winning split hands, tips to the other punters, he was drawing as much attention to himself as he could possibly engineer.

He was pretty sure it would all be over when the players at the table, with his guidance, had collectively won so many chips that the dealer had to radio the cage for more to be delivered. But, no, in the end all that happened was that more chips were delivered.

Lucas had begun to think that his monk-like avoidance of casinos for fear of getting caught was a waste of time and that he could quite easily have made his money in this way instead of dealing in forgeries and heists until...

"Lucas, keep doing what you're doing." It was Zoe's voice in his head, and he couldn't reply lest they find the earpiece and assume it was electronic instead of mental powers that were influencing his winning. "We've lost contact with Violet and Katie and we think they've been..."

"What?" asked Lucas.

"What, what?" the dealer asked Lucas with a smile. "I didn't say anything, sir."

Lucas waved his hand to dismiss the line of questioning and turned to a waitress to order a very large drink.

"We think they've been taken by the security team for the casino," Zoe said.

Lucas nodded to the dealer, who plucked a card from the shoe and placed it in front of them. He went bust and lost a thousand pounds.

"Keep doing what you're doing. I've got a handle on their location and Barry has an idea to cause a different type of distraction. It should give them a window of opportunity to let them complete their mission."

"Right," said Lucas, to the dealer and to Zoe. "Deal me in."

*

"So what is it that's happening?" Barry asked, trying to take an interest in what Zoe was doing. He basically had two options; sit in the front of the van and stare at the pigeons in the car park or sit in the back of the van with Zoe and all her computers and occasionally ask a polite question.

If she furrowed her eyebrows and *harrumphed* he knew it was a bad time and to shut the hell up. If she started chattering and pointing to the screen and using words he'd never heard before then that meant it was a good time and to continue pestering her.

The furrowed eyebrows had been in place for the best part of fifteen minutes and, in spite of the previous evidence, Barry was fairly certain that Zoe wanted to be asked what was going on.

Zoe let out a long, slow, sigh then ran her hands through her hair and pointed to one of the screens. As far as Barry could tell it was gibberish, but it must have meant something because Zoe was staring intently at it.

"I've got the security-camera feed." Zoe gestured to one of the monitors that displayed alternating pictures of deserted corridors within the bowels of the ship and was punctuated by views of the gambling floor. "But it's analogue."

The way she said that word, as if it had taken a dump on her tongue and forced her to swallow it.

"And analogue is a problem?" asked Barry. He understood analogue. He liked it. Vinyl sounded better than digital.

Zoe shifted her gaze away from the screen to look at Barry. "Not inherently, no," she said. "A digital system like the one the banker has, you can properly hack it, make it do your bidding. But this, you're waiting for the feed to come around. I mean, there are some aspects of it where they have their own circuit where I've been able to isolate them but..."

The image on the monitor changed. It was a security guard with a shotgun walking down a corridor below deck.

"But what?" asked Barry, sensing his input was required.

"But there was another circuit. It was weird. Like a doorbell or something. Not a video feed." Zoe gave up on that and flicked all four monitors to video feeds. "You see the guy with the shotgun?" Zoe asked.

Barry nodded.

"Tell me if you see him go into room 512."

On the monitor to Zoe's right, Violet came into view, closely followed by Katie.

"Violet, Katie, do you read me, over." Zoe tapped furiously at her keyboard but there was no response. "They're going in circles. We need to get comms back up," she said to Barry, who nodded appreciatively. "The tech Katie's wearing acts a bit like sonar, so I've been able to get a good portion of the ship mapped while they've been wandering about."

"But if you can't talk to them..."

"Then I can't help them."

"That bloke with the shotgun's just gone in to room 512," said Barry, a big, dumb smile spreading across his face as he finally got the chance to help.

"Fuck," said Zoe, instantly bursting his bubble. "They're on to us."

"What?" asked Barry. "How do you know?"

"Violet, Katie, there are five security guards in room 512. Can you hear me?" Zoe's voice was beginning to crack, the nerves setting in.

"It's okay, Zoe," said Barry, putting his hand on her forearm.

Zoe looked at it as if he'd just placed a live octopus on her.

"Whatever happens, we'll deal with it. Okay?" Barry's tone was softer. Zoe flicked a smile on and off, then started at the keyboard again. "Look, they've stopped."

Zoe turned to the video feed to see Violet and Katie standing at a junction, looking around. They were definitely lost. Zoe tried to enhance the image, zooming in to try to discern where in the hell they were. It was blurred and partially obscured by Violet, but there was no mistake.

"Violet, Katie, please respond. You need to move on now. In room 512 next to you there are five guards, probably heavily armed, ready to take you. I repeat... Five security guards waiting for you in room 512. Please acknowledge."

A green light suddenly appeared in the corner of Zoe's screen.

"Yes!" said Zoe, turning to Barry. "We've got them back online!"

Barry pointed at the screen. The door to room 512 was open and a shotgun was levelled at Violet and Katie.

"Shitbags," said Zoe and turned off the mic. "Barry, what can we do? We need to do something, what can we do?"

Barry stared at the screen and scratched his stubble. "Take a breath, Zoe," he said. "Katie's pretty fucking handy, so they aren't going to get shot. But we need a backup plan for them, you're right there."

Zoe looked at the reams of information that were appearing on her screen. Katie had responded and the system was harvesting all the data she'd inadvertently been gathering.

Barry was watching the scene between Violet, Katie and the ambushers silently play out on the monitor. The bloke holding the sawn-off was moving, letting a guy with what looked like a knife come out into the corridor. There was talking. Violet looked worried but Katie didn't.

The security guard with the knife came to Katie's back.

"I've got an idea," said Barry. "You say you can pinpoint their location?"

"Yeah," replied Zoe.

"Even if they can't hear us?"

"Yeah."

Barry and Zoe's eyes both flicked to the monitor at the same moment sawn-off threw his arms wide.

Zoe winced as Katie exploded into violent action.

"Holy shit!" said Zoe, as Katie's blows connected and sawn-off bounced off the wall like a rag doll.

"I know, she's quite a woman, isn't she?" said Barry.

It was over as quickly as it had begun as another of the security guards waded in with a pistol of some description.

"Right then," said Barry. "Tell them to stay alive for five minutes then we'll have a distraction for them."

"Okay," said Zoe. "What?"

Barry grinned. "I'm going to blow a fucking big hole in the side of the boat."

"Katie, Violet, if you can hear me, hold tight." Zoe was keeping it together, the adrenaline was coursing through her but she felt in control. "We have your location. If you can stay alive for five minutes we can give you a distraction. A big one."

There was no response from either of them. Zoe just stared as the owner of the gun shoved the barrel into Katie's mouth.

"Oh, she's going to fucking punish him for that," said Barry

"Can you last five minutes?" Zoe asked as calmly as she could muster.

Finally the response came through from Katie.

Yes. They could last five minutes.

Zoe exhaled.

thirty six

"So where's the boss?" knife-boy asked, putting what few possessions they had stripped from Katie and Violet onto the desk that dominated one side of the room. A backpack with a couple of bottles of water and Violet's lock picks weren't of much interest to him, so he drew his knife once more and began staring at his own smudged reflection in the blade instead.

"Which one?" knuckle-duster replied. "I ain't seen either of them all day."

The Baldoni brothers ran a tight ship. Tight enough that they didn't feel the need to actually be on board for large chunks of time. The security guards had carefully herded Violet and Katie into the captain's quarters and sat the pair of them on chairs under one of the portholes.

The reason for this, it had become apparent, was that none of the five guards wanted to be anywhere near either of them. Sawn-off sat behind the Baldoni brothers' desk, the imprint of Katie's knuckles blossoming as a bruise under his skin. The shotgun lay on the desk in front of him, but he was much more preoccupied with his face and seemed presently to have no intention of going toe to toe with either Katie or Violet.

Katie rolled her sleeve and glanced at her watch. Three minutes had elapsed since Zoe's warning. Their captors were beginning to relax slightly. The initial excitement over, they were settling in to the geography of the room. Katie maintained a careful map of where all of them were and, at least in general terms, what she was going to do to each of them the next time she got to her feet.

Especially snub-nose. That cocksucker was going to get some special attention.

"I've left them a message," snub-nose said. "We wait to find out what they want to do."

"I can't wait much longer," sawn-off grumbled. "That bitch broke my jaw, I need to go and see a doctor."

"And one of the dealers has been bitching about some bloke winning a shit load of money down on the floor," said knife-boy. "I reckon that might be more important than two crazy women breaking and entering."

The five of them stared at Violet, weighing up two or three of their ranks leaving the room. Then they looked to Katie and decided that the other problems could wait just a little longer.

"Try calling the boss again," said sawn-off.

"Which one?" knuckle-duster asked.

"I don't fucking care which one. Either one. If someone can't get them on the phone in the next five minutes I'm going to bury these two fuckers at sea." Sawn-off stomped across the room towards a fridge, opened it and took out a bottle of water. He tried to unscrew the cap, failed, then just held the cold glass of the bottle against the side of his jaw.

And then it started.

A metallic *clang* from somewhere outside. Something hitting the side of the boat. Violet and Katie glanced at one another expectantly. This was their chance.

The second *clang* was less of an actual *clang*, more of a *kerthunk* with an overtone of *clangyness*. Whatever it was, it got the attention of the security guards, who all looked at the wall – perhaps hoping for it to suddenly become transparent and reveal what was happening.

The third time was definitely more *kerthunky*, the *clang*-factor probably just the sound of the impact as whatever it was hit the side of the boat.

"What is that?" Knuckle-duster got to his feet and walked toward the porthole above Violet and Katie's heads.

"Just ignore it," sawn-off said, still rubbing the bottle of water against his jaw. "It'll just be kids. This side of the boat is against the riverside, they throw shit up here all the time, tennis balls, footballs, you know, shit like that. Fucking kids, man. Ignorant little bastards."

"You two," said knuckle-duster. "Up on your feet and into the middle of the room. I want to look out of this window."

Violet nodded; both she and Katie slowly stood and moved to the centre of the room. A smile invaded the corners of Katie's mouth.

There was a loud *crack*.

"What in the name of shitting Christ was that?" knuckle-duster blurted, cupping his hands around his eyes to look out of the porthole.

There was a second, louder, *crack*. The boat rocked slightly.

Violet and Katie both took the opportunity to crouch down into the brace position.

"Can you see anything?" sawn-off asked, absently. "We could–"

The third *crack* happened just outside the porthole, punched the round window from its house and sent it flying into the room.

Unfortunately, the trajectory of the air-bound porthole was blocked by knuckle-duster's face and it slammed into him, shattering his cheekbones, flattening his nose and knocking him to the ground in a cloud of vapourised blood.

The porthole continued, apparently unperturbed by the interruption, coming to rest once it had embedded itself in the opposite wall.

For a moment there was a pause, the only sound a high-pitched ringing in their collective ears. Knuckle-duster just lay, his knuckle-duster fallen from his hand on the floor, and a small pool of blood began to form, flowing steadily from his injuries.

Katie made eye contact with Violet, reached out her hand and, with splayed fingers, pushed slowly toward the floor.

Stay down. Violet wasn't about to argue.

Katie balled her hand into a fist and exploded upwards.

Immediately in front of her was the security guard carrying the other knuckle-duster, the one with the knife moulded onto the end; and standing just behind him was knife-boy.

The element of surprise finally back on their side, Katie sprang upwards, her powerful thighs and calves giving her instant, enormous momentum. The security guard closest to her didn't have time to cry out, but even if he had he would have been immediately silenced by the rising right hook to his jaw.

Follow through, just like in golf. The results of her attacks were perfectly transparent to Katie. Knuckles connected to the security guard's chin, driving bottom teeth into top teeth, either loosening them or smashing a few if he was lucky. If he was unlucky then his bottom teeth would ram into his upper lip, possibly dislocating his jaw and bursting his top lip in the process.

Keep extending the punch. Follow through, the muscles in her upper body taking over from the momentum that had carried her this far. Result; security guard is propelled into the air and the ceiling is not too high so the top of his head smashes into it. The downward force exerted in the equal and opposite reaction will slam him back down onto her fist so important to pull back as he peaks.

Two down.

Katie was on her feet now, and the three remaining guards had begun to react. The two closest to the guns were the two farthest away from her. No matter. They were already running scared, the panic on their faces feeding Katie's confidence.

Pulling her arm back, she changed the shape of her right hand, her fingers sliding out of a fist but the tips staying tucked under. Knife-boy had taken out his weapon but she could see two things; that he wasn't ready to swing it and that his reach was considerably shorter than hers.

Taking a beat, she shifted her feet to a better stance and struck out, punching him in the throat. Result: partially collapsed windpipe, knife dropped on the floor. Secondary results: cabin filled with the gasping, rasping of knife-boy as he struggles against that horrible drowning feeling. The fear that it instils in the others is priceless especially as he drops to the floor and begins gagging. The appearance to the layman is that he is having some sort of fit.

Three down.

Knife-boy hit the ground at the precise moment the bottle of water sawn-off had been holding bounced to the floor. He had dropped it in favour of sprinting back across the room to the desk to grab his sidearm. Katie swung round her arm to clothesline him; he saw it coming and ducked, making it to the desk and grabbing the gun with both hands.

Katie lunged forward and hooked her arms under sawn-off's, locking her hands behind his head in a full nelson. He bucked and writhed, but Katie lifted him off the ground to use him as a human shield as snub-nose fumbled with his pistol.

As she swung him around she thought for a moment that he might actually try to shoot them both with the sawn-off. But as she exerted more pressure on the back of his head, he began to concentrate more on trying to stop Katie from pushing his head so far forward that she would snap his neck.

Finally he dropped the shotgun on the floor, but snub-nose had got his act together and was pointing the gun at Katie's human shield as he dangled in front of her.

One second turned to two, turned to three. Katie could smell the cheap aftershave and sweat on the man in her grip. She stared coolly at snub-nose.

"Put him down!" snub-nose squeaked. All manly posturing was thrown aside as he bleated at her. "Put him down and put your hands up... or... or..."

"Or what?" asked Violet, who had, in the confusion, armed herself with knuckle-duster's dropped knuckle-duster. She gripped it tightly in her hand and punched inexpertly forward.

Whatever level of expert she was, a punch to the back of the hand is going to bloody well hurt, and snub-nose felt it, squealing as it impacted. Result: the gun's trajectory is changed and snub-nose fired. The smell of sulphur and cordite filled the air and the gun clattered to the ground and span off towards the wall. Snub-nose followed as he clutched at his wound.

Katie dropped sawn-off from the full nelson into a choke-hold and dragged him forward three paces, then landed her foot down hard on snub-nose, somewhere in between his arse cheeks.

Result: bruised or, if she had gotten enough force behind it, broken coccyx. Snub-nose howled, the pain shooting up his spine.

This also bought Katie a little time, which meant that as she squeezed the choke-hold harder the result would be unconsciousness, not death, and soon she achieved it as sawn-off went limp in her grip.

By this time snub-nose had crawled to where the gun had come to rest. He grabbed it and turned, struggling to get the thing into his grip. Katie dropped sawn-off and he hit the ground with a meaty *thwack*.

One left.

She advanced on him, staring him down as he turned over. His eyes came up to meet hers and she was picking up pace, running across the room towards him. He turned onto his back, trying to prop himself against the wall, and his broken tailbone touched the floor. Again the pain shot through him and he shoved his pelvis forward, away from the floor, leaving his legs wide apart.

Katie planted a kick of enormous force right between his legs.

Result: if Katie's calculations were correct then snub-nose's balls would have been pushed against his pelvic bone with such force that he would experience a testicular rupture.

Snub-nose made a noise like a dog slowly dying, rolled onto his side and vomited. Katie kicked the gun out of his reach.

"Right then," said Violet, clapping her hands together. "If you've finished flirting with these boys we've got a painting to recover."

thirty seven

Lucas stood up and thanked the dealer. Things were getting ridiculous. He had continued to follow the plan and beat the casino to draw attention to himself. And that had only half worked. After winning and winning he had thought that helping the other players at the table would spark some sort of intervention.

Except it hadn't. And now he had amassed sixty thousand pounds and helped his fellow players to, at a guess, ten thousand a piece. This obviously wasn't working. Time to cash in his chips and check in with Zoe. He slid a generous tip across the table to the dealer, but as he walked across the floor to the cashier, Zoe wasn't answering.

"Lucky night tonight, sir?" asked the cashier, counting out his winnings.

"No, it's a talent," said Lucas, then caught himself and rounded it off with a smile.

The cashier handed over the bundles of cash and Lucas shoved them in the various pockets of the suit jacket he was wearing and wandered towards the bar.

"Zoe, can you hear me?"

There was an odd *thump* that seemed to resonate throughout

the boat.

"Zoe, is that you?"

Another *thump*.

"Zoe?"

And a third *thump*.

Was it a thump? It sort of sounded like a firework. Lucas ordered a pint of lager and surveyed the gaming floor. At the far side he spotted that the Baldoni brothers had just arrived and were beginning to do the rounds of the tables.

"Lucas? Can you hear me?" It was Zoe.

"Ten-four, good buddy. Reading you loud and clear," said Lucas his hand in his trouser pocket stroking the edges of a pack of twenty-pound notes.

"What are you talking about?" Zoe sounded flustered. "Are you in trouble too?"

"What? No. The opposite actually. That was just like trucker talk. Like in the movies, you know, *Smokey and the Bandit*?"

"This is going to be one of those things I have to Google to find out what the fuck you are gibbering about, isn't it, you prat?"

"Listen," said Lucas. "I won a fucking shit ton of money and nobody batted an eyelid. But the Baldoni brothers just arrived."

"It never rains but it pours," Zoe sighed.

"And the attention you were looking for me to garner is about to start raining down on me," said Lucas, looking over to where the taller of the two brothers had rounded on the dealer Lucas had just tipped. There was a quick exchange and then the dealer raised her index finger and pointed it at Lucas.

"Ooh," said Zoe, excitement creeping into her voice. "Head for the exit now and look out for Barry coming in. I've got a brilliant idea."

*

Katie pointed to the desk in the office and Violet looked over. On the other side was an old safe. Bolted to the floor, it lurked beside a filing cabinet and was perhaps a half a metre wide, the same in height. It was obvious from the peeling black paint that the thing was ancient.

Violet vaulted the desk and landed in a crouch next to the safe.

She ran her hand against the cold metal of the door, then reached up to the desk and grabbed the backpack that contained her lock picks.

"Bet they're in here," said Violet, staring unblinking at the safe. It was old-school, with a lock rather than a dial. She could hear the sound of movement behind her but, recognising the footsteps as Katie's, she didn't budge, instead selecting one of the lock picks to get the feel of the inside of the safe's lock.

Katie's footsteps got closer. A frown flickered across Violet's brow as she tried to concentrate and her friend distracted her. Katie tapped Violet on the shoulder with something.

"What?" Violet snapped, turning to face Katie, who held the courier tube in her hands. "Oh," Violet sighed. "Are they in there?"

Katie nodded.

"Oh," Violet said again, her eyes darting back to the safe. "Where were they?"

Katie gestured to the corner of the room; there was a filing cabinet with a gap down the side.

"I wanted to crack the safe," said Violet. "I was looking forward to it."

Katie shrugged.

"Ah, but the tablet!" said Violet, less convinced but still hopeful. "That could be in there!"

Katie shook her head slowly.

"No?"

Katie pointed first to the desk drawers, then to sawn-off's prone body. She lifted her left hand flat in front of her and started tapping the fingers of her right hand on it.

"You saw him using it?"

Katie nodded and opened a couple of drawers. The third one held Zoe's tablet.

"So we're done then?"

Katie nodded and gave her friend a sympathetic smile.

"But the safe..." Violet turned to look at the safe, one of the lockpicks drooping out of the lock. Suddenly she brightened. "We need to cover our tracks! Need to make it look like we haven't just come here for the paintings and the tablet. So really, I need to break into this safe. The job depends on it."

Katie glanced at her watch and nodded, but Violet wasn't looking; she already had the lockpick back in her hand and was beginning to rake for the tumblers.

*

"I'm not going in there," said Barry from the front seat of the van. "Not with the Baldoni brothers on patrol. It's just asking for trouble, isn't it?"

"I want them to catch you," said Zoe with an evil grin. "That's the whole plan."

"What are you talking about, you idiot?" said Barry, looking a little hurt. "Why would you want them to catch me? In case you've forgotten I still owe them a shitload of cash and I just nearly sunk their casino."

"Because Lucas has just won a serious amount of cash on the tables and what could be more poetic than paying them back with money we won from their own casino?"

Barry thought about it for a second. "In general, I like the plan."

"Just in general?"

"Well, the specifics, the small print if you like, I'm a little hazy on."

"Hazy how?" asked Zoe.

"Well, let's say, just for shits and giggles, that I walk through the door and one of them shoots me straight in the face."

"It is a possibility, I won't lie," Zoe said. "But given the number of regular pundits I'd say that they would be more likely to call security."

"And then I'll have a crowd of Neanderthals kicking the living shit out of me. I don't like the sound of that either."

"Ah, but you're forgetting something," said Zoe.

"And what's that exactly?"

"Katie has rendered casino security inactive."

"Eh?"

"She's beaten them all half to death," said Zoe. "So grab that empty gym bag and meet Lucas in reception. He'll give you the cash, you give it to the Baldonis."

Barry continued to protest, but knew that it was an opportunity he couldn't really turn down. Although the thought that he could just take the winnings and run briefly danced across his brain, he dismissed it. They were a team now. If today had proved anything it was that they could pull off the impossible in the face of overwhelming adversity and the plan turning to molten shite in front of their eyes.

He grabbed the bag and headed out of the van.

*

Lucas had made it off the gaming floor before the Baldonis intercepted him. He wasn't hugely keen on Zoe's plan; there was something in his criminal make-up that made handing over huge sums of money and getting nothing in return something that he was ill-equipped to deal with.

He knew what it was. It made him feel like a mark. And he didn't like that one little bit. But as he turned the corner into the deserted entrance corridor he knew he had to do it. Also, there was the voice in his head. Zoe's voice. Telling him he had to do it.

Barry came into view, pretending to jog the last few paces. Lucas immediately dipped onto one knee and, emptying his pockets, placed £50,000 into the bag.

Barry slapped him on the shoulder then zipped the bag and strode off down the corridor toward the floor of the casino. Lucas reached into his inside pocket and rifled the edges of the last wad of notes. Ten thousand. He'd earned that much. At least.

*

"Fuck me, you've got some balls, son."

The Baldoni brothers had been chasing Lucas out of the casino, but came to an abrupt halt when faced with the spectre of Barry looming onto the gaming floor. The brothers stared at Barry; the shorter of the two rubbed his overhanging belly and panted with the exertion.

"I've got your money," said Barry, deciding to open with that fact in the hope that none of the horrendous additional scenarios he had conjured in his mind would come to pass.

"And the vig?" panted the shorter Baldoni.

"The what?" Barry and the taller Baldoni chorused.

"You know – the vig?" the shorter Baldoni repeated.

Barry looked to his taller brother, who shrugged in response.

"The vig. The vigorish. The juice. The *interest*."

"Fuck's sake, Chris, you've read two books and you think you're Chili Palmer. You can't talk like that in Kilchester, it just makes you look like a cunt."

The pair looked at Barry, who shrugged. Definitely not getting involved in that one. "I've got the money. With interest."

"How much?" snapped little-Baldoni.

"How much?" asked Barry, suddenly realising he had no idea. He put his finger in his ear. "How much money do I have in the bag? Well, that's a good question."

"How much is in the bag?" Zoe's voice boomed in Barry's ear. He flinched. The Baldoni brothers stared at Barry. "Lucas, how much is in the bag? Fifty. Fifty grand."

Barry's eyes widened and he allowed himself a little smile.

"Fifty grand," he said and held out the bag.

"That'll do." Little-Baldoni grabbed the bag and started rooting around inside. He pulled out the bundles of cash and flicked through them.

"Satisfied?" asked large-Baldoni.

Little-Baldoni nodded.

"Want the stuff we took from you?" asked large-Baldoni.

"Nah, couple of autographs. Worthless. And the computer thing didn't even work – belongs to my sister and my nephew. Keep 'em. There is one thing…" Barry trailed off.

Large-Baldoni jerked his head back in a half-nod, questioning.

"You could try not to kill me again. That'd be grand."

"Then we're done, Barry," said large-Baldoni, nodding as he did so. "Unless you fancy a few rounds of roulette before you go?"

Barry looked over the tables and was about to answer when the voice boomed in his ear.

"The answer you're looking for is 'no', in case you're wondering, Barry," Zoe said.

"Better not," Barry said to the Baldoni brothers. "Been a pleasure doing business with you fellas."

"See you on the flip side," said little-Baldoni.

thirty eight

It didn't take long for the five members of the crew to extricate themselves from the floating death trap that was the Princess Casino. Lucas jumped in the back of the van, and the second he closed the door Zoe called shotgun. When Barry returned he drove the three of them to the meeting point in a booth at the back of the Crow and Crown pub.

In spite of Katie's fidgeting, foot-tapping and constant pacing up and down, Violet had stuck with the safe.

"It took me five minutes," she explained.

Katie tapped one of her long index fingers on the wooden table.

"It took me nine minutes," Violet said, a tiny bit of the enthusiasm ebbing from her voice.

"I don't understand," said Zoe. "Why is that a bad thing. Isn't nine minutes to crack a safe practically Guinness Book of Records territory?"

"It's a bad thing," Lucas interrupted, "because Violet is terribly, terribly vain..."

The crew all laughed – except Violet.

"Listen, do you want to hear the rest of this story or not?" she said, pouting.

"I think I want you to go back to the part where Katie tore the place to shreds like some sort of shaved Wookiee on a murder spree," said Barry, reaching over and squeezing Katie's bicep.

Katie drew herself away from him and cracked her knuckles

"Whoah, there," said Barry with a smile. "That is one of the most impressive feats I've ever witnessed. I am in awe!"

Katie smiled and shook her head.

"So the safe..." said Violet monotonously. "I was picking the lock remember?"

"I hear it took over ten minutes," said Zoe. "How long did it take Katie to clear the room?"

"Less than thirty seconds." Barry did a mock salute.

"Well, piss off, then. I'm not telling you if you're going to be like that." Violet pushed out her lower lip and looked out the window.

"Oh come on," said Lucas. "Let her tell her story. She listened to my counting cards bit so it's only fair."

There were groans from the others.

"So I got into the safe in *nine* minutes," said Violet. "And wasn't that surprised to find that the thing was full of cash, casino chips and various important looking papery-contracty type things."

"So you filled your pockets and you're going to share the spoils with us all now?" asked Lucas.

"Hardly," replied Violet. "The chips were still factory-fresh. Plastic-wrapped."

Lucas shrugged, the cogs in his brain turning, trying to work out what she would do in a situation like that. He knew what he would do, but Violet was so different in her approach. After the job she'd just orchestrated he was beginning to think she may have a touch of genius about her. At the very least she seemed able to pull a golden egg from a bag of turds.

"Opened them up," Violet continued. "Shoved some in the pockets of all those lovely, welcoming security guards that Katie had so kindly left sprinkled around on the floor..."

"Like a bloody pile of hundreds and thousands?" Zoe laughed, and took a swig of her drink.

"So when the Baldoni brothers get to the office they'll find the safe open and the chips in the guards' pockets," said Lucas, finally joining the dots.

"Exactly!" said Violet, banging her hand on the table. "I mean, whether they'll actually get blamed for anything –"

"Because when they wake up…" Lucas was staring into the middle distance, concentrating. If he'd had a pad and paper he would have been making notes. "Their story will be 'We grabbed two women. One of them was a giant and the other one was a ninja. They beat us senseless and then left without stealing anything.'"

Violet clicked her fingers and pointed at Lucas. "At the very least we muddy the waters."

"But what about the security footage?" asked Barry, certain he'd found a chink in the armour. "You said it wasn't digital, didn't you, Zoe, so doesn't that mean you can't – you know – delete it or whatever?"

Katie reached into her jacket pocket and withdrew a VHS video cassette.

Zoe grinned. "With the help of my beautiful assistant we retrieved the tape in… oooh… let's be kind and say 'under five minutes'."

Violet sat back in her chair, picked up her vodka and coke and took a swig. She had assembled a fine crew. Of course, she'd had her reservations about some of them, that was inevitable. A find like Katie was…if it wasn't one in a million it was one in a couple of hundred thousand. Everyone came with baggage, that was true, whoever you worked with. But today she had watched the wheels spin off and the plan crash into the wall – and in spite of that, they had won. In fact, this didn't just feel like they'd won, it felt as though they were ready for the real job.

Taking another slug of her drink then flicking it with her index finger, Violet tried to bring the crew back to order for a moment.

"Can I say," she said, "you were all magnificent today. It has been an absolute pleasure seeing you all do your thing and…"

The rest of what Violet had to say was lost in the cheering and catcalling that ensued. She gave up and waved over to the waitress for another round. This was going to be a long night and she intended to get very, very drunk indeed.

Three hours later and the crew were, to all intents and purposes, completely shit-faced. The first hour had consisted of what could generously be called playful banter, but had rapidly descended into the four speaking members of the crew putting the world to rights.

Katie had sat, stoically observing the proceedings whilst knocking back single-malt whiskies, while Violet, Zoe, Lucas and Barry had engaged in some sort of punishing alcohol-based endurance test.

Zoe was the youngest and, as such, it wasn't a huge surprise that she was the first one to fall. First her head had started to nod, then she was propping it up with her palm, and finally she just crossed her arms on the table and used them as a pillow.

Lucas and Barry had got to the point where they were arguing with each other – but both of them were arguing the same side of the argument. Violet, who was something of a happy drunk, had just left the conversation at the end of the second hour and was happy to sip and watch the world go by.

Eventually last orders were called at the bar and four of them left on foot; Violet on her own, Lucas and Barry with their arms slung around one another's neck, as much for support as for the friendship quotient, and Zoe... well Katie had picked Zoe up and slung her over her shoulder. Zoe had hardly noticed, her light snoring occasionally peppered with the odd bout of gibberish.

"Need a lift?" Barry asked no-one in particular. He fished his keys out of his pocket and spun them around his index finger.

"There is no way you are dr–" Violet began, but stopped short as the keys flew off Barry's finger.

Barry darted forward to retrieve them, instantly lost his balance and landed inelegantly on all fours on the tarmac of the car park.

Violet sniggered and Barry crawled forward, squinting at the keys through the fog of drink. He reached his hand out to pick them up but a booted foot stamped down on them.

"Hello, boys and girls," said a voice. "Having a lovely little piss up are we?"

Barry's gaze snaked up the boot to the trouser leg to the suit jacket. It didn't take as long as he expected. About half the time it would usually take, in fact. Barry dropped his gaze back to the keys under the boot and blinked before trying a second time. This time, when he reached eye level with the person his head lolled back and he frowned.

"What the fuck are you staring at, you little piss-pot?" asked the person.

Barry reached up and scratched his forehead. His brain was trying to send him a message and the alcohol was stopping it from getting through.

"Err," was all he could manage.

"Err?" the person sneered. "Fucking *err*? Jesus Christ, are you lot a bunch of fucking robbers or a bunch of donkey wankers?"

The person took his foot from the keys and hopped forward, landing his weight on Barry's left hand.

Barry howled in pain.

"It wasn't me!" said Zoe, snapping into consciousness but muffled by the back of Katie's coat.

"Big Terry," said Violet in a dull monotone. "It's been too long."

Big Terry nodded toward Violet and stepped off Barry's hand. "Violet," Big Terry nodded in acknowledgement. "So this is your crew then?"

Violet nodded slowly. "So it would seem."

Katie had begun to lower Zoe to her feet and Lucas was helping to keep her upright. Zoe, in turn, was trying to keep her head level and burping in a way that seemed to indicate she might very well vomit at any moment.

"What a pathetic bunch of sloppy shites they are," Big Terry laughed, his gaze flicking across the five of them.

Katie drew herself up to her full height and began slowly to move in the direction of Big Terry.

"I see your golem is in attack mode," said Big Terry with a laugh like a punch in the gut. "Call her off before she gets someone killed."

Katie continued to advance until Violet whispered her name.

"It says a lot about the fucking rock rattling around in that bulbous head of yours, knuckles," Big Terry continued, "that you believe I would put myself in a situation where I couldn't deal with you or any of these dirty little wank-stains."

"Terry," said Violet.

"Big Terry," Big Terry corrected.

"Big Terry," Violet continued. "We're all friends here, Katie just didn't recognise you, that's all. We've had a skin full tonight, listen can we catch up tomorrow when—"

"Shut the fuck up."

"Sorry?" Violet frowned, staring down at the angry little bastard. The adrenaline was rushing through her now, sobering her to a degree, but she couldn't for the life of her work out why Big Terry would be pissed off at them.

"Sorry's a good start," said Big Terry. "Your little crew have made me look like a cunt and, to be frank, my dear, I'm not a man who's fond of looking like a cunt."

"I'm sure it's just a misunderstanding, Big Terry." Violet tried to take the psycho off the boil but she could see he was working himself up even without any input from her.

"Shut up. I don't want to hurt you but I will if you make me," he sighed. "Do you remember an X-ray you lot sold? Marilyn Monroe?"

Violet nodded. No point in denying it, no point in explaining who was or wasn't involved. Take your medicine. Big Terry would have men positioned around the car park. If they had been sober maybe they could have controlled the situation, but...

"Who's that little boy?" Zoe slurred from behind Violet, but was quickly shushed by Lucas.

"So those two suits..." Violet began.

"Belong to me. You conned them so, by inference, you conned me." Big Terry had begun pacing up and down in front of the crew and kept absently tapping at a bulge in his jacket pocket. "Well, only one of them belongs to me now. I had to let the other go."

He stopped pacing.

"I'm implying I killed him," said Big Terry.

"Yeah, I got that part," said Violet.

"Took quite a bit of research to track you all down. You've been busy little bastards, haven't you? Planning your little plans. I even spoke to Fegan," he continued. "Your loyal fence."

Violet felt sick. It felt like there was a jigsaw in the bottom of her stomach and Big Terry was systematically removing every piece.

"Everyone has a limit, though, don't they? Fegan's limit was his little finger. Snapped it like a twig." Big Terry barked a pretend laugh. "He cried like the fucking pussy he is. But he spilled the beans. Spilled them all over the table. I let him keep his other nine fingers cos I'm generous."

Violet nodded again. All that was left of the jigsaw were the pieces around the edges.

"And I'm feeling generous tonight." Big Terry clapped his little hands together and walked to Katie's feet. The two of them stared at each other for a few seconds, but Katie didn't make a move, knowing what was coming. "So I'm going to give you a choice. This job is a big old score for you lucky fuckers, isn't it? Set you up in the good life for a while?"

Big Terry stepped away from Katie, circling back to Violet. "Course it is. Small time wankers the lot of you. But I can see talent. I can fucking smell it. So you can do the job for me and, like I say, I'm a generous fucker so I'll give you... I dunno... ten per cent of what Fegan was going to give you."

Barry began to protest but Violet cut him down.

"Go on," she said. "We're listening."

And so Big Terry laid it out. They owed him for the X-rays. They owed him for what he called the 'emotional damage' he had suffered. All they had to do was do what they were already doing. Only instead of delivering it to Fegan – who had bankrolled the whole thing and was promising them a ton of money – they would need to hand the painting over to Big Terry.

Of course, Violet knew he was never going to let it be as simple as that. And as Big Terry paced and talked she felt the last of the pieces of the jigsaw fall away inside of her until all that were left were the four corner pieces. Fegan hadn't deserved this. They had brought this on him and now – they owed him...and Big Terry...

Big Terry underlined where their priorities lay when he described to them what a drawn out and unspeakably painful death each of them would have to endure if they chose not to do exactly as they were told.

"So what's your choice, then?" asked Big Terry finally.

"We'll do the job for you," said Violet firmly. "Then we're even?"

Big Terry thought about this for a second. "Yes. I don't care if all of you get arrested or shot or maimed. As long as someone hands me that painting, I will give them the money. Then, and only then, we're even."

Violet nodded.

"Good," said Big Terry. "I like art. Proper fucking collector me."

He started walking away. "I'll be watching you until the job's done too, you slippery twats. And don't forget, no second chances. I'll probably start by cutting the young girl's nose off. Bet she's a screamer."

Zoe whimpered and puked all over the pavement.

25th September

~~2 ½ weeks to go…~~

24 hours to go...

thirty nine

Lucas dry heaved then winced, the noise playing havoc with the hammering in his head. He glanced at his car keys, then took his mobile out and called a taxi. If he was going to puke it would be in someone else's car.

He ditched the taxi about a mile up the road, partially to keep their secret overground lair hidden but mostly for the fresh air. He wanted the wind to blow on him and take the cobwebs with it. Unfortunately it was triggering some sort of migraine-level headache. He decided to stop when he drew level with a lamppost and placed his left hand against the cold, smooth metal and his right hand on his knee. Bending forward looking at his shoes seemed to do some good so he resolved to stay like that for a while.

Flashes of yesterday hammered past as he closed his eyes. The casino. The money. All that money. Gone. Most of it gone. And Katie. And Violet. And the paintings. And the bombs.

And the shots. And the pints. And the cocktails. And Big Terry.

Lucas gagged again. There was nothing left in his stomach, that much he knew, but his body was trying to reject itself. Turn itself inside out. Maybe that was a better way to go than what Violet was leading them into.

Last night, after the others had gone, after Barry and Katie had bundled Zoe into a taxi, Violet had asked Lucas to hang back. To go with her. So the pair of them got into a second taxi and went to a motorway service station. Got coffee. Talked about Big Terry.

Lucas thought she was going to confront him about the ten grand in his pocket. Confront him about... well, he was hungover now and felt slightly depressed. Guilty. What was he doing?

But she didn't know about the skim. So they talked about the job. The confrontation with Big Terry and the consequences. He liked the way Violet talked. And when she was drunk she talked in circles. Talking about Big Terry. And her ex-boyfriend Percy.

But after a while the circles got smaller and smaller and she talked herself out. And he thought that was it. They stared out of the window at the sporadic cars that were hurtling past.

"Thanks Lucas," she had said. And touched his hand.

Lucas stared at his hand now, resting on his knee, and thought he might have to be sick.

Even now he wasn't entirely sure if it was the hangover or the fear of being beaten to death by a psychopathic dwarf.

*

"So did you and Lucas..." Barry nudged Violet with his elbow and gave a little cheeky whistle.

"Did we what? Do an impersonation of a chaffinch?" asked Violet. At the request of Zoe she had turned out most of the lights in the warehouse, but through the office window she could make out the clock. Five to eleven.

"No," said Barry, placing a cup of something strong and black in front of her. "I'm asking did you two... you know...?" Barry made a sound like the horn on a clown's car.

Katie stood in the middle of the warehouse with her hands in the air and a very weary look on her face while Zoe fixed some sort of corset-type affair around her waist. Neither Zoe nor Katie spoke, and the effect was made all the more bizarre by the fact that Zoe wore a dark purple dressing gown, large sunglasses and oversized slippers with bunny faces, complete with overhanging ears.

Barry pointed at the two of them then looked back to Violet, raised his eyebrows and shrugged. "Bit of a girly makeover then? We got time for that?" Then he remembered what he was talking about a moment ago and drew breath to speak.

Violet lifted her index finger and placed it over his mouth. "I didn't screw him, if that's what you're asking."

"Spoilsport," said Barry through Violet's finger.

"He should be so lucky," Violet laughed. "I wouldn't normally fraternise with the staff." Violet opened her eyes wide and pushed her chest out. She stared at Barry and kept her finger on his mouth. "You have awakened a passion in me that I thought had long died. You..." she paused and took a long, deep breath. "Go and get me some milk for this tea, you silly arse."

Barry stood up. As he did, the door opened and in stepped Lucas.

"Big Terry's got at least two cars watching this industrial estate, you know?" he said, looking left and right outside before quietly closing the door.

"Yeah," said Barry. "He's had people on and off watching all of us. Cuppa?"

"Please," said Lucas, walking past the performance-art makeover that Zoe and Katie were still engrossed in.

"Am I actually awake?" he said as he passed Zoe, looking her up and down. "The sunglasses, I'm with you. The dressing gown, I understand. But the bunny slippers? Why bunny slippers?"

Zoe winced as she turned her head to face him. She lifted the sunglasses and balanced them on top of her head. "Because fuck you is why," she said before lowering the sunglasses once more and turning back to adjust whatever it was she was putting on Katie.

"Coffee," said Barry, returning with a cracked cup. "And milk," he said to Violet, handing her a plastic bottle.

Violet nodded her appreciation and sloshed some milk into the tea.

"Right," she said firmly. "Stop pissing around playing dress up, you two."

Zoe hissed in response and Barry and Lucas laughed.

"You too, Sleepy and Dopey." Violet got to her feet and swigged a mouthful of tea. "In the office. Now."

forty

The clock in the office ticked surprisingly loudly, but none of the crew were paying it any mind as it scraped past eleven in the morning. Violet laid out the forgery of the painting on the desk which she had dragged to the middle of the floor.

"So this is it then?" said Barry, squinting at the signature in the corner of the canvas.

"This is, as you say, it," confirmed Violet. "From the surveillance Zoe gathered..."

Zoe had retreated and was now sitting on the comfortable chair that usually sat at the owner's side of the desk. She nodded her head forward an infinitely small amount.

"...it would appear that Lucas' forger friend has a damn sight more artistic skill than he has social skills," Violet continued. Lucas nodded and perched himself on the only other chair in the office. "In fact, both copies he made are completely indistinguishable from the real thing. I *really* hate to admire the handiwork of that goon but..."

"I'll never breathe a word," Lucas smiled.

Katie coughed. Everyone looked at her. She shuffled slightly.

"We've been planning this for weeks and–"

248

"Seriously Violet," said Barry. "We could walk away. We could go to ground. Leave Kilchester. There's no shame in that. Big Terry wouldn't find us."

Everyone stared. Barry saying out loud what they had all thought about, however fleetingly.

Violet slowly put her cup of tea down on top of a filing cabinet.

"Here we are," Violet went on. "Dragging ourselves into *work* at the crack of noon. Hungover. Beaten down by a tribe of arseholes. Doesn't it make you feel alive?" Violet laughed her staccato laugh, this morning sounding more like the death rattle of a terminally ill car exhaust. "Yesterday we had a plan. Yesterday–"

"Yesterday the job went to shit and then we got hijacked by a three foot high loony," Barry snapped.

Violet was still staring at the mug of tea she had placed on the filing cabinet.

"Yesterday we ripped off a casino with virtually no planning. Yesterday you lot showed me why I'd picked you for this job." Violet was slowly raising her gaze and slowly raising her voice and Barry had, at last, stopped talking. "Yesterday this crew shone. We walked in there and we kicked it into gear and blew the fucking roof off."

Violet was almost shouting and when she stopped her words echoed from the empty walls.

"We were a goddamned machine when we had little to no planning. We have a job tomorrow, and that we've been planning for weeks, haven't we?" Violet was staring at Barry, who felt compelled to nod in agreement.

"We've got the tools." Violet gestured towards some of the computer equipment. "We've got the skills, we've got the motivation and, my friends, we have the fucking brains to pull this job off *and* get paid."

Zoe took off her sunglasses and nodded firmly.

Katie was smiling.

"Yeah, I thought so," said Barry with a shrug. "I was just checking."

"Yeah, well I want this to go by the numbers, people. Understand?" Violet nudged Lucas' foot as she walked past him. "Now let's run it from the top. Zoe, did you get everything you needed from the tablet we recovered?"

"Yes," Zoe croaked. "Affirmative."

"So," said Violet. "You're up first, Zoe, what's the first play?"

Zoe sucked air through her teeth, seemingly requiring additional oxygen to kick-start her mouth.

"And no barfing this time," Violet smirked.

Zoe winced and began. "Well," her voice was thin and hoarse, "I'll access the security cameras for the shared spaces externally through the bug I planted. Research shows the guard who'll be on likes his coffee and pretty much every hour and a half he'll top up. Wait till he goes for a piss, then..."

Zoe waved her hand in a forward motion.

Violet repeated the motion. "Then..."

"Then I nip in and put the stuff in his coffee," said Zoe.

"He comes back," Violet interjected. "He drinks, then his bowels open. Pretty soon he's going to call for his replacement and when he makes the call..."

"I intercept it." Zoe was sounding a little stronger. "I intercept it and tell him his relief is on the way."

Violet nodded and turned to Lucas.

"And I swoop in all dressed up with somewhere to go," said Lucas. His coffee was hitting the spot. "All the while little miss Z will be disabling the first round of the security system." He looked to Zoe, who had put her sunglasses back on.

"At that point I make the call–" Lucas began.

"Zoe, are you even awake?" Barry interrupted.

"Ten-four," said Zoe. "It's just so bright in here. But I think there's probably a one in three chance I'm done with the puking."

"Now that's progress," said Barry. "So Lucas makes the call and I'm outside. First defence against the dark arts of the short arse. You lot are a pile of fucking lightweights and no mistake. When we are done with this job I am going to drink you–"

"So Zoe has control of the systems and Lucas is in place. Katie and I get in the lift and descend to the flat, get inside and get the party started on stealing the painting," Violet continued, shutting Barry's shit down. Then, in an exaggerated, jokey voice, "But – what – if – someone – turns – up – someone – who – isn't – us?"

"Head's up from me," said Barry. "Because I'm the perimeter, bitches!"

Violet raised an eyebrow. "You are the perimeter. Bitch."

"Well there's no need to be like that," Barry sulked.

"And if Barry here turns up as pissed as he was last night?" Violet blew Barry a kiss.

Katie moved her hands in a tying motion then smacked her fist into her palm.

Violet nodded to Katie. "Tie him up," she went on. "Give him a bit of a smack and *if* he runs?" Violet was getting more and more exaggerated, stalking around the room slowly and over-extending her strides.

Katie lifted her hand in the shape of a gun, let her thumb fall as the trigger and then grabbed her stomach, leaning backwards with her mouth open.

Violet slapped her on the shoulder. "Damn right," she said. "So by now..."

"I've got the security system down." Zoe's voice cracked as she spoke, but there was an energy returning to her. "The next layer I mean. The one for the painting."

Violet danced over the room to Zoe. "Yes you do, my clever little prodigy. So the painting is stolen and the forgery put in its place as I get my arse out of there."

"Everyone's getting out of there," added Barry.

"And I'm putting the security back in place level one," said Zoe.

"I'm out of the lift," said Violet.

Katie knocked on the wall dramatically.

"Level two, the front door, is restored," Zoe continued.

"I place the call to the security firm," said Lucas, caught in the momentum. "Telling them I'm sick and they need to send a replacement and the call gets through because–"

"Because I've restored the telephones," said Zoe.

"Does that have a level?" asked Barry.

"I lost track of the level analogy," said Zoe. "I've got a fucking headache, alright?"

"Aw, diddums," said Violet. "I scoop up lightweight here and we exit stage left."

Zoe stuck out her tongue at Violet.

"And I sit there and wait until the replacement security guard arrives," said Lucas with a sigh.

Katie laughed softly, the two puffs of air escaping from her nostrils laugh. Lucas looked over and she waved.

"Yeah, well excuse me for not feeling very reassured," Lucas went on. "If any of that shit with security goes wrong... I'm the one on the desk, aren't I?"

"If everything goes as smoothly as we've planned there'll be no reason to suspect anything. Don't forget to retrieve the bug Zoe planted," said Violet. "Zoe, can you send him a picture of what it looks like?"

Lucas looked petulant. "I'm perfectly capable of–"

"None of us know what that crazy shit Zoe plumbs in looks like, sweetie," Violet interrupted. "Don't feel bad." Violet reached over and tapped him on the cheek. "So Lucas, you retrieve the bug then–"

"Then," Lucas interrupted right back at her. "We get the fuck out of there, deliver the painting to Big Terry and all sail off into the sunset without a single one of us taking a bullet to our forehead."

"Cheerful thought," said Zoe.

"I thought it was the right note to end on," said Lucas and the two of them burst out laughing.

There was a collective exhale, with everyone realising that they could rely on each other. That they all had each other's backs. Violet clapped her hands together, then paused for a second as she caught Lucas' eye.

"I think we're ready, but..." she began.

Everyone groaned.

"Just one more thing, Columbo?" asked Barry.

Violet nodded. "Yeah. There's something else I've been thinking about. Just one more thing I want to go through."

26th September

~~2 weeks to go…~~

The day of the job…

forty one

Zoe zipped up the last two inches of her bomber jacket and crossed the road towards the reception of the banker's house. It was exactly ten thirty in the morning; she had just watched the security guard make his mid-morning coffee, put it on the front desk and then wander off toward the toilet.

There were no cameras back there, of course, but she still had to hurry. The game was afoot. She shoved her hands in her pockets to ward off the chill in the air.

She had thought about costumes, but the blonde wig and glasses she'd worn on her last visit would single her out as the same person. If there was anyone there who would recognise her. And her usual choice: the school uniform. Somehow she felt like she had outgrown it.

Her fingers wrapped around a small, smooth glass bottle Barry had given her. Two drops in the drink. No more. No less. Barry had been *very* insistent on that point. Any less and he'll just have a very bad stomach. Any more and there would be more significant internal problems.

Of course, Barry hadn't put it as politely as that. He'd said, "Don't give him more than two drops or he'll shit himself inside out."

As a result, Zoe was paranoid about getting it on her fingers and having to run the whole technical operation from the ladies toilet.

It was the nerves getting inside her head and jumping up and down. She felt... well, she felt like she was a fraud. As the reception door loomed in front of her, and her moist palm wrapped around the handle, she just felt she shouldn't be there. Zoe stared at the door. In her heart of hearts she knew the truth, believed in herself. She had the skills, the ability and the intelligence to stand shoulder to shoulder with the rest of the crew. But the nerves jumped up and down and there was that feeling again, like she was just pretending. Like she was going to fuck this up.

She walked up to the door, instinctively expecting it to slide open. It didn't. Zoe froze, her reflection in the glass suddenly coming into focus – and then she remembered. The guard had to open it. She reached into her pocket and pulled out her phone, accessed the computer system, and the door slid silently open.

A smile made the slightest appearance at the corners of Zoe's mouth. The guard wasn't at his post. This was how it was supposed to be. She wasn't going to fuck this up. She was in control. She strode across the polished floor, eyes scanning the desk at the point the cameras had shown the guard had placed the cup. It was there. Waiting.

Carefully she plucked the bottle from her pocket and, coming to a halt first, she unscrewed the dropper from the top and began to exert the gentlest pressure on the rubber teat at the end.

Nothing.

Her eyes flicked to the door behind the desk. She imagined she heard him coming. Or perhaps she did hear him coming. Her eyes darted back to the dropper and she squeezed a little harder. A drop formed at the end but nothing actually dropped.

Zoe's heart pounded in her chest. Whether she could hear him or not, he would be back at any moment. She squeezed a little harder and one drop fell into his drink. She squeezed again and three more fell in rapid succession.

She screwed the lid on as she began striding toward the door.

Four drops. Was that too many? Would she permanently damage him? As she stepped back out into the cool air she heard the actual sound of the guard's footsteps moving across the reception floor.

She whipped her phone from her pocket and glanced at the video feed coming to life on the screen. He was craning his neck to look at her walking away, but he was unconcerned. Fantastic. He looked down to the desk and picked up his cup and then, sitting back in his chair, he took a long gulp.

Zoe winced and hoped for the best.

*

Lucas ran his finger around the collar of his light blue shirt then touched the embroidered badge on the breast pocket.

"Guard drank the coffee and just ran off to the bathroom." Zoe's voice came through his earpiece as closely as if she was sitting on his shoulder. "Hope you're in position, Lucas."

"All dressed up and nowhere to go," replied Lucas.

"I never did ask," Zoe continued. "Where did you get the uniform from?"

Lucas groaned.

"Did Violet tell you to ask me that?" Lucas asked.

"What? No. Why?"

Lucas picked at a bit of lint on the neatly-pressed line ironed into his trouser leg.

He shook his head. "You're not the only one who can find out stuff, you know."

"I know that. Apparently in the olden days you could find things out without using a computer," Zoe laughed.

"In the olden days?" Lucas sighed. "Great, kid, don't get cocky. I did it the old fashioned way. I followed one of the security guards home then went through his bins."

"Why the hell did you – oh, hang on a second, he's picking up the phone. I'm going to have to answer it. I'll keep you on the line if you like."

Lucas shrugged. The sound of a dial tone echoed in his inner ear, but was broken by the discordant melody of the numbers being dialled. There was a ringing.

"Watchmen Security," Zoe answered the call. She sounded

259

posh. Probably putting on her phone voice, Lucas thought.

"Yeah, hi, listen, this is guard 187 slash 2411 at location 657."

"One moment please," Zoe tapped at a keyboard. Lucas had a mental picture of her sitting at a computer filing her nails whilst playing a sound effect of a keyboard being tapped. "Confirmed. Password please."

"Blodwen."

"Blodwen?"

"Blodwen. It's my niece's name."

"Confirmed," said Zoe. "What can I do for you, Neil?"

"I'm ill. Really ill," the guard continued.

"Are you going to be able to continue to the end of your shift?" asked Zoe.

There was a low rumbling noise in the background of the call.

"No. You need to get a replacement over here. Fast. I – well, something has disagreed with me and I keep – it's just that..." He fell silent for a second. "I keep going to the toilet. I'm very unwell."

"I understand," said Zoe. "Hold the line please."

There was some hold music playing in Lucas' ear.

"Lucas," said Zoe. "I'm going to tell him ten minutes. You reckon that's about right?"

"Yeah," replied Lucas. "Should be. I'm just round the corner so—"

"Shh," replied Zoe and cut the hold music. "Neil? Are you still there?"

There was a groaning at the other end.

"We can have a replacement there in ten minutes."

The security guard hung up.

"So you were going bin diving?" asked Zoe matter-of-factly.

"Yes, princess. It was necessary," Lucas groaned.

"Sounds like I'd rather stick to computers, to be honest."

"Well, before I dived straight into the bin I found out that he didn't have a computer," said Lucas, with more than a little smugness.

"He didn't have a computer? Where did you do the surveillance? The 1970s?"

"I found out from going through his rubbish that he got his uniforms dry cleaned. So I robbed the dry cleaners."

"Petty crime? Good job there, skip rat."

"Piss off. I got a uniform didn't I, geek girl?"

"You know I can electrify your earpiece and shock you, right?" asked Zoe.

Lucas laughed. Then he stopped laughing. "Not really?"

"Nah, not really," Zoe laughed. "Now get your arse in gear, you're up."

forty two

"Thank God you're here, mate," said the security guard – and retched.

Lucas smiled warmly and under his breath said, "Jesus, Zoe, how much of that stuff did you give him?"

"What? Why?" Zoe sounded panicked. "Exactly the amount Barry told me to give him."

"Are you new?" the guard asked Lucas, standing up and putting on his overcoat.

Lucas nodded. "Pretty new, but I've been on shift here a few times. They put me all over Kilchester."

The guard nodded and staggered from behind the desk. "Did the same thing to me when I first started. Listen, thanks for covering for me. I'd probably ditch the milk in the fridge if I were you. Just in case this is food poisoning."

Lucas nodded and made his way behind the desk. "Food poisoning, eh?"

"It's pouring out both ends, mate."

Lucas picked up the cup he knew contained the drops, then paused as he called to mind where the kitchen was. Zoe had rendered the whole thing in 3D and Lucas had been playing the bloody thing like a game. He had to admit it made things a whole lot easier than blueprints and schematics.

He turned around and walked through to the kitchen.

"Security guard has cleared the perimeter." Barry's was the first voice to come through as Lucas sat down at the desk in reception and adjusted the security monitors. "We're good to go, people."

"Confirmed, everything is A-Okay in here," said Lucas.

"I know we're good to go, dumbass." Zoe's voice was in his earpiece but also approaching him in his actual ear. Lucas raised his hand in greeting as she strode across to the desk, his gaze dropping back to the monitors as Violet and Katie strode across the car park toward them.

"Good morning, skip rat," said Violet as she entered reception.

Katie ducked her head as she approached the door, returning to her full height as she came inside. Smirking.

"Oh piss off, all of you," said Lucas. "Sometimes you've got to do what needs to be done."

"Quite right," said Violet. "Now Zoe, you best get your shit together – otherwise when we get downstairs we're going to make quite the spectacle of ourselves, aren't we?"

"I'm on it," said Zoe and jogged towards the door behind the desk. Reaching it, she tapped at her phone once more and the lights on the card reader to the side of the door changed from red to green. Zoe smirked, pushed it open and continued through to find the junction box she had located on her previous visit.

"After you, my dear," said Violet to Katie and gave a little bow.

Katie walked to the lift and pressed the call button. Violet walked over to stand by Katie's side.

"Good luck," said Lucas.

Violet and Katie stared at the lift doors. There was a *bong* as the lift signalled its arrival, followed by a grinding noise as the lift doors slid open. Violet let Katie fold herself into the tiny box. She looked on as Katie bundled herself in there, not really sure if they might have to take two trips. When she was sure Katie was packaged securely she joined her inside, then turned back to face Lucas and pressed the button marked '–1'.

"I'm too fucking talented to need luck, Lucas," she said as the doors slid shut. "And if you stick with me, one day *you* will be too."

She winked and the doors closed in front of her.

The lift's lights blinked and it began to slowly descend.

"I'd turn around and face you, but..." Violet said.

Katie gave her a dig in the back with her index finger.

"You all set with everything you need?" asked Violet.

No response.

"Thought so," said Violet. "This lift is slow, isn't it?"

Violet edged around to face Katie, who was contorted from crouching her great bulk in the tiny box. Violet smirked. Katie rolled her eyes.

"Can you still hear me?" asked Zoe. Her voice was different, it had a more tinny quality, but the signal wasn't broken.

"Affirmative," confirmed Violet. "How are you progressing?"

"All cameras in public areas belong to us," said Zoe smugly. "Can you check the tablet I gave you? I can't get a signal from it."

Violet opened the top of a canvas satchel she was carrying and fished out the tablet computer Zoe had given her.

"That's the one," said Zoe.

Violet glanced up at the camera in the corner of the lift. "Should I be disturbed by your omnipotence?"

"I am a benevolent God if you appease me," Zoe replied.

Violet turned her attention back to the electronic device in her hand. She pressed the power button and it began to boot up.

"It was turned off," said Violet. The lift shuddered to a halt, shaking the mirrored walls and creating a frightening spectacle of Katie in the reflections.

The doors slid open to reveal the long corridor leading to the banker's flat. Violet jogged down the corridor with Katie striding behind keeping pace.

"I've picked it back up on the system. It'll take me a minute to configure."

*

Zoe sat cross-legged on the floor of the tiny kitchenette, a laptop on her knee and a very, very sore arse. She had planned every aspect of the technical assault. But she'd not had the foresight to bring a cushion.

The screen of her laptop flickered as she scrolled and clicked, occasionally hammering some code in through the keyboard. This was the hardest part.

What was it the secretary had said? That the system attached to the front door would silently call the authorities if it was triggered. Although she had also said there was no picking the lock.

"Right, Violet," said Zoe, shifting what little weight she had to try to stop her legs from going to sleep. "Plug the cable into the bottom of the tablet then slowly slide the card until it reaches halfway down the card reader."

"Acknowledged," said Violet. She sounded more serious than Zoe was used to. Was this Violet getting nervous?

Because Zoe certainly was. She watched the screen as Violet did as she was instructed. The decoder activated and began running through combinations and – there it was – the red flag, the system realising something was wrong.

Zoe tried to buy some time up front, feeding the system conflicting messages about the presence of an internet connection, testing it until…small victory. She convinced the system that it had lost its internet connection completely. Which felt like winning, but really if there were any backup algorithms in place then they would be kicking in right about now. But it bought them time to–

"Zoe, the light's gone green!" Violet shouted down the line. "That's good, right?"

"Yes, that's good," Zoe confirmed. "But DON'T. OPEN. THE DOOR. YET."

"Zoe?"

"Violet?"

"I started opening the door."

"Fuck."

Zoe stared at the screen. It was going absolutely mental. Warnings, red boxes flashing. The system was fighting back.

"Fuckfuckfuck," said Zoe. She couldn't handle this. There were too many ways it was trying to notify the outside world. Any second now it would connect and the police would be called.

And then it came to her. She took the laptop and placed it on the floor beside her.

She stood up. Not as fast as she would have liked to, because her left leg had gone to sleep. And then, with a scream, she dived over to the junction box and unplugged the master socket for the comms for the building. There was no way a signal was getting in or out of there with no internet connection.

"Zoe? Zoe?" Violet was panicked in the earpiece. "Zoe? Are you alright? What happened?"

Zoe waved her leg in the air and rubbed at it. "I'm good, it's fine, it's..." she sighed, knowing she would suffer for this later. "I had pins and needles."

She took a deep breath. That was a schoolgirl error; she had let herself get lost in the tech. But she was still winning. Today was a good day.

Bending down slowly, Zoe picked a small plastic box from the gym bag that she had left on one of the counters, plugged the main line for the building's internet connection in one end and then connected the other end to the outside world.

The door to reception opened a crack and Zoe glanced up in time to see Lucas hurling a cushion at her. It bounced off her shoulder and onto the floor.

"Aren't you supposed to be making a phonecall or something?" Zoe shouted at Lucas.

"I was, but someone pulled the plug on the phone system," Lucas called back.

Zoe shook her head and returned to her laptop. The security system was calling out, looking for a response, but the box she had installed was acting as a firewall.

Zoe adjusted her posture on the cushion and set to work again. Soon she'd found what she was looking for. The red flashing boxes and streams of data calmed to a trickle and then stopped completely.

"We now have control of the secondary system; you can enter the flat without the police coming," she said sheepishly.

forty three

"Pins and needles?" said Violet. "Really?"

She pushed open the door and the lights inside the flat came on automatically. Violet and Katie swung their heads around, surveying the vast underground residence. They began to move quickly.

There was no wandering the corridors or getting lost this time; both women had studied the floorplans and rendering Zoe had created. Both knew exactly where they were going and what they had to do.

At the archway that served as the entrance to the den, the pair stopped. Violet nodded at Katie, who reciprocated the gesture, and Violet entered the den alone. There, over in the corner, was the prize. The Dali canvas had yet to be moved; it was where Zoe had seen it originally on the same wall as two other paintings and a mounted, stuffed fish.

Violet darted over to it and deposited her satchel on the floor next to her.

"I have eyes on the painting," she said to everyone and no-one.

"I see you still have a gift for cheese." Barry's voice blundered into the conversation. "I have eyes on the prize, Mr President," he said, adopting a fake American accent.

"Piss off, retard," Violet laughed. "What else should I have said?"

"I dunno," said Barry. "It says more about you than what is actually going on. You see, if I had something important to say then I would say something like 'Rollo Glass's car just passed me so you lot better have your shit together' and I think it would encapsulate all it needed to."

There was a silence in all the earpieces.

"Rollo Glass's car just passed me so you lot better have your shit together," repeated Barry.

"Fuck," said Violet. "He's early. Masks, people." She reached into her satchel and pulled out her mask.

"Yeah," Barry's voice once more came drifting thinly through their earpieces. "About the masks..."

"You aren't going to panic me for no reason, Barry," said Violet, tossing the white ball of fabric from hand to hand. "I've already got the mask out of the bag."

"Oh, don't worry about that," Barry continued. "I didn't forget to distribute the masks. We've all got one. It's just—"

Violet opened the ball of white material. One side of it was smeared with black ink.

"Barry..." said Violet slowly. "Why has my mask got graffiti on it?"

"I had them in the bag," Barry replied. "With a permanent marker. And I suppose the lid came off."

"You suppose that, do you?" Violet sighed. "Nice white stocking masks to look professional. That wasn't too much to ask, was it?"

It was Violet's mask of choice. No need for eyeholes because you could see through, so no-one who saw you even got your eye colour. And now Barry had managed to fuck that up. She pulled her own mask on over her head. The marker pen wasn't particularly evident. It didn't obscure her view. It could have been a lot worse.

Violet stood up and looked at herself in the mirror. The ink wasn't scribbled on the mask, rather it had seeped. An ink blot. That looked like an eagle with its wings spread.

"Mine looks like a butterfly," Zoe giggled across the airways.

"Awww. Sweet, Barry."

Katie stepped into the den and walked up to Violet. She pointed at the ink blot on her mask and then pointed at her fist. Violet nodded half-heartedly. To her it looked more like two people joined at the head than a fist.

"Well, I really can't wait to find out what face-wrong you have prepared for me but, as I'm presently pretending to be a security guard, I might give it a miss for a few minutes," said Lucas. "Also, they're approaching the door, which means they'll be at the lift in the next forty-five seconds."

Violet ran her fingers around the edge of the frame of the Dali painting. "Zoe, how are we going on the security on the paintings?" asked Violet anxiously.

"It's slow going, to be honest with you," said Zoe. "I need more time, otherwise they're not only going to know we've tried to get the painting, they're going to know which one we tried to get. I'll shut up and get on with it, shall I?"

Violet growled under her breath. Everything had been going so well and now the banker was on his way downstairs, the masks were ruined and Zoe still hadn't disabled the security system. Talk about leaving things until the last minute.

"Three targets approaching the lift." Lucas' voice was quiet as he whispered his update. "Zoe, could you trap them in the lift?"

"I *could*," Zoe snapped. "But I only have one pair of hands and right now that pair of hands is working on a security system, okay?"

"We planned for this." Violet stood up and spoke calmly to the crew now. "Barry, close the net to the exterior. In the car park. No-one comes in or out. Got it?"

"Check," said Barry.

"Zoe," Violet went on, walking out of the den and into the main living area of the cavernous flat. "Keep doing what you're doing; update me when you have something to say."

"Will do, captain," said Zoe.

"Lucas?" Violet began.

"They're in the lift and it's descending," replied Lucas. "I know what I need to do, I'm already on the stairs coming down. And in case anyone is interested, my mask looks like two women's feet.

Barry, these masks are fucking cool, man."

"Cool?" Barry's voice invaded their heads once more. "Erm…"

"Yeah," said Lucas, his breathing beginning to become heavier. All Violet could hear was the sound of his shoes clattering on the stairs as he took them two, three at a time. "Like Rorschach."

"Yeah, they're ink blots, you clot," Violet sighed. "Wasn't it called the Rorschach test?" and then, quieter for Katie's benefit, "I'm *very* well read these days, don't you know?"

"No, no," said Lucas. "Like in *Watchmen*, the graphic novel. Rorschach was a character in that. Had a mask like this. Proper badass. Fucking cool. It'll scare the shit out of these jokers, you wait and see."

"Speaking of which," said Violet to Katie. "We better get into position."

Violet stared as Katie nodded. The masks did look pretty terrifying. And perhaps if they were pure white someone might have seen a connection between them and the canvas. Like they were some sort of calling card.

*

Rollo Glass bellowed as the lift juddered to a halt at the bottom of the shaft. The lift was small enough that it reminded him of how fat he was every time he got in it. To be inside of it with two burly bodyguards was, frankly, insufferable.

"I ought to have made you two take the stairs," he puffed as the doors slid open.

"Sir, we are contracted to protect your person and that would not be something either of us could execute if we were not in the same room."

It was a statement. These burly steroid-filled halfwits didn't respect him in the slightest. Well, the next two he employed might. Glass made a mental note to have them reassigned to somewhere ghastly as soon as he returned to the bank.

"Come on then," Glass barked, and stepped out onto the deep pile carpet of the corridor. The familiar journey home was making him crave a stiff whisky but he would have to resist. Once heads had rolled here he would have to return to the office. Too many things that needed his attention.

What was it the security guard on the front desk had said? That the people had come to remove the paintings and take them into storage. Early. And that he had only let them into the flat because they were 'on the list'. On the list? ON THE BLOODY LIST?

This wasn't the first security guard he had had fired, and it most certainly wouldn't be the last. The banker waddled quickly down the hallway toward his front door and, reaching it, he scanned his key card.

A little red light flashed up on the plastic housing. Rollo growled under his breath.

"Sir," the bodyguard said, plucking the card from his hand. "Allow me to try that for you."

The guard breathed on the card, most likely fogging up one side of it with his stinking breath. Rollo shuddered at the thought and took half a step back away from him.

The bodyguard leaned forward and swiped the card a second time. This time a green light flashed up and the door made a satisfying *clunk* as the locks freed themselves.

The bodyguard pushed open the door to the flat.

forty four

"We are going to need that painting off the wall, oh great and mighty Oz," Violet hissed.

"Nearly there, hang on, one... more... minute," Zoe responded.

"Because things are about to kick off down here," Violet continued.

There was a heavy *clunk* and the front door began to open. Katie adjusted the courier tube that was slung around her shoulder and flexed and unflexed the muscles in her arms. They had the element of surprise – but the bodyguards would still be wary, so they had to be ready.

"Hello?" the first bodyguard called out. He padded slowly into the flat.

"Hello?" Violet responded, calling from the den but keeping herself firmly out of sight. "In here."

The bodyguard beckoned and Rollo Glass stepped into the flat too. Katie waited enough time for him to be clear of the swing of the door and then launched herself into a run, covering the distance between where she had been hiding and the entrance in a couple of strides and then slamming her foot into the heavy door.

Glass made a noise like a chicken, a sort of shocked *buh bawk* as he spun around to lay eyes on his attacker.

But Katie was already in attack mode. The door had achieved the desired result as well as its secondary objective as it hammered into the second bodyguard. She had hoped that she'd hit him hard enough that he'd be knocked down into the corridor and the door would lock shut, but no such luck.

The noise that she had heard, apart from the squawking of Glass, was a softer contact. Katie predicted that the door had caught the bodyguard in the arm and crushed him in the doorjamb. Still not a bad outcome. Although, having said that, the odds were still most certainly in the bodyguards' favour.

Katie lunged forward to scare Glass and he flinched, jumping backwards into the first bodyguard and knocking him off guard. Reaching forward, Katie grabbed the door handle and opened it wide. The second bodyguard was beginning to recover himself. Katie let go of the door handle and pulled back her fist.

A look of panic flashed across the second bodyguard's face and his hands instinctively flew up to protect himself, but it was too late. Katie's fist connected with his cheekbone and jaw, slamming his head into the door frame. Result: closed fracture to the cheekbone, dislocation of the jaw. He dropped to the floor, unconscious.

The banker howled like a frightened chicken once more, but the first bodyguard was more prepared, moving himself in between his employer and the masked behemoth that was Katie.

"I am going to enjoy this," the bodyguard said and readied himself in some sort of martial arts stance.

Katie didn't reciprocate but stood, ready for his attack.

The bodyguard came forward hard and fast, using his weight and height to his advantage and raining punches in Katie's direction. Unfortunately, and as she usually found in these situations, men who were drawn to trained fighting and were, as the bodyguard was, over six feet tall, were rarely faced with an opponent who was taller and stronger than them.

And fighting someone who was six foot ten was not something most people had any experience of. Katie easily deflected his blows with her enormous hands and he jumped back, bobbing on the spot as if he fancied himself as a modern day Bruce Lee. And he was grinning.

Katie hated it when they were standing long enough to get cocky. She drew back her right arm then propelled it forward, her flattened palm connecting with his sternum. The result should have been to catapult him backwards, ending with him sliding across the polished floor on his arse.

But it didn't happen like that. Somehow the bodyguard was ready for her and managed to take a great deal of the force out of the blow. Instead of skidding across the floor, the bodyguard was simply knocked off balance. Or so Katie thought. The cunning little bastard used the momentum she had given him and swung around, dropping down as he did and extending his leg to sweep Katie's legs from under her.

Much to her surprise, it worked.

Katie toppled, the world shifting ninety degrees clockwise in slow motion. Over the bodyguard's shoulder Katie could see Violet running out of the den, then she hit the floor with a *thunk*. Katie stared at the cocky bastard, he was doing the Bruce Lee dance again.

"You done then, mate, or you getting up for another fall?" the bodyguard taunted foolishly.

Katie grimaced behind her mask and popped herself up into a sitting position. Her eyes fixed on Violet, the bodyguard firmly monitored in her periphery. Violet's hand was dipping into her satchel, pulling something out and –

The bodyguard danced on the spot before bringing his foot up and forward to connect with Katie's head. This time, however, Katie was ready. She caught his foot and twisted it. The end result was much more to Katie's liking. The bodyguard spun in mid-air, the one leg he had planted on the ground shifted from vertical to horizontal and then Katie brought the whole weight of him crashing to the floor whilst simultaneously tilting his feet up slightly.

The final result: the full weight of the bodyguard came down on his own nose. And blood. Lots of blood.

The banker squealed. It appeared the bodyguard was down and out, but both Katie and Violet knew better than that. A hardcase with a busted nose just made for an angrier opponent. In the time it took for Katie to down the bodyguard, Violet had retrieved the item she was looking for in her satchel and slid it across the floor toward Katie.

The bodyguard let out a guttural noise, something akin to *hnnnnurgh*, then sprang to his feet, sending blood flying as he did.

"Hnnnn-you b-baaaaastard, grnnngh… I'm going to k-kill you for thaaat," the bodyguard screamed, causing the banker to recoil further toward the front door.

Shifting her enormous frame, Katie readied herself to spring up, but the bodyguard was faster and bore down on her again, coming in close, ready to strike. Katie lifted the item Violet had slid across the floor and slammed it into the bodyguard's crotch, firing just shy of five million volts into him. She watched the taser work its magic, disrupting his body's ability to communicate with its muscles, causing him to drop to the floor like a sack of rocks.

Katie drew herself up to her full height and stared down at the banker through her mask.

The banker bolted out the front door and into the corridor.

forty five

Lucas reached the bottom of the stairs and had to stop. His lungs burned, the polyester of the uniform was chafing his legs. He had to keep going, but not before he put on his mask. Whipping the crumpled bundle out of the inside pocket of his blazer, he unfolded it slowly to reveal... his Rorschach mask. He smiled, picturing himself momentarily as the fictional character, then wiped the sweat from his brow with his sleeve, rolled the mask over his face and burst out into the corridor.

And, judging by the noises that were echoing down the hallway, he had arrived at just the right moment. Lucas took his time, padding towards the flat silently. Enjoying a moment of fantasy.

But not too far into fantasy. He moved quickly past the half-open door, trying to sneak an eyeful of what was going on, but could see nothing past the bulk of the banker. He pulled out the zip ties he had brought with him. He would need those in a second.

There was the sound of a grown man squealing. Lucas laughed out loud; he couldn't help picturing Katie pounding the bodyguards. He edged forward, waiting for his cue.

And then it came. The banker ran, if you could call it running, out of his front door toward the lift. Lucas moved forward fast, hooking his right foot in front of the banker's and pushing his shoulders forward.

Rollo Glass dropped to the floor, his hands going out to stop a repeat of what had happened moments earlier to his bodyguard. Lucas dropped quickly but lightly on top of him, his knee in the small of the banker's back.

"Hands behind your back please," said Lucas.

The banker groaned but offered no resistance, moving his hands behind him for Lucas to secure. Lucas took his time; this was important and he had to get it exactly right.

"You know the police will have been called when you entered the flat, don't you?" was all Rollo Glass said.

"Erm, I don't think so," Zoe's voice suddenly invaded Lucas' head.

"I'm afraid not, Mr Glass," said Lucas as he helped him to his feet. "Not this time."

*

Rollo Glass walked back into his flat, followed by Lucas, who had been careful to stay out of the banker's line of sight. Sitting on two of his dining chairs were his two bodyguards, both neatly trussed and both sporting black canvas bags over their heads.

Lucas guided the banker to a third chair, separate from the bodyguards, and pushed on his shoulder. The banker sat. Looking over to Violet and Katie, Lucas pointed upwards. Violet nodded and Lucas left before the banker could lay eyes on him.

"So this is a kidnapping then?" Glass addressed Violet and Katie.

Violet walked into the den and out of earshot.

"The security system?" she said, addressing the question to Zoe.

"We're all good," was Zoe's response.

Violet walked back into the main atrium of the flat.

"Speak to me." The banker was becoming more agitated. That was probably a good thing.

Violet stood next to Katie and stared at him through her mask. She took a deep breath in and out.

"What the hell are those masks supposed to be?" Glass continued. "I mean, what sort of kidnappers have silhouettes of porn on their masks?"

Violet stared at him from behind the mask. He was squirming in his seat. Getting madder. Time to get down to business.

She turned to Katie and, with her right hand, pointed two fingers toward her own eyes and then turned her hand, pointing her index finger at the banker. Katie nodded.

And then the banker exploded into motion. For a man of his size it was quite a feat. Jumping to his feet, he looked for a moment like he would run straight into them.

"I am not a victim," he shouted and then, with fierce effort, he pulled his hands apart, snapping the zip ties that held his arms, but instead of running toward them he dived into the nearest room, his bedroom.

Violet tapped Katie on the shoulder and Katie began to move forward toward the entrance to the room he was hiding in. One of the bodyguards groaned as she walked by, and she absent-mindedly cracked her knuckles. She stopped in her tracks, however, when Rollo Glass appeared at the doorway to his bedroom with a gun pointed at her.

"I am not a victim," Glass repeated. He was sweating, his grip on the gun loose and his hands shaking.

Violet moved behind a counter. "Put it down," she said, trying to introduce a lower tone to her voice, perhaps to disguise it a little if he was asked to describe it after the fact. "Put down the gun. You've seen what will happen to you otherwise. Same thing that happened to your boys there."

Katie began to move slowly, but the banker spotted it and shouted at her to stop.

"Don't move a fucking muscle," he screamed. "I am in charge here, not you."

Katie laughed her delicate laugh, the air escaping lightly from her nose. The banker heard it and flew into an absolute rage.

"Nononono!" he screamed. The arm that was holding the gun was waggling about madly now; he seemed to be using the gun to point rather than to threaten. "I. AM. IN. CHARGE."

Katie inched forward. She was almost close enough to make a lunge to disarm him.

The sound of the gun firing inside the flat slammed the ears of all those present like someone jumping from a plane and hitting the ground after their parachute failed to open.

It was one shot; the noise hit them all but the bullet only hit one of them.

Katie's hand touched her stomach as blood soaked through her coat.

The ringing in the ears of the occupants of the flat was almost immediately replaced by the sound of Violet's voice as she rushed forward shouting one word.

'No!'

Katie dropped to her knees in front of the banker, and he dropped the gun on the floor, staring at what he'd done.

Violet ran forward to her friend, but Katie was dropping, onto her hands, onto the floor, clutching at her stomach as she bled and bled.

The banker didn't stare for long. He ran for the door, out into the corridor and into the lift at the end. All that was in his head was... Get out. Now. Get clear. Call someone. Someone to clean things up. Get out now.

forty six

"Watchmen Security," a bored female voice answered Lucas after one ring.

"This is guard 187 slash 2411," said Lucas, glancing at the piece of paper in front of him where he'd scribbled the information. "I'm at location 657."

There was the sound of a computer keyboard being tapped at and then a silence at the other end of the line. Lucas looked up as the door to the lift slid open.

"And can I take your password?" the woman on the phone asked.

The second the lift doors were wide enough, the banker barrelled across reception. Lucas wondered for a moment if he should try to hide himself but Glass didn't even give him a second glance. A security guard held the same interest as a lamp or a potted plant to the banker.

"Blodwen," said Lucas.

The banker shot through the outer doors and out of Lucas' view. He followed his progress on the monitor in front of him.

"And how can I help you today, Neil?" the woman on the phone continued.

"I'm ill, really ill. I'm not going to be able to make it to the end

of my shift, going to have to get to a doctor straight away," Lucas
lied.

"I see," said the woman with as much sympathy as a handgun.

Lucas watched the monitors as the banker jumped into the car
he had arrived in, gunned it and drove off.

"I'll send a replacement right over," the woman said. Lucas
thanked her and hung up.

"Front desk is clear," said Lucas to anyone who was listening.

There was no reply.

The door to the stairwell opened and Violet appeared.

"Katie's been shot," she said.

"Just finishing off back here," said Zoe simultaneously.

Lucas winced, struggling to multitask. "What?"

"Come on," said Violet. "We have to go."

Lucas checked the desk, making sure he hadn't left anything
incriminating behind. Violet strode past the desk, her satchel
flapping at her side and the now-familiar courier tube in her left
hand.

"Big Terry has eyes on us." Barry's voice drifted through the
earpiece from outside.

"Where?" asked Lucas, as he and Violet covered the ground
over the carpark toward Barry.

"Red car, parked opposite," Barry gestured and the pair of them
turned. There were two men inside.

Arriving at Barry's car, Violet gently threw the courier tube in
through the open window.

Barry looked at the two of them, the seriousness on their faces.
"What's going on?" he asked.

"Katie was shot," Violet said. "The banker's gone. Zoe's closing
down in there and–"

While Violet was talking, Lucas checked out the car containing
Big Terry's goons one more time then opened the driver's side door
and got inside. Violet was still talking to Barry as Lucas turned
the keys in the ignition and, after a momentary check to make sure
the courier tube was on the passenger seat, he slammed the car into
reverse.

"What the fuck are you doing?" Barry shouted, jumping out of the car's way.

Lucas said nothing, just swung the car out of the car park, hammered it back into gear and accelerated away from them.

*

Of course, leaving behind the crew meant picking up new friends. Lucas had put a good ten minutes between himself and the banker's flat before he pulled over to the side of the road.

The driver of the red car mistakenly believed that he had been taught to tail cars at spy school. As a result, he had driven a little further down the road then inexpertly veered to the side of the road.

Lucas got out of his car and walked over to them, tapping on the driver's window.

The window slid down and a man whose I.Q. could be measured in sausages stared out.

"You're following me for Big Terry?" Lucas did them the courtesy of asking, in spite of the fact that he knew the answer.

The driver looked confused, opened his mouth to speak and then closed it again.

"I've got the painting in the car," Lucas gestured.

"I know," the driver said, with a voice like a slap in the ear with an uncooked pork chop. "I watched the clever one throw it in."

"You want to give Big Terry a call then? Cos I want my money." Lucas flashed the driver a grin and then walked back to his car.

Two minutes passed, then the passenger got out of the red car and walked to Lucas.

"Boss says he'll meet you in half an hour," the goon said, then told Lucas where. It was some abandoned piece of ground halfway across town. Lucas nodded his acknowledgement then gunned the car and took off, leaving the goon running to get back to his own car.

One stress-free drive across town later and Lucas had had enough time to convince himself that what he had done was insane. Not only that, but the situation he was about to place himself in was almost certainly going to result in his untimely demise. His stomach was doing somersaults and he was half convinced that he may need to evacuate his bowels before the meeting – but something made him press on.

And at that moment, that very same something hopped out of the passenger seat of a black convertible and walked over to Lucas. He was followed by the two goons from the red car and someone else. Someone he recognised. It was Violet's ex, Percy.

"Alright, thundercunt," Big Terry said, staring unblinkingly at Lucas. "Where's those other fuckers?"

Percy stood behind Big Terry, a look of confusion on his face.

"Well, originally this was between me and you," said Lucas. His mouth was drier than he ever thought it possible to be. "So I wanted to deliver the goods. And apologise."

Big Terry nodded.

"I'll be honest with you, it was always my intention to stab them in the back," Lucas went on and then, looking directly at Percy, "I even went as far as to line up a fence to shift the painting. But after the situation developed with yourself I thought I best make good on my debt and at least make a few quid off the back of that."

Big Terry stared at him. Then he burst out laughing.

"Oh, that's priceless," he said.

Lucas shifted from one foot to the other as he stared down at the midget.

"And Percy here asked especially to come and see Violet come grovelling to me." Big Terry barked another laugh. "I was going to make her beg. Shall I make you beg, you dirty little shitpipe?"

"I'd rather not. I just want to give you what I got for you, get my money and go," Lucas said, being as careful as possible not to say anything that would inflame Big Terry's sense of offence.

"You'd rather not?" Big Terry repeated, putting on a high-pitched voice. "And what makes you think I'm going to give you anything at all after you stole from me? Eh?"

"You're a man of your word," said Lucas.

"I've got two words for you," said Big Terry. "Fuck off."

The two goons and Percy laughed. Big Terry waved a hand in the air and the driver-goon started walking to where Lucas' car was parked.

"This is how it's going to go down," said Big Terry. He reached up a stubby digit and scratched at the corner of his mouth. "He's going to get the painting from your car. If it's not there, I'm going to shoot you."

"It's there," Lucas bleated.

"Good, I thought it would be," replied Big Terry. "You're a treacherous bastard but you don't strike me as stupid."

Lucas shook his head.

"Once I've got that painting we're straight. You can walk."

"No money then?" asked Lucas, his voice flat.

"Course not. For a clever person, you're fucking stupid," said Big Terry. "At what point did you think I would pay you?"

"If you pay me, I've got something else for you," said Lucas. His eyes flicked to Percy for the briefest moment. Percy just looked pissed off.

Big Terry stared up at Lucas, weighing him up.

"You've got balls as big as me, haven't you?"

"You brought the money?" continued Lucas.

Big Terry raised an eyebrow. "I have the money," was all he said.

The driver-goon walked past the two of them carrying the courier tube.

"Get rid of those three," said Lucas.

"If you try anything at all..." Big Terry began.

Lucas was playing at being confident in spite of the fact that he thought he might throw up. "With respect, Big Terry, your reputation precedes you and I am fully aware that I don't have the slightest chance of taking you down."

Big Terry smiled wide.

"Fair enough then," he said. "Fuck off you three."

The two goons and Percy reluctantly withdrew to a reasonable distance.

Lucas took out his phone and tapped the screen a couple of times until an image of himself appeared.

"If you show me a picture of your cock I swear I'll cut it off." Big Terry shifted around to Lucas' side and Lucas tried to surreptitiously stoop to give him a better view of the screen.

He tapped the play button and the video began to play.

"Listen to me." Percy's voice could be heard before he could be seen, he was leaning in close to Lucas. "Big Terry is a big fucking moron. He wouldn't notice a turd if you smeared it on his top lip. I've been skimming off the top of practically every deal I've ever been involved in for him and he doesn't notice any of it."

"Really? How the hell do you manage that?" Lucas heard his own voice and wondered if he actually sounded like that. Finally he watched himself move out of shot so Percy could now be seen fully.

"Well," Percy continued on-screen. "Maybe it's because I'm skimming off the top. So he can't see it!" Big Terry drew breath sharply as Percy laughed in the video.

"I don't get it," said on-screen Lucas with a dumb smile. "What do you mean?"

"Have you met Big Terry?" asked Percy.

Lucas shook his head.

"He's a dwarf. A midget. Whatever the fuck. He's a short arse. So if I'm skimming off the top then he can't see it because he's too fucking short. Geddit?"

"Oh I see," Lucas nodded but didn't laugh.

The video ended. Big Terry said nothing.

"So..." said Lucas eventually.

"I'm not going to ask why the fuck you were recording this, because frankly I couldn't give a shit," said Big Terry quietly. "That you brought it to my attention is enough."

Lucas nodded, then realised Big Terry was still looking at the screen. Big Terry pressed the play button again and watched it in its entirety once more.

"It's not doctored," said Big Terry.

"No," said Lucas.

"I wasn't asking."

"No."

"I'll pay you," said Big Terry deliberately. "And I'll keep the phone."

"Of course," said Lucas. "And thank you."

Big Terry walked over to his car and Lucas followed at what he considered as safe a distance as possible. As they drew close one of the goons popped the boot of the car open and took out a small bag. Big Terry took the bag and gave it to Lucas.

"We're done," he said. "Now fuck off."

Lucas nodded.

Big Terry beckoned Percy over to him and pressed play on the video.

As Lucas walked away he could hear Percy's protestations, accusations, excuses bubbling over into gabbled pleading. Lucas turned as he reached his car and saw the glint of something sharp in Big Terry's hand.

Percy screamed as whatever it was plunged into his thigh, but his scream was short-lived. As Percy doubled over to clutch his leg, Big Terry swung up and punched him hard in the face. Lucas got into his car and shut the door. He turned the key in the ignition as one of the goons shoved Percy's shoulder, toppling him into the boot of the car then slamming it shut.

Lucas stared at the bag of money he'd just conned. He wanted to feel happy about it but the terror was still overwhelming. Instead he dropped the car into gear and drove away from Big Terry.

2 weeks later...

forty seven

"I was sorry to hear about your finger," said Violet and nodded towards Brad Fegan's bandaged hand.

Fegan's bushy black eyebrows collided in a frown as he stared at it. "Given the person who did this I can only think that I came out of the conversation pretty well."

"Well, I suppose so, yes," replied Violet.

Fegan had requested they meet in Kilchester's winter garden, a huge glasshouse standing over three stories high. It was like an indoor jungle and housed thousands of species of plants that it would otherwise be impossible to see in Kilchester, or indeed this hemisphere. And it was warm. Really warm.

"I heard that you lost one of your crew," said Fegan quietly. "I'm sorry."

Violet shook her head and stared out of the windows at the pond and fountains outside. A single jet of water shot out of the mouth of an algae-encrusted stone lion.

"Oh?" said Fegan. "So what happened?"

"I'm sorry," said Violet, and smiled. "I'm a bit tired. It's been... intense."

Fegan stared at the fountain too, both of them leaning on a

handrail. "You're milking it," he said eventually.

"I am," said Violet, with a familiar laugh. "I really am."

"So..." Fegan badgered. "What happened?"

"Where do I start?"

"At the risk of sounding clichéd... at the very beginning?"

Violet nodded. "A very good place to start." She ran her fingers through the leaves of an overhanging fern, gripping it tightly so that the chlorophyll stained her fingers. "After I got your message... I knew I had to make a decision."

"After what had happened with your ex?"

"Exactly. I mean, time had passed and I suppose it was obvious that, either through lack of interest or his own ineptitude, it was unlikely I was in any danger."

"You know, maybe you could just tell me what happened with the robbery? Did you get the painting?"

"Maybe I did. And maybe I'll tell you if you let me tell you the *whole* story."

Fegan sighed and rolled his hand forward. "Spill the beans, then."

"I knew it was inevitable our paths would cross if I came back for any length of time, and so I made a decision."

Fegan stared out at the rapidly setting sun. "And what decision was that?"

"That I would destroy him for what he did to my friend."

"Harsh but fair."

"I thought so, given the circumstances."

"And what were the circumstances exactly? You..." Fegan paused, giving himself some time to contemplate the right words. "You were circumspect with some aspects of the story, I felt."

"You're right," said Violet, staring off out into the park beyond the lake. "It's hard to say it. She died. My friend. I tried to save her but she died. And he didn't do it. But it was his fault."

"And you wanted to... what? Make amends?"

Violet shrugged. "In my own way, I suppose, yes. Selflessly in part. Selfishly too, of course."

"So..."

"Yes?"

"Stop stalling."

"Fair enough. Well, after we met I set about putting my crew together. It wasn't hard. Most people are incompetent so the list of possible people wasn't long. But I met up with people I used to know and everyone wanted me to tell them what happened *that night.*"

Fegan nodded and dabbed at the perspiration on his brow with a handkerchief that was now almost soaked through.

"I came back to Kilchester because the balance of power had shifted back to me." Violet turned her back to the great windows, leaning against the railing, staring up high at the palms that towered over them. "Now was the time to take action and your kind offer was the motivation to take back that power. The more people I talked to, the more I heard about him. Percy the success. Percy the womaniser. Percy who worked for Big Terry. So I made a decision... The job was always the number one priority but revenge would be the icing on the cake.

"I went to work, recruiting the crew I'd chosen and making my plans for how to get the painting."

Violet heard a noise and stopped talking. Coming through the indoor undergrowth was Zoe. She smiled widely at Violet and Violet reciprocated.

"Do you want to know how it played out?" asked Violet.

"It's a good story," added Zoe. "The parts I know, anyway. The rest... I'm intrigued to know more."

Fegan nodded and extended his hand in invitation; Zoe shook it.

"I recruited Zoe first," said Violet.

Zoe smiled with pride but said nothing.

"And we set a trap, of sorts, to recruit Barry."

"I was in the back of the car and..." Zoe began.

Fegan and Violet stared at her and she faltered. "I'll just listen then, shall I?"

"I went in to help Lucas close a deal," continued Violet. "And when I arrived, the two men he was conning... I recognised them. Not straight away but it itched at the back of my brain until I finally remembered who they were."

"And who were they?" asked Fegan.

"Associates of Big Terry. Part of some of the restaurants he runs."

"How did you know them?" asked Zoe.

"Long story," said Violet. "I've been around longer than I care to admit. But the point was that we had a connection to Big Terry. One that we could exploit."

Fegan let out a half-laugh and rubbed at the bandage on his finger. "You decided to factor Big Terry into the plan?"

Violet nodded.

"I'm not sure who's the bigger psycho. Him or you?"

"It's her," said a voice. Its owner padded along a nearby walkway and appeared from behind a miniature waterfall wearing bright white trainers, pressed jeans, a polo neck jumper and crimson jacket. "She's a maniac."

"Barry," said Violet.

"Your majesty," said Barry.

Violet ignored his jibe and pressed on. "People talk. Especially to mister white-shoes here. Barry the geezer. And Barry found out that a certain forger was a good friend of Percy. We had two or three options, but that swung it for us. I visited him with Lucas and made a big display. Making sure he knew that someone had arrived back in Kilchester. It was inevitable he would tell Percy."

"That's true," said Barry. "But who set Big Terry on us? Who told him that Lucas had ripped him off?"

Violet stared at him for a moment, pushing a strand of hair behind her ear. "I did," she said. "Phoned him myself."

Barry stared at her for a second. "If you'd told me that at the time…"

"Which is exactly why I didn't."

Fegan laughed.

"Well, that backfired," said Violet with a sigh. "No pun intended. Big Terry went straight to the guys Lucas had conned – that I had helped Lucas to con – and he blew one of their brains out."

Zoe stared at Violet, her mouth hanging open ever-so slightly.

"Well," said Fegan blithely. "You go into business with Big Terry, there's always the chance you're going to get your brains blown out. Or…," he held up his bandaged finger, "sustain other injuries. On with the story…"

"This was when I got Lucas in on the next phase of the plan. He was the professional con man, and if anyone could con Big Terry, the forger *and* Percy it was him. I mean, I could have done it but it was an easier sell to make it look like he'd betrayed us."

Fegan gave a quiet whistle of amazement.

"Because by now Big Terry would be tracking you down, there would be surveillance on its way…" said Fegan, the penny finally starting to drop.

"And I SOLD that performance to Percy." Lucas stepped out from behind an enormous palm leaf. "When he confessed to ripping off Big Terry on camera. That was the clinching moment of this job, really. Wasn't it?"

"Meh," said Zoe. "More likely it was my mad disguise skills."

"Lucas," Violet nodded and smiled. "Good to see you, sir."

"And you lot," Lucas replied.

Barry gave Lucas a pat on the shoulder.

"Did I tell you I nearly didn't record it?" asked Violet.

Lucas, Barry and Zoe frowned in unison.

"I'm not as good with the tech as I pretended," said Violet, quickly. "Anyway, we got it, so I think I'll just move on. There was a minor blip."

"We had to rob a casino," Zoe explained to Fegan.

"What? That was you?" Fegan goggled.

"There was a thing," Barry muttered. "But we sorted it."

"And then Big Terry descended for real," said Violet. "We were celebrating."

"You were… drunk?" asked Fegan.

"One or two light ales might have been consumed," said Zoe.

"So your plan to piss off Big Terry came to a head when you were blind drunk?" Fegan waved his bandaged hand in the air. "I wish I'd been drunk when he came to see me three hours earlier…"

"I bet you'd like some good news right about now?" asked Zoe. "Like we've got the painting for you?"

"The thought had crossed my mind. Do you?"

Barry, Lucas, Zoe and Violet all shook their heads.

"This better have a happy ending," said Fegan. "So what happened on the day?"

"I mildly poisoned the guard," said Zoe. "This stuff would make you lose your shit. Literally."

Lucas nodded. "Then I replaced him at the desk."

"And I knocked out the security system," interrupted Zoe.

Violet coughed. "Katie and I went downstairs to get set up."

Lucas and Zoe looked a little shamefaced.

"Oh, hi Katie." Violet gave a wave to Katie as she arrived, looming out of the heat and the moisture. Katie nodded a salutary hello and ran her two thumbs down the straps of a backpack she was wearing. "So almost the first thing I did was go into the banker's bedroom and replace the bullets in his gun with blanks."

"While she was doing that, I was phoning him up to tell him the company had come to move the painting early," said Lucas.

"He did *not* like that," said Zoe. "I was listening."

"So he arrived with his security contingent, who Katie dealt with," said Violet. "Then Lucas made sure that Glass was tied up."

"But not so tied up he couldn't escape," clarified Lucas. "The idea being that if he believed it was a botched kidnapping then he wouldn't even look to see if we'd taken the painting."

"Exactly," said Violet. "And when he escaped he shot the woman who was attacking him."

"Bang!" Zoe shouted.

Fegan jumped.

"Don't worry," Zoe continued. "I put a corset-type-thing on Katie and it was just squibs. Katie just had to Helen Mirren the shit out of that performance whilst remembering to press the button to pop the blood bags."

Zoe shot an accusing look at Katie, who gave her a thumbs-up before miming pressing the button with her thumb.

"Of course, it's easier to pull the trigger than it is to come to terms with the fact that you killed someone in your own home," said Violet. "The banker did exactly what I knew he would, which was to drop the gun and run for the hills. So while I took one of the fakes upstairs and threw it in the getaway car, Katie swiped the original and replaced it with the second fake."

"There were TWO fakes?" Fegan barked.

"Did we not mention that?" asked Lucas.

"I made sure we had two," said Violet. "One for the banker."

"And one for Big Terry," said Lucas.

"So while Katie cleaned up, I finished putting the security system back together," said Zoe.

"I had to go and see Big Terry," said Lucas.

"My God, man," Fegan grinned. "You must have balls as big as…"

"There are three women and two men in this crew," said Violet tersely. "Balls have nothing to do with it."

Lucas looked a little deflated.

"But yes, Lucas," Violet conceded. "You pulled a blinder."

"I delivered the fake to Big Terry," Lucas started to explain.

"So you really did get it?" said Fegan, cutting Lucas short. The relish he had for the victory was tempered by the knowledge that the tale was not yet at its end.

Night had begun to fall, the sun setting behind the trees, and a single light was turned on in the pond, shining up under the fountain's single jet.

"We really did get it," said Violet.

"But have you still got it?" asked Fegan, nervously.

"It wasn't over," said Violet. "There was still the matter of Percy to deal with."

"And Big Terry," added Fegan.

"Oh yeah," said Violet. "But Lucas delivered the painting and, as we expected, Big Terry was ready to give us nothing."

Fegan nodded.

"He was ready to kill me," Lucas muttered.

"But he didn't, did he?" laughed Barry. "More's the pity. I could have had your share."

Lucas raised his middle finger toward Barry.

Lucas picked up the story. "After Big Terry offered us nothing, he'd taken the fake, accepted it as real. But that wasn't enough for Violet…"

Fegan raised an eyebrow. "The video?"

"Of Percy," Violet confirmed. "We gave it to Terry…"

"*I* gave it to Terry," Lucas confirmed.

"*Lucas* gave it to Terry," Violet conceded. "And somehow managed not to shit in his pants. And when he handed it over the net closed and Percy was dealt with."

"Dealt with?" asked Fegan.

"Big Terry stabbed him in the leg and threw him in the boot of his car," said Lucas.

"And will he... kill him?"

Violet nodded. "I sincerely doubt Big Terry will kill him, he still has value to the little psycho, but he will punish him. Probably *literally* to within an inch of his life. If he kills him... Well, let's just say I'm at peace with my decisions. If he doesn't. I suppose we're even."

A silence fell over the group as they stared out at the pitiful fountain spewing its single jet into the near darkness.

"But why did he pay you?" asked Fegan, after a moment.

"He thinks it motivates us to do a better job, if he ever decides he wants to work with us again," said Barry. "We're all criminals, but by not calling the police, by honouring at least a part of the deal, in his twisted mind at least, it demonstrates the hatchet is buried."

"If it wasn't for you," Fegan turned to Violet, "the hatchet might well have been buried in the back of someone's head."

"I love it when a plan comes together," said Violet with a grin.

"So let me get this straight," asked Fegan, shaking his head. "You recruited your crew, phoned Big Terry to set him on your own trail then dragged your treacherous ex into the mix, got *two* copies of the painting forged, robbed a casino, staged a fake kidnapping *and* a fake murder. All to steal a painting and wreak your revenge on you ex?"

Violet nodded.

"Which means that you have it?" Fegan said eventually.

"Absolutely," said Violet, then nodded to Katie, who took off her backpack and removed a carefully wrapped canvas from within. Katie handed it gently to Fegan, who took it with a smile.

"So this is the original then?" he said.

Katie nodded.

"After Katie cleaned up the blood from the squibs there was plenty of time for her to take the original out of its frame and put one of the fakes in there," said Violet.

"But if Big Terry has already paid you, you won't need paying a second time now, will you?"

Violet raised an eyebrow in Fegan's direction. "I told you a story about a woman who died. Big Terry's payment is going to her family. An anonymous gift from a mystery benefactor. It can't bring her back, but... I knew you wouldn't mind."

"No, of course. I suppose," said Fegan, sighing as he wiped the sweat from his brow with his sleeve. "And there's no need to worry about the dwarf finding out about the other copies. My buyer always had the intention to keep this painting in a *very* private collection. Which was why they requested the switch in the first place. So it's unlikely he'll ever be any the wiser."

Violet nodded.

"I'll arrange the transfer of your fee in the morning," Fegan continued. "You should consider sticking around in Kilchester, you know?"

Violet stared out at the fountain then let her gaze pass over the crew. Her crew. "I was thinking that maybe I would stick around in Kilchester for a while."

Katie grabbed Violet and hoisted her up, hugging the air out of her.

The sound of laughter echoed around the enormous glasshouse.

"Well, in all likelihood I'll be in touch with you soon," said Fegan. "Just one thing that would have been the icing on the cake."

"What's that?" said Violet, now safely returned to earth by Katie.

"The diamond heist," said Fegan. "The one you left Kilchester after. Such a shame you didn't grab any of the diamonds."

He sighed and turned to make his way out of the winter garden.

Violet grinned at him. "Who said I didn't grab any of the diamonds?"

acknowledgements

It's difficult to know where to begin or end when paying tribute to the people who have been instrumental in helping me bring this book to life. I'm lucky to have all of them in my life, whether I paid them to be there or not, so forgive me a little sentimentality.

Most of all my wife, Eve. Your unwavering belief, unerring support and oceans of love are a constant source of inspiration to me. I love you now and always and my life would be much duller and have much less laughter in it without you.

James Whitman, my writing spirit animal. Thank you for your support through every stage of this novel. From the long, convoluted conversations about outlines to arguing over sentence structure and changes in tense you are infuriatingly, irritatingly correct more than anyone has any right to be. Thank God I ignored you as often as I did.

My co-editors Sam Hartburn and Elaine Jinks-Turner, for all the hours and hours (and hours) that you have put in to bashing the book into shape, thank you both.

Matt Austin and Mark Young for your eagle eyed insistence that time operates in a linear fashion and, as such, should be adhered to when writing fiction. Both of your input has helped to ensure this most convoluted of tales has remained understood on non-quantum levels.

To my family and friends for all their advance input; Mam, Brenda West, Michael Brett, Claire Aberdeen, Roz Wyllie, Margaret Field, Oliver Kinsley, Martin Greatbatch, Richard Heslop. I'm grateful to you all for the questions, pointers, clarifications and encouragement.

The cover illustration by Mute. How you crowbarred those images out of my head and rendered them in colour and shape I do not know. Neither do I know how to remove the scars from my temples.

To Damien Walter from The Guardian for being kind enough to write a blurb to help me convince people to take this journey with me.

Lastly I'd like to thank my advance team expert loungers who volunteered to read this. You kick arse. All of you:

Kristy Linderholm, Jesse Fowler, Krissy Lee, Gary, Paulo, Ian, Amber, Nessa, Jenny, Stephen, Kryste, Peg and Graham.

- A.M.

Made in the USA
Monee, IL
15 October 2020

45203811R00182